On This Side of Heaven

On This Side of Heaven

For Wendy
Grace & Peace
Pamela Jackson

Pamela Jackson

www.ivyhousebooks.com

PUBLISHED BY IVY HOUSE PUBLISHING GROUP
5122 Bur Oak Circle, Raleigh, NC 27612
United States of America
919-782-0281
www.ivyhousebooks.com

ISBN: 1-57197-466-0
Library of Congress Control Number: 2006903398

Printed in the United States of America

For my husband, Dale,
and my children, Juliette, Jeffrey, Cameron, and Annaleigh,
with much love

Acknowledgments

FOREMOST, I ACKNOWLEDGE that it is by the grace of God that I have written this book. For without Him, I am nothing.

It is such a privilege to thank all those who have made *On This Side of Heaven* possible. I begin with my dear friend, Lee Chadwick, who held my hand and walked with me through the entire process. Without her this book would still be collecting dust on a shelf in manuscript form.

I owe much to the following people for taking time to be part of this project: Denise Jacob, my best friend and soul sister. She is always there with a cup of tea in hand . . . for me! And her husband, Jay, who was among the first guinea pigs to read *On This Side of Heaven.* I am especially grateful to Andy Stanley, Lanny Donoho, The Reverend Joe Bowen, and his lovely wife Harriette Bowen (whom I secretly aspire to be like!) for their support and generosity of words.

I am grateful to all the people at Ivy House Publishing Group . . . Anna Howland, Tami Stoy and Janet Evans. It has been delightful working with you.

I thank my family from the bottom of my heart with love that shall transcend eternity. Again, I thank God for allowing me to be the mother of Juliette, Jeffrey, Cameron and Annaleigh. How blessed I am! I use the words 'thank you' for lack of a better word to express my feelings for you. I thank my mother, Caroline Allen, for always being available to 'help' with whatever was needed, usually meaning she spent time driving the car, and for multiple times editing. My father and step-mother, Ken and Jo Allen, cheered me on with avid enthusiasm and support. I also thank Daddy for his attention to details! Now I know where I got my perfectionist attitude!

My deepest love and gratitude go to my husband, Dale, for the endless hours of listening, advising, and encouragement. I am deeply grateful for his perspective, insight, patience, and for just loving me. And whether he realizes it or not, he is truly my spiritual mentor!

Chapter One

THERE IS A common misnomer that the church is all about God. Well, at some point that may be true, but . . . not at this level. Tuesday morning was a ritual for the Reverend Bob Buck during the spring and summer. The aroma of the freshly-cut grass heightened his sense of smell. The green stains on the sides of his well-worn tennis shoes were like a picture of his youth to him. Mowing the grass to some men is as tedious as scrubbing floors, but the way he saw it, this was a gift to him, and he cherished every moment of it. It was his time with nature. Seeing the beautiful blue sky above him brought a reality that all the fullness of God was abundant in this life. The drone of the lawn mower shut out everything except the flood of memories of his life as he encountered God along the way.

He had never wanted a riding lawn mower. When he played football in high school his coach made all the guys mow their lawns with push mowers. "It builds the shoulder muscles," his coach always said. Well, if it was good for him then, it must be good for him now. As a kid, he only had a city lot to mow; now he had the equivalent of four. But, he figured he was now almost four times the age, so he needed almost four times the work in order to keep the same physique.

Buck was not a frail man—not by any means. He had turned sixty-nine on his last birthday, which meant he would be turning seventy on his next. But, to look at Buck, you would think he was not a day over fifty-five. His hair was silvered in the front and around his ears, and his blue eyes were still as bright as ever. And the grass mowing had certainly paid off. He felt quite confident that, if required, he could hold his own against any twenty-five-year-old kid. Often there was speculation in the pews about the smoothness around his eyes and forehead. Julia Matthews, who wasn't afraid to tell anyone what she thought, would whisper to whomever might be sitting next to her on any given Sunday morning, "I suspect there's a mighty fine plastic surgeon somewhere out there." Most of the congregation agreed, but Julia was the only one that actually came out and said it. Of course, she never spoke a word of it to Buck.

Mowing the lawn was Buck's time for prayer and meditation. Every week he started the task with the same phrase: "Lord, thank you for another week in Your garden."

Buck always cut his lawn in a criss-cross pattern. He thought it showed the infinite variations in the palette of green. There is a fine art to mowing grass, one that he seemed to think he was close to perfecting. It was an expression of his artistic vision, which could not be broken. That was, until the poop.

"Son of a . . . ," Buck mouthed out loud.

The Bucks had new neighbors, Betty and Ron Silver, in the house next door to the parsonage. They hadn't met officially yet, but Bob Buck had met their dog. And by all accounts, the Silver's dog had claimed Buck's front yard as his own.

"Poop," Buck cursed out loud.

Reverend Buck preached about pride as one of the roots of evil on a regular basis. Pride is what causes us to do things for our own benefit and not in service to the Lord. However, there are exceptions to everything, and proud he was of his landscape work. But, the vision of poop—not to mention the aroma that wafted through the air—was enough to push even the godliest of men over the edge.

It was probably time that he meet his new next-door neighbors. After all, they had lived there for close to a month now. He did have a tinge of guilt that he hadn't been over to say hello and invite them to church. And, while he was there, he didn't suppose it would hurt to mention the poop.

• • •

WHEN THE DOOR opened, a clean-cut man appeared smiling—and there was the dog at his feet.

"I'm Reverend Bob Buck. Welcome to the neighborhood," Buck said. He glanced at the dog, which appeared to be smiling, too.

"Please come in. I'm Ron and this is Angel." The man gestured to the four-legged creature at his side. *Angel?* Somehow it was not the name he was expecting. *Lucifer would be more fitting,* Buck thought.

"I have been meaning to come over for weeks," Buck proclaimed. "Time is something I've never gotten a handle on, and it always gets the best of me."

"Well, glad to finally meet you," Ron returned.

Ron Silver was a young looking fellow, probably somewhere around forty, with dark hair, olive skin and brown eyes. He was a real estate attorney with a law firm in Salem, which was more like being a banker with a law degree. *Boring,* Buck thought silently. The young man smelled like most of the young men in his congregation—flowers and musk. His polo shirt was a pale orchid, his blue jeans had creases down the front and although he was wearing loafers, there was a glaring view of his bare ankles. The real estate business was booming in Salem and the surrounding areas, which provided Ron and his family with a very large income. So, they were easily capable of buying the extremely expensive, beautiful white farmhouse next to the parsonage in Wakefield.

Wakefield was a transitional community that was once a little country town, where gentleman estates sit next to small homes; like the parsonage and Ron's house. Buck saw this as a plus, because whoever lived in the beautiful white farmhouse was sure to be well off financially. That meant if he could get them to join the congregation at First Covenant Chapel, it was sure to be a good source of tithing income.

They walked through the foyer, to the rear side of the house and into a sunny room, which Buck knew well. It overlooked the little pond that the two neighbors shared. He had spent many evenings in this room with his former friend and neighbor, Edward Tarken, who had passed away about six months prior. Buck had presided over the funeral for Edward; he had not only lost a parishioner, but also a very close friend. Edward had been one of the most prominent members of First Covenant Chapel, where Buck served as senior pastor. Edward's wife had passed away five years earlier, just before Buck had been assigned to First Covenant Chapel and just before Buck and his wife, Peggy, had moved into the parsonage that sat between Edward's home and the church. Feeling that the sunset was one of God's greatest creations, Buck and Edward would sit in the back room overlooking the pond and watch the sun go down. Usually, this admiration ritual included Scotch and cigars.

Buck listened to Edward tell stories for hours about his life and the precious time he spent with his wife. Edward also talked about times that were not so precious. Much of their time together could be summed up as pastoral counseling. Edward had not always done things the "right" way, but, as Buck would assure him, what man has? Buck felt the guilt with which Edward Tarken was afflicted. And he knew that finding a place in the church was healing for the soul. Edward had been well off financially, and tithing seemed like penitence to him, which Buck made no effort to dissuade. Tithing, coupled with counseling from Reverend Buck, seemed to be just what Edward's soul needed to find its final peace on this earth.

"Have you settled in?" Buck asked Ron. Being awash in the torrent of memories, he couldn't think of anything else to say at the moment.

"We're getting there. It's a big change from city life to here. My wife and I like it, but the children, well . . . it will take some time."

It's hard not to be settled when you are living in the country. There is a real sense of tranquility that takes over when your roots are planted where there are wide open spaces.

Strong fences make good neighbors, Buck thought, trying to remember who said that quote. Fearful that his neighbor might be able to read his mind, Buck blurted out, "Why don't you and your wife join us for church on Sunday? We are the United Covenant Church of America." His mind was focused on the poop, and he was certain he had just convinced his new neighbor that Covenant ministers used the "rope and tie 'em" approach.

"Thank you," Ron said, still smiling, "but my wife, Betty, and the children have been going to Spring Rock Church. I go with them occasionally, but I was raised in a Jewish home. We were non-practicing, although we did celebrate all the holidays, especially those that involved great Jewish cooking."

"I know what you mean," Buck replied. "A good corned beef sandwich can be a religious experience."

They both laughed, and then Ron began to whisper as if the phantom rabbi might hear him. "So when I do go to church, it's something I do for Betty and the children. Our kids seem to have connected with the children's program, and Betty loves Uriah Jonah." When Ron said "loves," it was long and drawn out. "I've even found that sometimes his sermons speak to me," Ron said.

"Uriah Jonah! What a great preacher! I am so glad you and your family feel at home there," Buck lied, being certain to hide the jealousy in his voice. "Well, the invitation is always open if you would like to join us."

Uriah Jonah was the bane of every other preacher for miles around. Not only was he good looking, he was also gifted at public speaking, and he always looked like he had just been cut out of the front cover of *GQ Magazine* and pasted onto his stage. His charisma reeled in the young crowd, particularly the singles. It was reported that his membership was up to nine thousand. Uriah Jonah was a well-respected preacher, and quite frankly, that irritated Buck.

Buck shook Ron's hand as he walked out the front door. He had now officially met his new neighbor . . . and Angel. Not a word about the poop was mentioned.

After the unsuccessful visit to his new neighbor's house, Buck went back to his lawn. He detoured to the little shed on the side of his house and retrieved a shovel. He was angry and tense. His muscular shoulders were now up close to his ears. *Uriah Jonah and poop,* he thought. One was definitely full of the other, but frankly, he just didn't want to think about both of them in the same day.

He carefully scooped up the poop. "Angel? I don't think so," Buck whispered to himself. He looked around to make sure his neighbor wasn't lurking in the bushes, and with a quick fling, the poop hurled through the air and landed back in its rightful yard.

Having now handled that situation, for at least the moment, Buck went back to mowing, hoping to calm his anger. But the bitter resentment of why he was in this tiny town, cutting this grass in the first place, came flooding back to him . . .

"GOOD LUCK" WERE the only words spoken by Katrina, the senior pastor's secretary. She had always been very sweet and kind to everyone that came her way. Katrina was a charming woman in her late fifties. She was tall, thin and wore her soft, silvered hair at shoulder length. When she smiled, it accentuated her high cheekbones. She looked youthful, despite the fact that her life had been difficult. She was a single mother who worked hard to give her son the very best she could. He was nearly thirty years old now, but he was still her pride and joy.

"Good luck to you, too. He's a hard man to work with," Buck said, referring to his now former senior pastor, Frank Maddox. They momentarily exchanged a knowing look.

Katrina knew there was resentment between the two men, but Maddox was a good man, and he ran a tight ship. The two men couldn't have been more opposite.

Katrina had known Buck for more than thirty years. She had been the church secretary at Buck's first appointment. They worked together for four years, until Buck was moved, as is usual with appointments in The United Covenant Churches of America. It was a quarter of a century later when they met up again at Holy Oak United Covenant Church. Katrina had been the secretary to the senior pastors at Holy Oak for the last twenty years, fifteen of which Frank Maddox served as senior pastor. Five years earlier, Buck had been appointed to Holy Oak as the new associate pastor. He had been extremely fond of Katrina, and it was always comforting to see a friendly and familiar face when coming to a new place.

Buck tried to bring new and original ideas to the ministry at Holy Oak. He knew how to slap people on the back and make them his friend. His ways may have been a little unconventional, but as far as Buck was concerned, Frank Maddox was a stuffed shirt, afraid of taking chances on things that can get you ahead. Buck was more of a marketer, and Maddox was an administrator. The two could have complemented each other, but Maddox didn't seem to think God needed a marketing director, and at the end of the day—regardless of anything else—what the senior pastor says, is what goes.

They worked together for three years. Buck headed the missions committee. The missions program at Holy Oak United Covenant was, without a doubt, the best program in the district. The money pouring into it was unbelievable. Holy Oak was giving large sums of money to the United Covenant Children's Home, homeless shelters, and food kitchens. They ran regular mission trips to Mexico and Paraguay to lay the foundation for churches and teach Vacation Bible School; they even adopted several single mothers with children who were on the verge of being homeless, and helped get them back on their feet.

As wonderful as these things were, they were expensive, and Frank Maddox began to wonder how the church was paying for all of these programs. After all, Maddox did know the budget, and Buck seemed to be stretching his funds beyond that which was believable. Maddox began to investigate, and it turned out that Buck had been requesting members to tithe directly to his mission fund. This was not necessarily bad, but the problem was that it pulled the money away from the general funds, and the operating budget was beginning to suffer noticeably. It was like robbing Peter to pay Paul—nothing that justified Maddox filing a formal grievance to the Administrative Conference—but Maddox didn't like Buck's unconventional ways of doing things. It was Maddox's opinion that Buck wasn't in the ministry for the greater good, even though Buck did have quite a following and many of the members applauded his religious zeal and ambition. Maddox wanted a transfer for Buck.

• • •

BUCK HAD BEEN lost in his thoughts about the past for quite a few moments. He shook his head, trying to snap the thought out of his memory. The grass was finished. Buck was hot and tired, and this particular Tuesday, the ritual had been emotionally draining.

He put the mower away in the little shed and headed straight for the refrigerator. He popped open the top of a lite beer and plopped down in his leather wing chair—the one thing that probably knew him better than anything else in the world.

"Finished?" His wife's voice approached from the hallway.

"Finished."

"What's on your agenda for the rest of the day?" Peggy asked with a raspy voice, the result of a cough she hadn't been able to shake since winter.

"I have to prepare for the council meeting tonight and go to the bank and sign the final loan papers; I'm going to try to talk to the zoning office; I've got my usual lunch meeting with

Tom at the Dixie Diner; and if there is any time left over, maybe I'll start on my sermon for Sunday." He also had an afternoon appointment with one of his parishioners, but he didn't share that information with Peggy.

Peggy looked at him blankly and then smiled. "I'm tired just hearing that."

"You've been tired a lot recently," Buck replied to his wife.

"I'm fine, Bob. Quit fretting. You know it's a sin," she said with a smile that turned into a bout of coughing.

"I met our new neighbors today," Buck commented.

"Ron and Betty?" Peggy responded.

"Yes. Well, I met Ron and the dog, Angel. Have you met them?" he said with a quizzical face.

"I went over a couple of days after they moved in," Peggy said as she moved toward the kitchen.

"Oh," was his only response.

"They are very nice. I invited them to join us at church anytime," Peggy said.

"Yes, I did, too. What did they tell you?" Buck was curious.

"They said thanks; they might take us up on the offer sometime."

Maybe Peggy should have been the minister.

"I'm going to take a shower." Buck pulled himself out of the chair and headed toward the bathroom.

He looked at himself in the mirror. He needed to shave. Catching a glance at his own eyes for a moment, he saw into himself.

Lord, he began to pray. *Please forgive me. I harbor such anger. I know I do, God. Why can't I let go? Why can't I move away from my own selfish space? Deep in my heart I believe that you brought me here to this little country church for Your specific purpose. You know better than I. I sin against You, and I feel anguish deep in my heart, but I can't seem to turn away. I always crave more. Your will be done, Lord, Your will be done.*

He turned the shower on to barely lukewarm and got in. Over and over he continued, *Your will be done, Your will be done.* The water beat down on the back of his neck and shoulders, which were still tight. He seemed to be living in the past today, something he seemed to be doing more and more the older he got. Buck was lost in his thoughts of the past, and he seemed to be trapped in every painful memory . . .

HE REMEMBERED CLEARLY the day when he first came to the little white clapboard church in the country. It was the middle of the winter. He remembered walking up to the front doors of First Covenant Chapel. The 150-year-old sanctuary, small as it was and rich with hand-hewn paneled walls and pews that spoke of generations of God's people, was cold and chilled him to the bone. Buck shivered as he looked around. He rubbed his arms to try and warm himself. *I don't deserve to be here,* he thought to himself. Looking at the wooden cross hanging behind the altar, he whispered out loud, "Why?"

Buck had been moved to this little country church by the district superintendent, but of course because it had been requested. "Maddox," he said out loud with vengeance in his voice. Buck was full of resentment that Frank Maddox had such control over him. As far as Buck was concerned, Frank Maddox was the sole reason he was where he was today.

Not only had Buck been demoted to a smaller church, but his new appointment to this little country church was as a chaplain—to complete the last chapter in the history book of the little church and close the doors of First Covenant Chapel forever. It would also be the end of Buck's career.

He remembered thinking his first Sunday there was coming too soon. He would meet his new parishioners and have to preach all in the same day. By his way of thinking, those were two events that definitely needed separate occasions.

FOR JUST A moment, Buck managed to return his thoughts back to his shower. He turned and let the water run across his teeth and into his mouth, then spit it at the drain. But, he couldn't shake thinking about the past. He remembered clearly that his strongest feeling on that first day was that he would need to keep his stomach empty . . .

WHILE GREETING EACH person with the obligatory handshake, certainly a few hugs—which, actually, he never minded—he would have to be formulating in his mind how to tell these people it was the end of their church. At least the sun was shining that day. The only thing that could have been worse was if it had been raining. He reached into his pocket for his key to what he now saw in his own mind as a prison cell. But the door was already open. Taking a deep breath, he walked in confidently, knowing he was going to meet his first parishioner.

Buck walked into the small musty room, which was not very well heated. There was a man sitting in a chair. "Are you Reverend Buck?" the man said.

"Yes," replied Buck, "call me Bob."

"So nice to meet you, I'm Doug Miles." Buck shook the hand of a very tall and gentle-looking man. Doug's hair was about the same color as Buck's, but somehow Buck knew Doug was a least ten years younger, if not more.

"Nice to meet you," Buck returned. It was an awkward moment.

"Well, I guess you've made yourself at home in the parsonage," Doug commented. "What do you think of our little house?"

"Yes, I'm looking forward to the days ahead," Buck responded. Somehow neither one seemed to be involved in the same conversation.

The front door opened and the ray of sunlight was a small gift to the chilling room. More introductions, more handshakes, more fake smiles—at least on Buck's part—and, of course, more being sized up, on every account.

Mary Fletcher was an elegant lady. She was very tiny and thin and wore a hat as if she were the Queen of England. It was quite becoming and her face was sweet. Buck was experiencing a wave of comfort for the first time since he had learned about his sentence to the tiny dying church. He had been told she was eighty years old, but she didn't look a day over sixty. She smiled at him from across the room and he smiled back.

BUCK CONTINUED TO sort through his memories as the water from the shower beat against his back. He reached for the soap and began to move it slowly, back and forth across his chest. His memory went on . . .

FOUR OR FIVE more people walked into the church. Pleasantries were exchanged, there was small talk and absolutely everyone who had entered seemed thankful for the sunshine. The small group of people walked into the sanctuary and took what appeared to be assigned seats. Buck stayed in the narthex, near the front door. If he had to be here, he was going to make the best of it and meet and greet each member personally that morning. The tiny room now smelled of a mixture of Old Spice and Shalimar perfumes, which he found nauseating.

Reaching out his hand to the new minister, an elderly man introduced himself. "Edward, Edward Tarken. Neighbor and member. Glad you're here, Reverend."

With relief in his voice, Buck replied, "So glad to meet you, sir."

"I saw you working in your yard the other day, but you looked deep in concentration, so I thought I'd save the honors until this morning." Edward had a deep, resonating voice with a definite country twang. He, too, was at least eighty years old with thick white hair, and although it seemed that age had taken its toll on him, he still gave the appearance of having once been a very vibrant, athletic young man.

"It is such a pleasure to meet you, sir," Buck responded.

"I've been going to this church for over fifty years—never miss a Sunday. Everyone knows that if I'm not here, you need to come 'a looking for me in the hospital," Edward said with a chuckle.

"I will keep that in mind," Buck said as he raised his index finger and waggled it at Edward.

"Look forward to your sermon." Edward walked on by and took his assigned seat.

A few moments later, Doug Miles came into the narthex. "Reverend Buck," he said with a slight stutter to his voice, "we're ready."

"Yes, yes," Buck said, "I am ready, too. But, today I would like to personally greet everyone first."

Doug had the oddest look on his face, Buck thought. This wasn't a look that had a statement behind it that was going to be positive one. "You have," Doug said very slowly, nodding his head toward the six other people seated in the sanctuary. Miss Mary's hat now stood out like a sore thumb. He had spent enough time in the ministry to know that God had a sense of humor. He didn't always understand God's sense of humor, but he accepted it. This must have been one of those times.

"I see." Reverend Buck conceded and began walking to the pulpit, trying to keep his shoulders low so the mass of people watching him from behind wouldn't know he was stressed, saddened, and even bitter. He took another deep breath; it was either that or hyperventilate. He turned and said in his pastoral voice, "This is the day that the Lord has made. Let us rejoice and be glad in it!" *Poppycock!* was his only thought, and he smiled.

AFTER THE LAST of the third degree was over and he had gallantly kissed Miss Mary's hand, he closed the door of her dark blue Mercedes. He looked around. The parking lot was empty. He took another deep breath. His shoulders were now up around his ears as he walked solemnly back into the sanctuary and seated himself in the back pew. How was he going to tell these seven lovely people that the Administrative Conference of The United Covenant Churches of America was closing their church? Especially Miss Mary; she had been born into this church.

He took another deep breath, but behind this one was anger and frustration that he didn't even know he had in him. *They* didn't know his heart. Sure, he had made some mistakes;

but let the man who lives in the glass house be the first one to throw the stone. This was not how he wanted to end his career, and he wasn't going down without a fight. He wanted more than this. He deserved more than this. And the way Buck saw it, it wasn't vanity.

THE SOAP WAS now an hourglass shape, he had held it so tightly in his hand. He quickly stroked it down his legs and swiped it across the rest of his body. He rinsed and then turned for one final swig of water and a final spit. Stepping out of the shower, he dried his arms and legs, ruffled his hair with the towel and then wrapped it around his waist and tucked it at the top. He opened the bathroom door.

"I was beginning to worry about you. That was a long shower," Peggy said as she was putting laundry away in a drawer.

"Just relaxing," Buck responded with a chiding voice.

She glanced back down at the drawer. She knew her husband better than this. Bob and Peggy Buck had been married for forty-five years. They had struggled together from church to church, raising four children in a pastor's world. "Relax" wasn't in the vocabulary.

He grabbed a pair of boxers from the stack of clothes in his wife's hand and stepped into them.

"Will you be at the council meeting?" Buck asked as he finished dressing.

"I'll be there," she replied with absolutely no enthusiasm.

Buck didn't notice the stillness of his wife's voice. He tucked his shirt into his pants, picked up a bottle of cologne from the dresser and splashed some on his face. The perfume filled the air in the room. It reminded Peggy of when they were dating; she always knew what their date was going to be like by whether or not he was wearing aftershave.

"You look handsome," Peggy said.

"Thanks." He kissed her on the cheek and walked out the bedroom door. "See you at the church at seven."

"Yeah, see you," Peggy whispered to herself, sitting on the edge of the bed and trying to fight the weakness.

Chapter Two

WITH ONE HAND on the steering wheel, he pushed the numbers on his cell phone with the other.

On the third ring, Doug Miles answered, "Hello?"

"Brother Doug, Reverend Buck here."

"What's doing?" replied Doug.

"Just checking on things for the council meeting tonight."

"I guess we're ready," said Doug. "Michael's done most the work, he'll make the presentation."

"Well, good then. He'll do a great job. See you, man. Blessings to you." Buck hung up the phone.

Michael Gillard was the son-in-law of Bob and Peggy Buck. He was married to Amy, their second daughter. Michael was a smart businessman. He always knew how to make things swing on the side of positive.

Buck never asked much of his children—just to be honest, work hard and love God with all their hearts. However, there were acceptable times when he felt it was okay for even a father to call in a favor.

All four of the Buck children lived in the surrounding area, which meant all his grandchildren lived there as well. Buck thanked God daily that his family had such close ties. And when he realized First Covenant Chapel had only seven members, he called his children for the favor. With children, son-in-laws, daughter-in-laws and grandchildren, he had an instant congregation that the district office couldn't ignore.

THE BRAKES ON Buck's car squealed. "Damn, a red light!" He stopped hard. For some reason, the day was haunting him. Why was the past so prevalent today? He couldn't shake his mind of it. He stared at the red light nearly hypnotized and slipped back into his memory of the past . . .

• • •

"I'm not closing these doors," Buck told his wife on his second Sunday of serving First Covenant Chapel. He seemed to be able to think of nothing else but his career, and he had a plan—a brilliant plan, if he did say so himself.

"What?" was Peggy's only response.

"I'm not closing these doors!" he said again, this time more firmly.

"I'm not sure I understand," Peggy said with a puzzled look on her face.

"With our children and grandchildren and you and me, we had twenty-eight people in the congregation today. Don't you understand, Peggy? This church doesn't need to be closed."

"I'm not sure that's your decision, Bob. You were assigned here for a purpose," she reminded him.

"Peggy, look at me." Buck gently grabbed his wife's shoulders and pulled her face close to his. "I have spent most of my life serving God. When the district sent me here, it was because of Frank Maddox. He wanted to end my career. I don't have to let Maddox control me anymore."

Peggy looked at her husband, not really sure of what he was saying. "But, Don Russell sent you here to close this church—not Frank."

Don Russell was the district superintendent for the area in which both Holy Oak United Covenant Church and First Covenant Chapel were located. Don had been in the ministry longer than any of them. He had a reputation for being a fair man, but he expected very high standards of the ministers in his district.

"Peggy, I made a deal with Don. I said I would come to First Covenant Chapel if he would allow me to stay here until the church was finally closed or I retired. I'm sixty-five years old." Buck appeared to be pleading to his wife. "I don't have to retire for five more years, and Don never put a deadline on closing these doors. You know I am good. I can build this church in that length of time," Buck said arrogantly.

Peggy looked blank. She was tired. She had worked to pay his way through seminary and then stood by her husband for forty years while he served in the ministry. She had sacrificed her own needs to the needs of other people long enough. The church and its people always came first. She felt like crying. Peggy saw First Covenant Chapel as a sanctuary to her, a place where she might finally be able to rest and be the center of her husband's attention once in awhile. "Why do you let Frank get to you like you do?" she asked.

"Peggy, stop! It's not Frank," Buck fibbed. "It's about not letting God and His people down. This community is going to be growing because of the development in Salem. This church is needed."

Peggy knew better.

FROM ALMOST ANY point where you stand in the little town of Wakefield, you can look around and imagine that you are in the French countryside. Wakefield is wide open, with green pastures divided by trees. It is still farm country, although the neighboring city is encroaching. You can still be awakened in the morning by your neighbor's rooster—that is, if they didn't eat it for dinner the night before. First Covenant Chapel sits right in the middle of town. The only other business is a feed store across the street. Of course, they sell milk and eggs, too. It is quaint that one can buy both milk and a wormer for their cow at the same register. But just ten miles down the street is the ever-growing town of Salem, which one might call a city at this point. Over the last five years Salem had gone from a population of 1,000 to 35,000. They now have a real mall, a multiplex movie theater; and you know you're in a metropolis when you have both a Home Depot and Wal-Mart at the same intersection.

Bob Buck had been around the block a few times, and he knew that the floodgates of Salem would have to give way soon, which meant that people would be spilling into the little town of Wakefield. When they did, he had every intention of being prepared. The only other church in Wakefield was an antiquated Baptist Church, and Buck didn't see them as competition. Of course, in Salem there was a church for every denomination, plus it was the home of the ever-growing church of Uriah Jonah, Spring Rock Church, which is the heavyweight of churches.

Buck looked deep into his wife's eyes as if he were a six-year-old boy asking for a new puppy dog. "Peggy, no man could ask for a better woman, and no minister could ask for a better wife. You have stood by me through thick and thin." He caressed her cheek with his hand. "You have been my strength when I didn't think I could go on. You encouraged me to continue." His eyes were deep. "Peggy, stand by me now, encourage me now. We have so much left to give God."

Peggy was confused. She loved Bob Buck, but she wasn't sure who was asking her to give more: God or her husband?

• • •

BUCK STARTLED FROM the wail of the car horn behind him. He was staring right at the light and never saw it turn green. His neck was aching and his shoulders were tight and hard. He picked up his cell phone from the passenger seat and dialed again.

"First Covenant Chapel, this is Margaret." Margaret was the secretary at First Covenant Chapel.

"Marge—hey, woman. How's it going?" Buck asked with his usual exuberance that never showed emotion.

"Reverend Buck, I'm fine," she replied. "How are you?"

"Can't complain. I'm on my way in. Had to run to the bank in Salem. I should be there in fifteen to twenty. Is Tom in?"

"He came in early this morning," Margaret replied, "but he's in Ben's office."

"Oh," Buck replied, a little curious. "Well, can I talk to him anyway?"

"Just a moment, I'll transfer you."

"Thanks. Blessings to you, woman," Buck replied.

Tom Werner was the financial officer of First Covenant Chapel and an old friend of Buck's. He and his wife, Lisa, had gone to Holy Oak United Covenant Church when Buck was associate pastor there. Buck knew Tom well; they had been through a lot together. They had worked on committees together, played golf together, laughed together and there were even times when they cried together. Most of all, Buck had been there when Tom's marriage to his wife Lisa was falling apart. Buck had counseled with Tom and Lisa for many hours, sometimes as a couple and sometimes individually. Tom trusted Buck with his deepest secrets—the kind of secrets only men could share, the kind of things only men could understand.

"Feelings *are*," Buck had told Tom. "They just *are*. We cannot be held responsible for what we feel. However, we will be held responsible for what we do with those feelings . . . and then we have to be willing to accept the consequences."

Tom and Lisa had been married for twenty years and had two teenage boys. They were married right out of college. He had earned a degree in accounting and she in marketing. The early part of their marriage had been dedicated to getting Tom established in the world of accounting. He was a smart man and was hired by a large, well-known firm in Charleston. He worked there for five years, until Lisa became pregnant with their second child. At that point, Tom decided to break away from the large accounting firm and start a practice of his own, hoping it would give him more time to spend with his family. They moved to the suburb of Salem, which was expected to be a boomtown. He set up a small office. Within ten years, Salem began to burst at the seams, and Tom had the largest accounting firm in downtown Salem.

Much of Tom's success was due to Lisa. She was lively and vivacious—not to mention very attractive—and she knew how to throw a good dinner party. Lisa used a lot of her marketing expertise to help Tom build his practice.

Tom loved Lisa with all his heart. They were made for each other. They would joke about being penguins: they had mated for life. Tom still felt for Lisa what he had felt for her on their wedding day when he was kissing his bride. Although she was now in her early forties, she was as beautiful as the first day he met her. Lisa was tall and had curves in all the places men seemed to want women to have curves, even during her pregnancies. She wore her blonde hair shoulder length with wispy bangs that framed her face.

Lisa had made a career out of building Tom's career. She was successful in helping Tom, and he now made an extremely good income, which allowed Lisa to stay at home and raise their boys. But the success of his business didn't leave much time for Lisa or the family. At first, Lisa made small jokes about him being a "ghost" husband. She would tease him by saying she had seen his shadow floating around the house at least once during the week.

One night Tom came home late after Lisa had already gone to sleep. He went into the bedroom, and in the darkness he saw the outline of a figure lying next to Lisa. Stopping dead in his tracks, he was unable to move for a moment. Never would he believe Lisa would be unfaithful to him. He felt a hole in the pit of his stomach, then a quick rush of anger. *In his own bed!* This didn't make sense to him. She knew he was coming home. In his anger, he threw the light switch on and forcefully went toward the bed and pulled back the covers. There, lying on his side of the bed with its head on Tom's pillow, was an inflatable blow up man that was labeled across its chest with the words "virtual husband." Tom let out a deep breath, blowing out the air slowly in relief, and as he did he heard a giggle. Lisa rolled over and looked at him with a most mischievous smile, and he knew exactly what the smile meant. "Point well taken," Tom said. He flipped the lights back off, stripped off his clothes, tossed the inflatable man out of the bed and moved into his rightful place next to his wife. Drawing her close to him, he pulled her nightgown over her head with one flowing motion and tossed it on the floor next to the blow up man.

They had nights of passion as time allowed, but Tom still placed his work ahead of everything else. For the rest of the time, they had become like two ships that pass in the night. Tom was too busy to notice it and Lisa was tired of telling him. She began to withdraw from Tom; even their nights of passion became less. Their only common ground seemed to be their children.

One night in early April, Lisa waited up for Tom to come home. She knew it was tax season, Tom's busiest time of the year, but she could no longer suffer the loneliness that she kept inside. Somewhere along the way during their marriage, she had lost herself and become a mere extension of Tom and, unknowingly, he was taking advantage of the situation. He took their relationship for granted, never really stopping to think what Lisa needed. Even though she had been telling him for quite a long time, he seemed to brush it off.

"Separation?" Tom was caught off guard. "Are you joking?"

She wasn't.

Tom slept on the sofa that night, never really falling asleep. He didn't want to lose Lisa. She was everything to him. Why didn't she know that? He knew he had put his work before her, but it wasn't because he didn't love her. He lay there drowning in a flood of memories. He thought of her teasing him about being a "ghost husband," and he now realized she had been serious and was never teasing at all. The night she put the inflatable man in their bed, he had viewed it as an erotic invitation for sex. Only now did he realize that what she really wanted was more of him. He desperately wanted to go back to that night, but not just to have sex. He wanted to make love to her.

Tom rose early the next morning and made a phone call.

The sun had not risen, but Tom knew that Buck would already be awake. When Buck answered the phone, Tom told him that his marriage to Lisa was in trouble and he needed immediate help. Buck suggested they meet in his office that morning to figure it out.

After the boys left for school, Tom made coffee for Lisa and carried it to the bedroom door. He knocked lightly. There was no answer. The knob was unlocked, so he turned the handle and entered. After all, it was his bedroom—at least it was the day before yesterday.

Lisa was propped up in bed, just sitting there.

"I'm sorry," he said. "I knocked and there wasn't an answer."

All she did was nod. Her face was as still as stone.

Tom set the coffee cup on the nightstand next to her. She raised her head slowly, and he could see a tear running down her cheek. He sat on the edge of the bed and reached to wipe it dry. She didn't push him away.

"I love you," he said in a very soft voice. She sat there and didn't respond. Tom continued, "I don't want to lose you. I called Reverend Buck this morning and asked if we could see him. I've left a message at my office that I won't be in to work this morning. Will you go?"

Lisa couldn't believe that Tom had cancelled his morning schedule at the busiest time of the tax year. Maybe she was important after all.

Very softly, his hand brushed across her cheek to detour another tear. He asked again, "Lisa, will you go with me?" His face was close to hers and his eyes were focused directly on hers.

She closed her eyes and simply nodded.

Tom and Lisa continued to counsel with Buck for several months. Lisa had even elected to continue counseling without Tom, to help build her own sense of self-worth. Lisa clearly was happier and full of life again.

Ultimately, Tom and his wife patched up their marriage, and Tom always credited their success to Reverend Buck. So, several years later, when Buck called Tom and asked if he and Lisa would visit First Covenant Chapel, Tom and Lisa gladly did.

With the addition of Tom's family, the congregation at First Covenant Chapel grew.

• • •

MARGARET BUZZED IN on the intercom to Ben's office. "Reverend Buck is on the phone for Tom," she announced.

Tom picked up the phone.

"Brother Tom! How's it going?" Buck's voice came through the receiver.

"I'm okay, Bob, how are you?" Tom replied with an emotionless and level tone.

Several years had passed since Tom and Lisa had patched up their marriage, and it seemed as though they had fallen into the same old rut. But now, Lisa didn't seem to mind his working late. Tom couldn't place his finger on it, but he felt that something was wrong. He had even speculated once or twice that she might be having an affair. Tom was in need of spiritual guidance, and he turned to Buck again. Buck reassured Tom that he was certain Lisa was not having an affair and that it was just Satan's way of trying to destroy their marriage. Buck told Tom not to let the Devil influence him; he needed to fight his irrational fears. Tom was uncomfortable with that thought, but he respected Buck and was thankful that he and Lisa could depend on him.

"I'm on my way in. Is the agenda for tonight's meeting finished?" Buck asked.

"The agenda's finished," Tom replied, "but, Bob," he hesitated, "I have some concerns about the numbers and how they are supposed to be presented to the congregation." Tom spoke as if he were totally drained. His voice was lifeless. Tom didn't want to trouble Buck with his problems right now. He knew that all Buck was capable of thinking about was this Member Conference. Besides, Tom didn't really want to talk right now anyway. He was happy just to focus on the numbers to keep himself distracted from his trouble with Lisa.

"Don't worry about the numbers, Tom. I have been in constant contact with Victor. He's a good Christian brother and believes in what we are doing. God provides, Tom. Keep your eyes focused on the light at the end, man."

Victor was the president of the bank where Buck had been negotiating the $8.5 million loan necessary to build the new sanctuary at First Covenant Chapel. He had known Buck for nearly fifteen years. Victor trusted Buck. The loan papers that Buck had provided were tight and the numbers looked great. That, coupled with Buck being a man of God, was enough to seal the deal on any loan.

"Well, hey, you're the boss. If you feel good, then I feel good," Tom said. He always deferred to Buck's better sense of vision, especially when it came to the Good Lord.

"How'd we do on tithing last Sunday?" Buck asked, purposely changing the subject.

"A little light, but par for this time of year," Tom answered with no emotion.

"Thanks for the info. I should be at the church in just a few." Buck hung up the phone.

The car was one of the best places to pray, as far as Buck was concerned—as long as you didn't close your eyes. He began to talk out loud.

"Gracious and loving Father, You have always provided so abundantly. I know this new church building is your will. I just don't understand why it is such a struggle. You have led me into dead end after dead end. What am I missing, God? What is it that I cannot see? I so desire to serve you. Lord, I need this Member Conference approval. I have a congregation that is beginning to grumble because nothing is happening and Lord, I'm less than a year away from having to retire. I asked that You provide for this church. Amen."

He parked his dark blue Mercedes in the parking lot on the office side of First Covenant Chapel. Two cars down, he saw the little gray Toyota that belonged to Ben Montague.

"Oh Lord," Buck said out loud, "I hope he's counseling in his office or something."

He felt guilty for feeling this way. Ben Montague was a good young man and was going to make a fine preacher, but Buck shouldn't have hired him three years ago. Reverend Montague was a true traditionalist, which was not meshing well with the new dynamic style that Buck and First Covenant Chapel had taken. Montague was also a stickler for details, and he did things exactly by the book, just like Frank Maddox. Ben Montague had become another thorn in Buck's side.

Buck glanced in his review mirror, ran his fingers through his hair, looked at his teeth and then walked into the church office.

"Hey, Marge, how's the newsletter coming?" Buck asked shyly, as he was trying to breeze through the room without being noticed.

Margaret, who was deep in concentration at her computer, said without looking up, "Don't worry, he's in his office with someone."

"That obvious, huh?" Buck asked.

Margaret was loyal to Buck. She knew he had his shortcomings, but she felt deeply that he meant well.

Buck lightly padded down the hall to his office, walked through his door and quietly closed it behind him. He rolled his head on his shoulders. His neck was killing him. As he walked over to his desk he put his hand on the back of his neck and tried to rub it to relieve some of the tension. The agenda for tonight's meeting, with all the pertinent information he had requested from Tom, was sitting on his desk. This was his final step. All the congregation had to do was approve the $8.5 million loan and the new sanctuary at First Covenant Chapel would be under way. It was just a matter of how the numbers were presented. They had plenty of members to support this building project. They had fifteen acres of land as collateral and nearly $2 million pledged to the building fund, not to mention $350,000 in cold hard cash in the bank, for this project. What else did they need? Buck sat down at his desk and stared at the paper. Leaning back in his chair, he placed his left hand on his chin and gently shook his head. *How have I gotten to this point?* he thought to himself.

It all started so simply only a mere four years ago . . .

WITHIN A FEW months of Buck's arrival at First Covenant Chapel, family and friends had come to support Buck, and attendance at Sunday worship was over sixty. The Covenant Women's Group, which had originally consisted of only Miss Mary and the three other elderly ladies, was now a small group of twelve. The ladies met every Wednesday afternoon at the parsonage to have tea with Peggy.

"You know that old oak tree in the front of the church?" Miss Mary asked. "Well, when I was a little girl, on the second Sunday of every month, we'd put up a couple of tables and the ladies would set them so beautifully with tablecloths and china plates. Everyone would bring a covered dish, and after the service, we'd all go out front and sit around and have supper together. Everyone was invited. This was the only street through town back then, so if you were passing through, you'd be passing by here. Sometimes people stopped just to see what we were doing."

"So what's your thought, should we start that again?" Julia Matthews asked.

"What a lovely idea," Peggy said. "I know Bob will think it is a great idea."

"Just yesterday, this church was practically dead. We are so thankful to you and Reverend Buck," one of the elderly ladies said to Peggy. "Without ya'll, who knows what would have happened to this church?"

"Bob is gifted," Peggy proclaimed.

"And it doesn't hurt that your husband's so handsome, either," Julia remarked, as bold as ever. "Some of the ladies have come just to see what all the hoopla is about."

Lisa Werner glared at Julia as if she had just thrown a shard of glass in her direction.

"Well, thank you Julia . . . I think," Peggy answered, with a questionable look on her face, "but, it is his heart that kept them here."

"Then we'll do a Sunday Supper next month," Miss Mary said quickly. She was old, but not too old to miss that the conversation needed to be diverted.

The meeting was running late and most of the other ladies had already left.

Peggy poured more Earl Grey for Miss Mary. Julia placed her hand over the top of her cup as she stood up. "None for me—got to run. Peggy, you'll let Reverend Buck know to announce the Sunday Supper from the pulpit. Everyone has to know. I'd say we should have sixty folks. That's a good little crowd."

"I'll take care of it," Peggy replied.

"Peggy, Miss Mary," Julia said as she pushed her chair back under the table, "it has been a delight. I'll see myself out. Enjoy the rest of the afternoon."

Julia walked to the front door and returned a little smile to Peggy and Miss Mary as she left.

Miss Mary turned back to Peggy. "She's a character, but a real blessing, too."

Peggy gave a noncommittal smile and her forehead did a little brow bounce.

Julia Matthews was in her mid-forties and had never been married. She was attractive in an unusual sort of way. She was well groomed, and her auburn hair always sported the latest trend, although it was never fitting to her age. Julia had an attractive figure and wore the very latest fashions . . . a size too small. She was very outspoken. If it was on her mind, it surely was no secret from anyone else. Julia meant well, it was just that she always had a definite opinion and felt strongly that it should immediately become everyone else's opinion as well.

"Is Bob doing okay, Peggy?" Miss Mary asked. "I mean, he just seems very tense."

"Oh yes, he's fine, Mary. Thank you so much for caring. You know, we have only been here seven months and in that time, the membership has quadrupled. And he's certain that Salem is going to start to spill over into this little community."

"It's hard to believe how things have changed," Miss Mary replied.

"And, for the most part, Bob is doing it all by himself right now. He's preacher, counselor, church administrator, music director and the janitor when need be."

"He's a good man," Miss Mary responded. "How are you doing here, Peggy?"

"I'm fine, too." There was hesitation in Peggy's voice.

"I know we haven't known each other for very long, but if you ever need somebody to talk to, my ears are about the only part of me that isn't worn out."

"*You* are an incredible lady, Mary. I think I want to be just like you when I grow up."

They both laughed.

Chapter Three

BUCK LOVED THE idea of a Sunday Supper. "What a marketing idea! We can make a banner and hang it out front: EVERYONE WELCOME! This might be the first of our newly formed committees. Miss Mary should chair it," Buck said with certain enthusiasm.

Peggy understood the excitement in her husband's voice. "The people at First Covenant are happy, Bob," she replied.

"When God shuts a door, He opens a window!" He couldn't remember who said that quote, but it was a good one. "Peggy, since we have been here, there have been three new subdivisions started down the street. God is preparing us for the boom that is about to happen here."

"You know, it's your birthday next week." She tried to change the subject.

Buck continued with his own train of thought. "I was next door visiting with Edward yesterday. He's looking for someone to help him mow his property. He says it's just gotten too hard for him to keep up with."

"You'll be sixty-six years old," Peggy said.

He walked over to the window and pointed past the pond. "You see all that property back there? There's fifteen acres that back up to the church property. Did you know that Edward owns that?"

"All the kids are coming for supper. Is there anything special you'd like?"

"Peggy, did you hear me?" Buck asked his wife.

She wondered if he had heard her.

"I have an idea," Buck said. "I know that with my gifts and grace, in no time we are going to outgrow this little chapel. We could use that property to build a bigger sanctuary."

Peggy wondered if her husband knew what he was saying. "Bob, the church doesn't own Edward's property. Edward owns Edward's property."

"Oh, Peggy," he said with irritation in his voice, "Edward is eighty-three years old and has as much money as he could possibly use. He doesn't need that property."

"But you're missing the point," she said with frustration. "It's still Edward's property."

"He could use the tax write-off," Buck replied. "Edward can tithe it to First Covenant Chapel . . . in his wife's memory."

She wondered if her husband realized that no one else in the church had talked about building a new sanctuary. And had he forgotten that only several months ago the plan was to close the doors of this church? She might understand what she was hearing, but she didn't know if she liked it. "Does Edward know about this?"

"I'm going to talk to him tomorrow," Buck said in a more than confident voice.

Chapter Four

HE SAT DOWN in his leather wing chair and picked up the telephone. "Edward, Bob Buck here."

"How's it going, Rev?" Edward replied in his deep voice with a Southern twang.

"Well, the Lord's been good to me today, Edward. He's given me some time off for good behavior. Thought you might like some company."

"That would be a mighty fine treat. And you did say the sunset was prettier from my side of the pond. Come on over. I'll pour us some Scotch."

"With an offer like that, I'll have to hurry. Be over in a minute," Buck said, and then he hung up the phone.

He stuck his head in the kitchen. Peggy was working on supper. "Smells good in here."

"It will be ready at seven," Peggy replied, looking over her shoulder at her husband.

"I'm going over to Edward's. I'll be back before then."

"Bob?" Peggy said with fleeting hesitation.

"Yes?" he replied.

"Oh, never mind, I know you always do the right thing," she said. Or at least he always did what he wanted, and nothing she said would really make a difference anyway.

HE WALKED OUT onto the front porch and looked over his right shoulder where First Covenant Chapel stood as if it were calling to him. Then he turned left and headed toward Edward's house. Fall was just around the corner. Although the South is still hot in September, there was something you could feel brewing in the air that let you know fall was on the way. There's one good thing about the country: nothing is closer to you than an acre's distance, which meant if you were walking, it gave you time to pray.

Father God,

I see, now, a plan unfolding. Thank you for the many opportunities that you have provided to me, and thank you for finding me worthy. You are my strength and energy. Please be with me during my visit with Edward. Please choose my words for me, so that I can help him to understand how important his land could be to First Covenant Chapel. Just imagine, Lord, how many of your children we could bring into this little church if we just had a larger building. I know how that would please you, Lord. Please help me in achieving that. Oh yes, and please give many blessings to Edward, too. Amen.

He walked up the front steps, pushed the doorbell and opened the door before there was an answer. *Good friends don't stand on ceremony,* he thought.

"Edward?" Buck called out.

"Come on in, Reverend," Edward called from the back of the house.

Buck walked back to the sunny room in the back of the house. "Perfect timing. Look at the sun." Buck motioned toward the window where the sun was setting across the pond. "If everyone would look at a sunset and see it as a gift from God, what a different place the world would be," Buck said.

"Amen, Reverend. Here's your Scotch." Edward reached his hand toward Buck. He took the glass and sat down in the peach colored, crushed velvet Lazy Boy next to the window.

"How about a cigar?" Edward held out a box of his finest, each in an individual light blue tube.

"Brother Edward, it wouldn't be a visit without one." Buck reached into the box and took one out.

They both sat back and quietly enjoyed the sunset. When all that remained was the rosy glow over the horizon, Buck swiveled his chair back toward Edward. "Tell me something new about Beverly. Something you've never told me before."

"Ah, Reverend," Edward let out a sigh, "you have no idea what it is like when you've been married to someone for what seems like all of your life, and then you lose them. Even the bad times, you remember as good. It may sound selfish, but you oughta start praying that you go first and not Peggy."

"I'd be lost without Peggy. I can't imagine the loneliness. And you can bet I'd never have matching socks again!" Buck laughed.

Edward laughed, too. Smiling, he said, "You reckon that's why all the young fellas quit wearing socks with their loafers? In preparation?" They both laughed, knowing there had to be a logical reason why the younger generation of men had quit wearing socks.

"I keep hearing that Beverly was a very important lady over at First Covenant Chapel," Buck said.

"She loved that church. She taught Sunday school there for over thirty years. And she used to sing in the choir. She had such a beautiful singing voice," Edward said while staring out the window.

"Edward," Buck said suddenly, as if he had just had an epiphany, "I just had an incredible idea! Would you like to have Beverly's memory live on in the church?"

Edward looked at Buck with a questioning face. "What do you mean?"

"Well, you know how just the other day you were telling me about how difficult it was for you to take care of that property of yours that wraps around the back side of the First Covenant Chapel? What if you donated it to the church? In Beverly's memory. I have had a vision, and I know that one day soon we are going to have to build a larger sanctuary, and we can dedicate the building to her. We'll put a big plaque outside that says: 'In loving memory of Beverly Tarken, who dedicated her life to First Covenant Chapel.'"

"Well, I don't know. That's an awfully big thing. I mean, I never thought of such a thing." Edward seemed a little distressed at the request.

"You just pray about it, Edward," Buck said with confidence. "The Good Lord won't let you down. He'll always let you know what to do."

The two men sat in silence and finished their cigars and Scotch.

"Well, Peggy's waiting with dinner. I guess I should head on back home." Buck stood up. "Thanks for the Scotch and cigar." He began to walk toward the door. "Oh yes, and thanks for the sunset!"

Chapter Five

"THIS IS THE day that the Lord has made. Let us rejoice and be glad in it!" Buck looked out at his congregation, and there must have been sixty faces. Family had brought family; friends had brought friends. News of the rebirth of the little white clapboard church in the country was spreading in the community. Neighbors from the newly developed subdivisions down the road were stopping by to visit. *Unbelievable!* Buck thought to himself. And Miss Mary still looked like the Queen of England in her Sunday hat.

"God is incredibly faithful. He doth provide. I look around this morning and I am so thankful for all the faces here." Buck spoke directly to his congregation, and it seemed he was able to make eye contact with each person at the very same moment.

"Blessings to all of you, and an especially warm welcome to those of you that are visiting with us for the first time. We hope that you experience the love and presence of The Lord, Jesus Christ." Buck continued, "There is a red and white card in the back of each pew that says 'Visitor.' Please fill out the bottom half of the card, tear it off from the nametag and drop it in the offering plate—along with your offering—as the plate goes by."

He smiled. "We have a lot of things going on in the church right now. Please read about them in the bulletin, but I want to make a special mention that next Sunday is the second Sunday of the month and we are starting a new tradition of Sunday Supper. Everyone bring a covered dish and a friend, and we will all 'break bread' together after the service, right here in front of the church under the old oak tree. If you need more information, call Miss Mary. Now, please turn your hymnal to number 223 and stand as we sing 'How Great Thou Art.'"

As the congregation stood, Buck moved over to the side of the pulpit. In the window, he caught a reflection of himself and he smiled back at it, full of joy, as the music rang out.

O Lord my God!
When I in awesome wonder
Consider all the worlds thy hands have made,
I see the stars, I hear the rolling thunder,
Thy power throughout the universe displayed.
Then sings my soul, my Savior God to thee;
How great thou art, how great thou art!
Then sings my soul, my Savior God to thee;
How great thou art, how great thou art!

As the congregation recessed after the service, Buck shook hands, hugged ladies an kissed the cheeks of little children.

"Fine service today, Reverend," said Doug Miles.

"Well, I couldn't do it without all of you!" They both laughed.

"Dad, we're all going to lunch. Are you coming?" asked Bobby, the Bucks' eldest son.

Buck slapped his grandson, Tyler, on the back, who turned and said, "Come on, Grandpa, you never come."

"I can't today. But we'll all be together on Tuesday. Grandma seems to be planning some big wing-ding for my birthday dinner. I'm looking forward to it." Buck winked at his grandson and then turned to Bobby. "Bobby, can you believe how many people we had here today?"

"Dad, I have never questioned your ability to evangelize! Watch out, Uriah Jonah!" Bobby was one of his dad's best cheerleaders.

Buck thought for a moment about Uriah Jonah. He privately dreamed that one day, First Covenant Chapel would be as big as Spring Rock Church. Then what would Frank Maddox say? He could finally prove that his "unconventional ways" weren't so bad after all.

"Reverend, you looked at little lost there," Edward Tarken said, breaking into Buck's thought process. "Enjoyed the sermon. I've been praying about what you asked me the other day."

"God is always faithful to answer prayers. Now, I'll be praying that He tells you 'yes!'" Buck smiled as if he were kidding.

"You have a good day, Reverend."

"You too, Edward. I'll see you across the field."

The last of the congregation had gone. Buck turned around and looked at the little white clapboard church. *Yes, indeed,* he thought to himself, *when God shuts a door, He opens a window. Who did say that?*

Chapter Six

BUCK STROLLED IN late. He carried guilt with him on nights like these. Quietly, he opened the bedroom door and peered in where Peggy lay facing the opposite direction. He could hear her breathing. She appeared to be asleep.

A pastor's time is never his own. When someone calls, it is his job to go. Peggy never questioned him and never seemed to doubt his faithfulness to God—or her. But he did need some time to himself every once in a while, and because a pastor's hours are not scheduled, he was able to steal that time without anyone suspecting.

Buck walked to the bathroom and took off his shirt. Looking in the mirror, he saw a face that he sometimes didn't recognize. He lifted his shirt to his nose and smelled it, then turned and threw it in the laundry hamper.

The day had been long, and he felt as if he had a film of filth covering his body. He needed to wash it away. Turning on the shower, he stared aimlessly as the water heated. He stepped in, hung his head and let the water fall down around his entire body, first hitting the top of his head and then washing across his face and rolling down his body. He was staring at the tiles on the shower floor, noticing the cracks in the grout that had come with age. Streams of water flowed off his body and he watched, foggy-headed, as it hit the tiles and washed down the drain forever.

He toweled himself off very methodically, as if there was a certain beginning and end to this process. Creeping into the bedroom, he quietly opened the dresser drawer and reached for a clean pair of boxer shorts. He stepped into them and climbed in bed next to his wife, leaving a space between them. He wouldn't kiss her, not tonight. He didn't want to disturb her.

Chapter Seven

DAVID BUCK WALKED into his dad's office on Monday morning. Another man followed behind him. David, the youngest son of Bob and Peggy Buck, was twenty-eight years old and as good-looking at his father. He stood six feet tall and had the same bright blue eyes that all the Buck men had and knew were a definite asset. "Dad, this is Ashley March, the man I have been telling you about."

Buck extended his hand. "A pleasure to meet you, Brother Ashley."

"A pleasure," Ashley said in a strong, but delicate voice. Ashley was about thirty years old and a striking man. He was well-groomed with very short blonde hair. He had fine features and was very well-tanned. He was wearing blue pants of a color somewhere between turquoise and navy, a shirt with wide horizontal stripes that looked like sailor garb and Italian slip-on shoes of black leather with no socks.

David and Ashley had met at the advertising agency where David worked writing jingles for commercials. Ashley had come to audition for work. They were both extremely gifted in music.

"Dad, Ashley has awesome musical talent and is a good Christian brother. He may be interested in helping out here at First Covenant Chapel."

"We can always use good talent and help," Buck said. "Sit down, let's talk."

"David has been proudly reporting to me everything that has happened in your church over the last seven months." Ashley spoke purposefully and meticulously. He pronounced every 't' hard. "I grew up in the Baptist church. Believe me, I know what the Lord can do. I understand you have about fifty members now."

"We had about sixty in attendance yesterday," Buck replied.

"So, how's your choir?" Ashley asked.

"I guess you could call it unimpressive." Buck gave a half grin. "We don't have one."

"Fifty, and no choir," Ashley said with surprise.

"Sixty," Buck corrected him. "Well, you have to understand, just months ago we weren't sure if this church was even going to be able to keep the doors open." He gave the impression that it was his job to resuscitate the church rather than close it.

"So what have you been doing for music?" Ashley asked.

"David's been leading the hymns."

"Yes, David told me he was," Ashley said in a very matter-of-fact tone. "I'd be interested in getting a choir started for you."

"What an answer to a prayer!" Buck said with a sort of "touchdown" expression. But Buck wasn't ready to start diving into the budget; money was still a little iffy. "We don't have any money, though. Would you do it as a service to the Lord?"

Ashley shifted in his chair and crossed his left leg over his right, his hands rested elegantly on the armrests of the chair. "Well, Brother Buck, we can build this church together and talk about money later."

"Then, it's a done deal." Buck and Ashley shook on it.

"Ashley and I have been talking about the direction we need to take the music," David said. "Dad, you and I have been talking about the city of Salem moving in this direction. That's a young demographic. We think we need to start moving into the contemporary music."

"The biggest church in the area is Spring Rock Church. Uriah Jonah pulls them in with the flash and the hip-hop," Ashley added.

Buck looked somber. "Have you been over to Uriah Jonah's church?"

"I've gone a couple of times," Ashley replied.

"What's the hoopla?" Buck asked.

"It's nothing we can't do," Ashley answered. "People nowadays want to be entertained. You have to give the people what they want. You know—big songs, big screen, big worship, big building."

"Well, church still needs to be church," said Buck, "doesn't it?"

"We can keep it reverent, but we've got to compete," Ashley came back.

"It's still church, Dad," David added. "It's just presented in a more exciting way."

"David's right, the old way of church is drab and boring. If we're going to keep up with the crowd, we've got to present the 'New Feel-Good God.'" Ashley was swaying both his hands with dramatic emotion. "When people leave feeling energized, they come back for more."

"And that's good for business!" Buck cut in. "I understand the idea, and for the most part, I like it. I will grant my blessings on moving in that direction, but we need to go slowly and carefully. We don't want to run anybody off, especially some of our older members—so take it slow."

The men continued to talk and discuss ideas and changes for the little church for over an hour. Buck was certain that God had handpicked Ashley and brought him here. Ever since Buck had come to First Covenant Chapel, he had felt like he had been flying by the seat of his pants, but now he felt sure he was soaring.

"We're having a potluck meal after the service next Sunday. We're calling it Sunday Supper. Come then," Buck said to Ashley. "It will be a great time of fellowship and you can start meeting the folks."

Ashley stood up and smoothed his hands down his hips. "Brother Buck, we'll be hearing the angels sing the 'Hallelujah Chorus' in no time." His hands were as purposeful as his speech.

Chapter Eight

IT WAS TUESDAY morning, his sixty-sixth birthday. Buck didn't feel a day over twenty-five. He looked into the mirror. "I look pretty darn good. Thank you, Lord," he said out loud. He put on his old shorts and a well-worn blue t-shirt that had a tear in the seam of the left shoulder.

Birthday or not, it was Tuesday morning, and that meant one thing. It was time to cut the grass. In the South, cutting grass was a chore that continued through the first of November. On his way to the garage he stopped for a moment at his old leather wing chair and picked up his well-worn copy of Oswald Chamber's *My Utmost for His Highest.* He rubbed his hand across the front cover and reminded himself of what that title meant. He flipped to today's date and he let himself fall to the edge of his chair as he began to read. He had read this page, on this day, every year for the last forty years. Then he closed the book and held it between the palms of his hands and prayed.

Lord God,
How grateful I am to have the gift of another year. Thank you for the many blessings You have given to me. Please

stay close to me throughout the day, protect me and guide me. In Your Holy Name, I pray. Amen.

He set the book on the table and headed toward the laundry room to get his grass-stained tennis shoes. As he passed the kitchen, the aroma of a bakery pulled him off track. He detoured through the kitchen to where Peggy was standing at the sink, scrubbing potatoes. "It smells incredible in here! If I had known turning sixty-six would get me this kind of cooking, I would have done it sooner." He kissed the back of Peggy's neck.

"Remember, sixty-seven is only a year away!" said Peggy. She smiled at him as he walked out the door.

He cut the grass in his usual criss-cross pattern, giving it that checkerboard effect he prized. As always, he used grass cutting time to think about his next sermon. He had decided he would preach on "being a joyful giver" next Sunday. When he finished with the lawn he put the mower away in the little shed and headed back to the house. He opened the refrigerator, grabbed a lite beer and headed for his leather wing chair.

"Katrina called while you were out," Peggy said as he walked by.

It took him by surprise. *Did she remember today was his birthday,* he wondered? "Oh, did she say what she wanted?" he asked his wife.

"Just that she had something she wanted to discuss with you. She did say that she has taken the position as secretary to Don Russell, the district superintendent. She starts next Monday."

"That's wonderful. I'll call her later," he said as he started to walk off.

"Do you want her number?" Peggy asked, wondering why he didn't seem to need it.

"Oh, yes, I guess I should have that." He took the small piece of paper from his wife's hand and stuck it in his pocket, trying to act nonchalant.

His mind was no longer focused on relaxing in his leather

wing chair, and he walked straight into the bathroom carrying his lite beer with him. He closed the door behind him, walked over to the vanity and stared at himself in the mirror. *What could Katrina want?* he thought to himself. Warmth ran through his body. It had been over a year since they had spoken, just before he left Holy Oak United Covenant Church. He turned the cold water on in the shower, then barely a little hot, and got in. He showered quickly; he was anxious to get on his way so he could return Katrina's call.

• • •

"I'LL BE HOME around six," Buck said to his wife in an overly calm voice.

Peggy was frosting his birthday cake. "The kids will be here by then. Don't be late."

"No, I won't," he said.

"Don't forget to call Katrina," she reminded him.

"Oh, thank you, I almost forgot. I'll call her from the car," he replied.

When he got in the car, he easily pressed Katrina's number into the phone—some things a man never forgets—then put the car in drive and headed on his way.

"Hello?" Her voice was soft.

"Trina, it's Bob. Peggy gave me a message that you called."

"How are you, Bob?" she asked.

"Can't complain," he answered. "How about you?"

"I can't complain, either," she said.

There was a slight lull in the conversation, and then Buck said, "Heard you're going to be working for the District Superintendent."

"News travels fast," she said.

"Well, this is good news for me," Buck replied. "Now when I need help from up on high, I can call on my old, faithful friend."

"Are you calling me old?" she said with a slight flirt in her tone of voice.

"Oh, no ma'am, as far as I know you're not a day over

twenty-three, just like the first day I saw you," Buck said with sweet sarcasm in his voice.

Katrina changed the subject. "I heard your church is growing."

"It's a miracle!" Buck said with jest.

"I doubt it's a miracle, I'm sure you've worked hard for it," she replied.

"I suppose I have," Buck said and then changed the subject. "What can I help you with, woman?"

"I was hoping maybe you'd do me a favor. For old times' sake." Her voice became serious.

"I'll do what I can. Shoot," he replied.

"You know my son, Ben, has been in seminary," Katrina began.

"Yes, how's he doing?" Buck questioned.

"He's doing great," she replied. "He's a third year student now, and he's looking for a student appointment. I would love to have him learn under you. Could you use him?"

Buck could use an associate pastor, and he knew student appointments were cheap. "I was always fond of Ben. I remember the day I baptized him. His little face stared at mine and there was something unspoken. I knew he would be a man of God."

"Yes, he's a good kid. I'm proud of him."

"Well Trina, I hardly think you can call him a kid. How old is he now? Isn't he the same age as Bobby? Thirty-three? As I recall, Ben was born three months after Bobby, right?"

"I suppose you're right, Bob, he is a man. But, he's still my son, and I am very proud of him."

"You've been a good mother, Trina. It's not easy raising a child alone, and you've done a beautiful job."

"Thank you," she said in a somber tone.

"Have you ever heard from Stuart again?" Buck asked.

"No, I never have," she replied.

"I have never understood how a man could leave his wife, knowing that she was pregnant."

"Yeah, well that's life, Bob. We move on. How about Ben?

Can you help him?" Katrina was tiring of the small talk and especially didn't want to talk about her ex-husband with Buck.

"Well, what a compliment. I'm honored. Let me lay the groundwork with a couple of the members of my church and let you know tomorrow?"

"That's fine."

"I do have one important question. Does Ben want to come to First Covenant Chapel?" Buck asked.

"I told him it would be good for him. I want him to learn the truth, and it's better to learn the ropes from the bottom up."

Buck took offense to the statement, which implied that he was the bottom, but he knew Katrina didn't mean it in a negative way. He responded with his usual form of positive attitude. "That's for sure!" Then he paused for a moment. "So, is everything going alright with you?"

"It's fine. Thanks for asking, Bob," she responded.

"Anytime, I'm always here," he said in a gentle voice.

"Thanks. Well, I'll talk to you tomorrow. And, by the way, Bob . . ."

"Yes?"

"Happy Birthday." Her soft sweet voice was music to his ears. It sounded the exact same as the first year she told him "Happy Birthday." He couldn't believe that was over thirty-five years ago.

When he hung up the phone, he had already reached the Dixie Diner. He stuck his cell phone in his pocket and hurried in to meet with Tom.

"Brother Tom" was Buck's usual start to almost any conversation. "What's doing?"

Tom was already sitting in their usual booth at the Dixie Diner in downtown Salem. It was close to Tom's office, and it was a favorite of all the old timers, before it became a big city. Some of the *nouveau riche* had started frequenting it as well.

Their usual booth was in the south corner by the window, which was dressed with blue and white café curtains. They met for lunch every Tuesday to go over the church's financial state.

Tom and Buck were the only two in the church with any knowledge about the finances.

"I ordered your usual tuna salad on toast. Hope that's okay," Tom said.

"Tom, you take good care of me, brother. So how do we stand?" Buck asked, getting straight to the point of the meeting.

"Things are good, Bob," replied Tom. "It's unbelievable what is happening at this little church. Tithing is up by forty-five percent over last month. That's unheard of!"

"God will provide, God will provide!" As always, Buck said this with enthusiasm.

"You know that, Bob, but it still catches us lay folk a little off guard. So, I guess you'd better thank Him for us," Tom said.

"You know I do, brother!" Buck said with his politician voice. "Listen, I've got two great things to share with you."

Tom looked at him with curiosity.

Buck continued, "I have two people that want to come and serve at this church. It's unbelievable! This church is anointed; don't you know it?"

"Reverend Buck, you're anointed. When you helped save my marriage, I knew that God was using you for incredible things. You don't have to convince me. I'm a believer!" Tom said with gratefulness.

"Blessings on you!" answered Buck. "Anyway, David brought a fellow to see me today. Ashley March—quite a musical talent. He feels led to serve First Covenant Chapel in music ministry."

"That's awesome!" Tom responded.

"But, that's not all. The District Superintendent's secretary called today." It sounded better than saying his "old secretary." "Her son is a seminary student and looking for a student pastor position, and she wanted to know if I would take him under my wing."

"Well, what did you say?" Tom asked.

"I told her I would be honored to," Buck replied. His chest

was puffed up. "I just wanted to run it by you first before I told her yes."

"This sounds like a great opportunity for us," Tom said with excitement.

"It is," replied Buck, "and student pastors are cheap. But, I have to go through the 'higher-ups' on this one, so there are some guidelines I need to follow."

"What do we have to do?" Tom asked. He always backed Buck on everything.

"Well, he'll have to be paid a salary. Can we afford it?"

"How much are we talking?"

"We can probably get by with eighteen grand a year," Buck said with a smile as he leaned back in the booth, signifying he had just scored big.

"What about the other fellow, Ashley March?" Tom asked.

"Oh, no," Buck said with the same tone, "I convinced him to serve as a volunteer. We've got him for service to the Lord alone."

Tom gave a little chuckle of amazement. "Either you are really lucky, Bob, or you're right—the Lord does provide."

"Sometimes I like to think that it's a little of both," Buck responded, not sounding a bit modest.

The waitress came over with the tuna salad on toast and turkey club sandwich and placed them in front of the men. "Can I get you gentlemen anything else?"

"Well, Cindy," said Buck, as he took her hand in his, "you could say Grace for us." Her hand was soft in his. Cindy had been waiting on Tom and Buck every Tuesday for the last six months. She was a single mom in her mid-thirties. She was attractive in a harsh sort of way, but her eyes were sweet and kind. What Buck liked most about her was the bright red lipstick she always wore. Every Tuesday, they took turns saying Grace.

"Reverend Buck, I said it last week. It's your turn this week. What are you trying to do, pass the buck?" She smiled at him with a half crooked smile of which some people might question the meaning. He smiled back.

"Let's bow our heads," said Buck.

"Holy and Gracious Father, thank You for the food that You provide to us. We ask that it nourish our bodies so we may use them for service unto You. Amen."

Buck purposefully squeezed Cindy's hand.

"Enjoy your lunch, gentlemen," Cindy said as she walked back toward the kitchen.

Buck watched her walk away. He was attracted to her. After all, he was still a man. Buck reminded himself there were consequences in life and with that, he steered his thoughts back toward his lunch and purposely tried to think about Peggy. Peggy was a wonderful woman and the best wife for which a man could ask. Sometimes he questioned why God gave men such an overwhelming desire, when by His design it is supposed to be one man and one woman. And he already had the best there was: Peggy. *But, does it really hurt anything to notice an attractive face?* he thought to himself.

"How are things with you and Lisa?" Buck asked with a curiosity that was almost obvious.

Tom gave a half smile. "I think they are good. We've settled back into a pattern. I am much more conscientious of the amount of time I spend with her and the boys. And Lisa has developed time for herself, which I think she needed." He gave a small laugh. "In fact, the tables were turned the other evening. I was home early in the evening, and Lisa didn't get home until very late."

Buck turned away to look at the crowd. They ate in silence for a moment, watching the groups of people come and go on their lunch hour.

While looking out the window, Tom asked, "Can you believe what's happened to Salem over the last year?"

"My thought exactly, Tom." Buck returned his focus to the meeting. "That's why it is so important to grab Ashley March and Ben Montague now. Salem is growing so fast that Wakefield will soon be a part of it. We need to strategically set ourselves up to handle the spiritual needs of the coming community. And we have to come up with a bigger and better plan than Uriah Jonah."

Tom looked up, but didn't say anything. He wondered what Uriah Jonah had to do with anything. There was another pause in the conversation. They continued to eat and watch the crowd.

"You know, the district office was not expecting First Covenant Chapel to still be open," Buck said, "but they underestimated me. We are still open, and we have a solid sixty members in less than a year."

If Frank Maddox thought he was going to push Buck into ending his career at some shriveled up old church, he was wrong. Buck knew the gifts he had, and it was going to take a lot more than some pious elder that out-ranked him to stop him.

Buck was tense, his shoulders tight. He tried to relax the tension by stretching his neck to the right and then to the left. "I've got annual reports due, and I don't even have a church council," Buck said. "We need to meet with some of the others."

"I'm right here behind you, Bob," Tom said. "What do we need to do?"

"We'll meet after the service next Sunday," Buck replied in a matter-of-fact way.

Buck stuck his napkin under the right side of his plate. "Is the church paying for this one, Brother Tom?"

"Every Tuesday's on the house," Tom reminded him.

"Blessings to you, brother." Buck stood up. "Ashley March is coming to the Sunday Supper. I'll call Ben Montague and ask him to come, too."

He turned and walked toward the door, leaving Tom to pay the bill. He smiled and made small waving gestures to the other patrons as he went.

Buck drove back to the office, detouring through some of the new subdivisions of homes that cost $200,000 and more. He saw this as a promise of new members to the church. The day was beautiful, and he was basking in the glory of all the good things to come. Yes, indeed, God had big plans for him and he knew it.

Buck picked up his cell phone and dialed.

"Hello?" Katrina's voice was soft as always.

"Hi, Trina," he said in a slow, deep voice.

"Bob," she said with surprise, "that was quick. It's not even tomorrow."

"I met with my church council after we spoke." Which wasn't really a lie; Tom would be part of the council when they formed it. And he knew he needed to form one quickly. "They all felt that Ben was an answer to prayer, ordained by God," Buck continued. "They gave me the go ahead to hire Ben on the spot."

"Wonderful!" Katrina said with excitement.

"I don't have Ben's phone number. Thought I'd get it from you," Buck said.

She gave him the number.

"Thanks, Bob. This means more than you know," Katrina said. Then she added, "For both of you."

"Yes," Buck responded, "I do believe this will benefit both of us."

There was a silence on the phone. Bob wanted to say something, but he wasn't really sure what it would be.

Chapter Nine

"HAPPY BIRTHDAY, GRANDPA! Don't let the old bedbugs bite tonight," shouted Mandy, the Bucks' youngest grandchild, as her daddy carried her to the car. Peggy and Bob stood on the front porch of the parsonage and waved goodbye to their children and grandchildren. His birthday celebration was coming to a close; it had been grand as usual. He watched little Mandy with her head on her daddy's shoulder. Ringlets of brown hair spilled down her back. Buck felt sad for a moment. Where had the time gone? It seemed like just yesterday he was carrying his own little girl, who was now Mandy's mother. He barely could remember the time in between then and now. For a moment he felt strangely removed from the scene, as if he were watching it from a far away place.

"Did you enjoy the evening?" Peggy said.

The chirp of the crickets was loud tonight, and although he sensed the murmur of Peggy's voice, he hadn't heard it.

She stepped closer to Buck and slid her arm behind his, locking their elbows together. She was warm and her touch got his attention. He turned and looked at her, and smiled.

"Did you enjoy the evening?" she asked again.

"It was fabulous, as usual," Buck replied. "You always make

me feel special." He moved his arm away from hers, placed it around her shoulder and led her to the front porch swing, where they sat silently and rocked for a moment, her head cradled into the crook of his neck.

"Did you talk with Katrina today?" she asked.

He didn't know why her question made him uneasy, but it did. He shifted his position, causing her to lift her head.

"Yes." His answer was blunt, and he said nothing else.

Peggy was still for a few moments, expecting further response, but obviously he felt his answer was a complete statement.

"Is that it?" Peggy asked, staring directly at his eyes, which were focused off in the distance.

"Is what it?" he said softly.

"Yes." Peggy said with a slight sharpness in her voice. "What I actually wanted to know was *why* Katrina called."

"Oh, I'm sorry sweetheart." Buck's voice was innocent and patronizing. "Her son, Ben, is a seminary student and looking for a student pastor position."

Peggy's eyes widened. "Ben?" she said. She placed her head back into the crook of his neck and stared off into the darkness of the night. "What did you tell her?" she asked.

"That I would consider it." He didn't want his wife to know he had jumped on the opportunity.

Chapter Ten

"MISS MARY, YOU have outdone the Colonel! This fried chicken is the best I've ever had!" Tom said while leaning against the old oak tree, whose branches reached out and created a green canopy of shade over the tables.

Buck, standing there too, with a drumstick in his hand, said, "Woman, indeed, you have outdone yourself. This Sunday Supper is a hit. And it's now a tradition. The second Sunday of every month will be Sunday Supper, thanks to you."

Miss Mary smiled. They all looked around. It was a sight of red and white-checkered tablecloths flapping in the breeze, children chasing each other and people smiling and laughing. Peggy was sitting with a group of ladies planning a mid-week Bible study, and the dessert table was an unbelievable sight. There were peach and apples pies, chocolate layer cake and lemon pound cake, and some of the softest, chewiest, melt-in-your-mouth chocolate chip cookies that you have ever tasted.

Carrying a plastic cup of sweet iced tea, Julia Matthews joined Peggy and the other ladies sitting at the table. She slowly leaned toward the lady to her right, and with a sly eye looking toward Ashley March, Julia said in a low voice, "He sure is a pretty boy, don't you think?"

"I think he's cute," the lady replied.

Overhearing the conversation, Susan piped in. "Who are you talking about? The new guy?"

"Which new guy," another lady asked, "Ashley or Ben?"

"They are both a sight for sore eyes," Julia said, "but there's something curious about Ashley. Those Italian slip-on shoes have a hidden agenda."

"Hidden agenda? They are shoes, for Pete's sake," Susan came back.

"Those shoes don't procreate," Julia said with a definite tone. She had everyone at the table listening to the conversation now. "There are three ways to judge a man on his character: by his shoes, his watch and his wallet."

There was a stillness that came from confusion. The ladies looked at each other inquisitively.

Susan picked up her iced tea and took a sip. She set it back on the table. "That's an interesting concept," Susan said with sarcasm, "but I'm not sure I fully grasp your drift."

Julia began to explain. "I have three rules before I will go out with a man. Number one, never date a man who wears a digital watch; number two, never date a man who carries a wallet that has Velcro on it; and number three, never date a man who wears clogs, or any other style of shoe that your sister might wear. Tennis shoes are an exception."

There was probably a reason why Julia Matthews had never married.

"Bob says that Ashley is blessed with musical talent," Peggy said, knowing she needed to create a diversion.

"I was talking with David earlier, and he said that Ashley was going to introduce some of the new contemporary music into our service," Susan commented.

"Bob feels that more upbeat music will bring in more of the younger crowd that is moving into the area," Peggy said.

"So, what's the deal with this Ben Montague?" Julia asked.

"Oh, Ben is a wonderful young man," Peggy said. "Bob and I have known him since he was born. His mother, Katrina, was Bob's secretary at his very first appointment."

"So, is he going to be our associate pastor?" another lady inquired.

"Yes, well, technically he is a student pastor," Peggy explained. "He is still in seminary."

"Now, he's a looker!" Julia proclaimed.

"Do his shoes meet your approval?" Susan asked with a jovial tone.

"Black leather lace-ups. Now that's a man's shoe! Haven't seen his wallet or his watch yet, but I'll bet you they follow suit," Julia said with excitement.

The ladies at the table giggled.

"Is he married?" one of the ladies asked.

"He's not. I already checked," Julia replied.

"He's ten years younger than you are," Susan was quick to say, directing her statement toward Julia.

Julia slowly turned her head and looked at Susan with threatening eyes. "And your point?"

IT WAS A lovely afternoon with the slightest bit of breeze blowing. Tom and Buck were still under the oak tree making small talk with Miss Mary and Ashley March, who had joined them.

"You know, Reverend Buck," Miss Mary said in her usual sweet voice, "we are forever indebted to you for what you have done here. I can barely stand to think what would have happened to this little church if it weren't for you."

If only Frank Maddox could have been here to hear that statement, Buck thought to himself. "Miss Mary," he said with a charming accent, "you flatter me. I am nothing but merely a servant of The Lord." As he spoke, his eyes focused beyond Miss Mary on Lisa Werner, Tom's wife, who was talking to a gentleman that was visiting the church for the first time that day. Buck noticed that the gentleman was young and attractive. His first thought was that their conversation appeared a little too friendly, and it bothered him. Then he thought about Tom, who was standing next to him.

"And I personally thank you." Miss Mary smiled. She was quite an elegant lady. She had grown up right here in

Wakefield, which, eighty years ago, was deep country. However, she was certainly refined for a country girl.

"Well, you just keep me in mind when you decide to sell that dark blue Mercedes of yours. You could cut me a good deal." Air blew through Buck's nose as he let out a small laugh, to let her think that he was kidding. *But it sure would be nice to have that car,* he thought to himself. "Miss Mary, would you please excuse us?" Buck asked. "Ashley, Tom and I have some things to discuss." Miss Mary smiled graciously and gave a modest but deliberate nod.

The men walked over to a table where Edward Tarken, David Buck and Michael Gillard, the Bucks' son-in-law, were deep in conversation. You would have thought they were planning something of monumental proportions, the way they were locked into the conversation, but it seemed to be something about a fish.

"How are my good brothers doing?" Buck interrupted. Ashley and Tom sat down. "Where's Bobby?" Buck asked. He saw his eldest son standing over at the dessert table and called to him, "Hey Bobby, come on over."

"Just a minute, Dad," Bobby answered back.

"How about Ben? Would you like for me to ask him to join us?" Michael asked.

"In just a moment," Buck answered. He knew his own agenda. "It's incredible what is happening here at First Covenant Chapel. Just look around. Edward, you were here eight months ago." He looked at the elderly gentleman, who donned a blue and white seersucker suit. "There were only seven people here. The Administrative Conference of The United Covenant Churches of America wanted this church closed. That's what I was sent to do."

The men were stunned. Even his own sons' faces showed shock. Bobby, who had come over to join them, bringing his chocolate layer cake along, was speechless.

"What do you mean, close the church?" Edward asked. His voice almost sounded angry. "Why didn't you ever tell us this?"

"I didn't say anything because we are friends," Buck

responded. "And I knew that I could keep the doors open, so I didn't say anything in order not to worry anyone."

"So what happened?" Bobby asked.

"I happened," Buck answered in a proud tone that could be defined as gloating. "God is using me to keep this church open. Not only keep it open, but grow it!" Buck was speaking with excitement. "We have sixty people here today. That's larger than some average churches. And more are on the way, I know it. God wants *me* to build this church." He placed a strong emphasis on the word "me".

"Amen," David said in a firm and steady voice. He was always a champion of his father.

"And I need you all to help," Buck continued. "The Administrative Conference is going to start asking for some accountability from this church. Up until now, we have been below the radar screen. But, we need to start giving the impression that we are making an attempt to follow the guidelines in the *United Covenant Book of Rules,* at least to the best of our abilities."

Buck shrugged his shoulders, indicating that the appearance of an attempt was all that was really needed. Buck despised the *United Covenant Book of Rules*, which is the official rule book for the United Covenant Churches of America. He felt that it was just a book full of inane rules designed by the bureaucrats of the church. But no one had ever asked his opinion, and he was willing to attempt the use of the book . . . as long as it didn't get in his way.

"We need a church council," Buck said, and then pointed at his son-in-law. "Michael, would you serve as chairman of the Board of Trustees?" It was obvious that Buck had already thought this through, and he knew who was going to be what.

"Bob," Michael said in a startled voice, "I'd be honored, but I . . . I," he stuttered, "wouldn't know what to do."

"Don't worry about that. A lot of this is red tape for the Administrative Conference. I'll be here to help you." Buck turned to look at Tom. "Tom, you've been handling our money," he said. "You'll be our treasurer. David and Bobby, you'll be the Staff-Parish Relations Committee."

"What about the fact that we're your sons?" David asked.

"Not a problem. You are also members of this church now. This is where I need you." Buck was not pausing for commentary or questions. He turned to Ashley. "Ashley, I know you're new here, but I also can see you're a team player. I'd like you to be my Lay Leader. You'll have to join the church; you can do that next Sunday. We all need to be Trustees."

Buck looked toward Edward. His emotion was calm and convincing. "Edward, I want you to have the most honored position, which is being the chairperson of my church council. You are one of the longest standing members of First Covenant Chapel, and you deserve this position."

Edward looked a little taken aback. "Why, Reverend, I don't know what to say."

"You'll say, 'YES!'" Buck told him. "Now, to make this all official, would one of you gentlemen make a motion that we accept this slate of leadership for First Covenant Chapel?"

"So moved," Michael said.

"Seconded," Bobby followed.

Buck said, "All those in favor, say 'Aye.'"

The vote was unanimous. Buck was relieved. Ever since it had become obvious that First Covenant Chapel was growing and not closing, Don Russell had been breathing down Buck's neck to institute United Covenant guidelines, and annual reports were due to the district in two weeks. Now, he had an official church council, at least as far as Buck was concerned.

Buck surveyed the fellowship. These people were becoming his flock. Indeed, he was a blessed man. He wished he could ask Frank Maddox what he would say to him now.

From the corner of his eye, he glimpsed Ben Montague talking with a group. He seemed to fit in well here. People were clearly enjoying his company.

Ben was a very academic young man, but full of personality—a rare combination. It made him perfect for the occupation of minister. His words were thoughtfully spoken, and he genuinely strove to seek God's will in everything he did. He was definitely a young man of fine character.

Now that Buck had completed his initial agenda, he called out to him, "Ben!" Buck was waving his arm in a "come here" motion. "Come on over and join us." Ben joined the circle of men sitting in white, plastic folding chairs.

"Ben," Buck continued, "I know you met most of these gentlemen earlier, but now you meet them as our church council. We were just getting ready to discuss a few things and want your input."

"Thank you," Ben said, "I am anxious to get my feet wet. Plus, my mother keeps telling me that I will learn more under Reverend Bob Buck than I could from anybody else."

Buck liked the fact that Katrina thought so highly of him. She hadn't asked Frank Maddox if her son could learn under him. *We're seeing who the better man is,* Buck thought to himself. "Your mother is a very wise woman, Ben," Buck said behind a smile.

The men were deep in discussion about church issues. Buck felt good about the group he had pulled together. This was a team effort, but it was important that all the team players were of one mind, which meant under Buck's control.

Realizing that the men didn't have any intention of breaking their conversation anytime soon, Julia Matthews headed over to interrupt. "Gentlemen," she said, announcing herself. Half the group stood up.

"Hello, woman," Buck said to Julia and then turned toward the men. "Ashley and Ben, have you all had the pleasure of meeting Julia Matthews?"

Ashley smiled and in a very soft voice said, "Hello, Julia, nice to meet you." He placed the tips of his right-hand fingers into the palm of Julia's right hand and attempted a shake. Julia considered bowing and kissing his hand, but she thought better of it.

"Nice shoes," she said to Ashley in a sarcastic tone.

Ben nodded toward Julia and said, "Yes, Ms. Matthews and

I met earlier. She delighted me with a good conversation about sanctification." He smiled.

"Well, gentlemen, I need to be going. I just wanted to come over to say goodbye and tell Ashley and Ben that I'm glad they'll be here." Julia looked straight into Ben's eyes and said, "You have lovely blue eyes. They look familiar. Have we met before?"

"I'm sure I would remember if we had, but thank you for the compliment." Ben smiled back.

Julia turned and began to walk away. She waved and called back to the group, "Enjoy the rest of your afternoon, gentlemen."

Looking at Ben, Bobby said, "Watch out for her, I've heard she has hooks."

"That doesn't scare me," Ben responded in his deep, calm voice. "Besides, I'm certain I'm not her type."

"Nobody has been able to figure out yet, what her type is," David added.

There was a pause in the conversation while the group contemplated what David said.

"I reckon I oughta be heading home," Edward said in a tired voice.

"I'll walk with you, Edward," Buck said. He stood up and turned to Ben. "Can you come by the office tomorrow morning at nine? That's when we have our weekly staff meeting. We'll get the process rolling."

"Yes, sir. I'll be there," said Ben.

Buck and Edward headed from the church, through the parking lot and across the front yard of the parsonage. The bright sunlight dappled the afternoon. The sounds of the Sunday Supper became muffled by the trees and bushes as they walked further away from the little church. They barely spoke as they continued on over to Edward's house, but good company is just fine, even in its quietness.

When they reached the front of Edward's house, he turned and looked at Buck. Buck could tell there was something on his mind. "Bob, I've been thinking about what you asked me about the property." Buck didn't want to hear what Edward might say right now, because he sensed that it wasn't what he wanted to hear.

Buck cut Edward off mid-sentence. "Don't worry about the property right now. Leave it to God." Buck lifted his right hand to his own shoulder that was aching with tension and began to rub it. He looked toward Edward with a certain pastoral face, but his eyes went over Edward's shoulder and off to the distance.

"Edward, my good brother," Buck began, "the prophet Isaiah said, 'Whether you turn to the right or to the left, your ears will hear a voice behind you saying, "This is the way; walk in it."' Meditate on those words when you're deciding what to do about the property."

"Thank you for the company on the walk home," Edward replied. "I'll think about what you said." He turned and put his right foot up on the step to the porch of his home and grabbed the railing to help pull him up. His age was getting to him. Climbing steps was not easy anymore. It was time he faced the fact that he was old. Maybe Buck was right. Maybe he should give the property to the church. *What do I need it for anyway?* Edward thought.

Buck smiled. He was wringing his hands. "Well, I better get back over to the church, to say goodbye to the rest of the folks."

Chapter Eleven

ROLLING OVER TOWARD his wife, Bob slipped his arm around Peggy's waist and curled his legs into hers. She was still asleep. He kissed the back of her shoulder; it was soft. With his fingers, he lightly stroked her arm back and forth from her shoulder to her elbow. He thanked God for giving him Peggy and thanked Him that Peggy had stayed with him all these years. Being a minister's wife is not an easy job, but Peggy did it with such dedication . . . and forgiveness. She led Bible studies and handled the prayer requests. She sang in the choir and taught Vacation Bible School. And when a late night call came from a single mother in tears, she would pray as Buck went to minister to the woman. Peggy was a very compassionate person and handled these situations well. Buck was grateful.

Peggy rolled over and faced her husband. There was a tear in her eye. Moments like these were rare. Bob was usually up by five and out the door by six-thirty. His side of the bed was usually cold, and Peggy had replaced him with an extra blanket for warmth. He placed his hand on her cheek and stroked her hair behind her ear. She was still a beautiful woman to him. Every soft line around her eyes told him of a story from their past. Many of those lines were because of him, he was sure, but she wore them well. If he could do it all over, there were so many things he would change. His heart was full for her. He softly kissed her lips, and she melted into to him . . .

"I LOVE YOU," Peggy said as she still lay next to him.

He didn't seem to hear her. "This is our town now," he replied. "There are good things getting ready to happen for First Covenant Chapel."

For a moment Peggy felt used, but she had been married to Bob for years, and she knew he loved her, too.

After he showered, he was drawn to the kitchen by the aroma of freshly brewed coffee. Coffee was Peggy's specialty.

"How about some breakfast?" Bob asked. Another rare moment. They had not had breakfast together for as long as either one could remember. He pulled the chair back from the breakfast table and sat down. His face clearly showed there was something very serious on his mind. His gaze was off in the distance. He played with the fringe on the blue and white checked placemat.

"What is it?" Peggy asked as she was pouring coffee into the cup.

His gaze was deep, and he was nowhere remotely close to being able to hear Peggy.

She turned and stared directly at him. "Hello?!" she asked. Nothing. "Bob!" she said firmly.

He looked at her. Not realizing he hadn't heard her, he said, "Is the coffee ready?" She placed the cup in front of him. He cupped the mug with his hands. "Within a year, Wakefield will be the outskirts of Salem," he blurted. She wondered if he actually thought that he had offered some conversation that led up to this statement.

Her only response was the obvious "Okay."

"Less than a year ago First Covenant Chapel had seven members and was getting ready to be terminated. Today, we have forty-five members." Then, with excitement, he said, "Peggy! I have a gift. I am reaching these people. I can grow this church. *We* can grow this church to be the largest church in this area."

Peggy had turned her back and pretended that she was wiping the counters so her husband couldn't see her face. The hope that they might ever have a chance of simply being husband and wife was gone. She had to muster a smile before she turned around.

Buck sipped his coffee, then pulled up the cuff on his sleeve and looked at his watch. "Oh my goodness! I didn't realize it was so late," he said. "No time for breakfast, I've got a staff meeting at nine." He pushed his chair back, stood up and took one more sip of his coffee. He walked over to Peggy, kissed her on the cheek and with a sly grin said, "I'll see you later . . . thanks for this morning."

Peggy didn't say a word. It wouldn't matter anyway; he wouldn't have heard it. As he walked out the door, she glanced at the clock on the microwave oven. 7:30. She turned back to the counters and kept wiping the already clean spot.

• • •

When he reached the office, it was still very early. He picked up a stack of leftover bulletins from Sunday, which were sitting on the corner of the table in the narthex, and tossed them in the trash, which was still full of styrofoam cups with traces of coffee. He walked down the aisle through the middle of the church toward the pulpit. The light green carpet was in need of a vacuum from the many people that had walked across it during the service on the previous day. He walked up to the altar and pulled a yellow daisy from the leftover arrangement and held it to his nose.

We really should start taking the leftover flowers to the hospitals and shut-ins, he thought to himself. He made a mental note to put that on the agenda. They did look pretty on the altar, though. Frank Maddox would have never allowed flowers to sit on the altar at Holy Oak United Covenant Church. Protocol stated that nothing was to sit on the altar except for that which was being offered to God, and protocol was always an issue for Maddox. That was part of what created the difficult relationship between the two men when Buck was associate pastor under him. Maddox was a "by the book" man, and Buck just didn't see the necessity of red tape.

He walked past the altar, carrying the daisy, toward the back hall that led to the church offices. He flipped the light switch in the workroom and then turned on the copier so it could warm up. Grabbing the pot from the coffeemaker, he rinsed it, filled it with cold water from the sink and poured it into the machine. He added some coffee to the paper filter and switched the machine on.

Buck headed on down the hall to his office, mindlessly flipping light switches as he went along. He stopped suddenly in the hall and focused more thoughtfully than he ever had on the portraits of the previous senior pastors that hung on the wall. They were clearly distinguished. In Buck's mind, part of what proves the success of a pastor is judged by whether or not his portrait hangs on the wall in a church somewhere. It was the highest form of a compliment. So far in his career, he still didn't have his portrait hanging anywhere; but with what he was doing at First Covenant Chapel, surely it was certain to happen soon.

He sat down at his desk, grabbed the latest copy of *The Covenant Review*—the official newspaper of the United Covenant Churches of America—and leaned back in his chair and began to read.

Margaret stuck her head in the door to Buck's office. "Everyone's here, Reverend. Would you like to join us?"

Margaret had come to visit the church about five months earlier. She and her husband had just moved into one of the new subdivisions down the street from the church. They were a young couple with no children—just the kind of people Buck needed in his church right now. Buck had asked Margaret to volunteer in the office one day a week. She hadn't found a job in Salem yet and was glad to get out of the house. One day of volunteering became two, which became three. Margaret now volunteered four days a week in the church office, and she was very valuable to Buck.

"I'm right behind you," he said, folding the paper and placing it back on his desk. He followed Margaret watching her hips closely as they moved in front of him. As he walked out of his office, he stopped for a moment to check in the mirror that hung to the right-hand side of the door. He made sure each hair was in place, checked his teeth and gave himself a big smile and a nod of approval.

Everyone was already seated around the table in the Sunday School room where they were meeting when he made his entrance. "Good Morning!" Buck said with exuberance.

"Good morning, Bob, how are you?" Tom asked.

"Can't complain," Buck responded, "but I didn't have time for coffee this morning. I made some. Would anyone else like a cup?"

"I would love some," Ben answered.

"That would be fabulous," said Ashley, stretching the word "fabulous" beyond the normal length of the word.

"None for me, thanks," came from Tom.

Buck turned toward Margaret. "Margaret, would you mind?" He smiled.

Margaret set down her pad and pen. Buck, noticeably, watched her walk out of the room.

While she was gone, the group made small talk—everyone except Buck, who was jotting notes onto a yellow legal pad.

Margaret walked back into the room carrying a copy paper box top that she was using as a makeshift tray to hold the coffee. She set it in the middle of the table.

"That's what I like, a creative woman," Buck said and then in the same breath continued, "let's bow our heads and go to the Lord in prayer."

"Gracious and Loving Father, we sit here humbled before You, as Your servants. We seek to follow Your will. Please be with us during this meeting. Help us to be productive and full of plans to expand Your ministry and grow this little church that You have called as Your own. You have ordained and anointed us with Your approval. In the name of Your Son, Jesus. Amen."

After the prayer, Buck continued to speak. "It comes to me as such a blessing that just last week, we were a staff of three: Margaret, Tom, and I. And Margaret and Tom volunteer their time and talent with such graciousness. Today, we sit here as five, most of us still volunteering. First off, I want to thank each of you from the bottom of my heart. We couldn't be doing this if not for your dedication. Believe me," he said with authority, "God will richly reward each of you." He paused for a moment and then continued. "Okay. What's on the agenda, Margaret?"

"Well, the first thing is the annual report to the district. It's due tomorrow, and I don't have numbers," she said.

"What numbers are you missing?" Buck asked.

"Pretty much all of them," Margaret said. She raised her eyebrows and lifted her hands to emphasize that she was empty-handed.

Turning in Tom's direction, Buck said, "Tom, you can give her all the financial info she needs, can't you?"

"I can do that," Tom confirmed.

"What else do you need, Marge?" Buck asked.

"I have no numbers for Sunday School attendance. The only class we have that meets regularly is the old folks' Celebration class," she answered.

"No, we have more than that, Marge," Buck said. "We can count all the folks that meet in people's homes." Buck was scratching out numbers on a piece of paper. He looked up at Margaret. "We have forty in attendance in Sunday School every week."

Margaret looked at Buck with a surprised face. "There are that many meeting in homes? There are only eight in the Celebration class."

"That number sounds very high," Ben said. "That is almost ninety-five percent of your congregation."

"We are blessed," Buck said, with a tone of finality to the conversation and an obvious irritation in his voice that Ben would question him, especially on his first day of work. Buck moved the meeting along. "Ashley, tell us what you've got planned."

Ashley stood up from his chair. His olive green pants were stiffly starched, and he wore a very tight fitting black t-shirt with a mustard colored pony and rider embroidered on the left side. His belt and slip-on shoes were an identical color. He lifted both hands so that the palms were visible to everyone sitting. "First off, I just want to say how moved I am that I have the privilege of being able to serve God at this church. What an incredible blessing. God is so amazing. If you just let Him have your life, He will make you soar."

His face transformed to a sculpture of pain as he continued. "It is so sad that so many people are lost children of God. First Covenant Chapel is in an incredibly unique position. We have the rich heritage of history with a gift of a growing community. And," he said with emphasis, "the community around us is a very young, affluent community, who, to a large extent, have made money and 'getting ahead' their god. Through a music program in this church, my goal is to save as many souls as we can."

Margaret was not exactly sure what she had just witnessed. Was she supposed to be taking notes on this? Was this for real? Was he for real? Her mouth was stuck half open and her eyes slightly bugged.

"Amen," Buck said.

Margaret tilted her head toward Buck with the same expression. *Was he buying this?* she thought to herself.

"Ben," Buck said, taking the lead in the conversation again. Ashley continued to stand, but moved his hands down to his hips. "I'm going to want you and Ashley to work closely together on the order of service. You'll do the welcome and announcements in the Sunday worship service, and then Ashley can blend into the music. Of course, this Sunday we'll be winging it."

"Have you got music already picked for Sunday?" Ashley asked, directing the question toward Buck.

"Yes. Sandy, the lady who plays the piano for us, is wonderful, but she likes to have some time to practice. I don't think we should throw something new at her for this Sunday," Buck said.

"Perhaps she could start coming to the staff meeting," Ashley suggested. "I think it would be very beneficial." Ashley's statements were precise and to the point.

Buck could tell that he and Ashley were going to hit it off. They seemed to have similar thoughts. Ashley was polished and refined and appeared to know what it was going to take to bring First Covenant Chapel to a competitive state, and Buck liked that about him.

"What is the plan for Sunday School?" Ben asked.

"That's something on which we need to focus," replied Buck.

"I'd like to take that on if it is alright," Ben said.

"Alright!" Buck responded with excitement. "It would be a blessing, brother. It's yours!"

"Who's the head of your Adult Education Committee?" Ben asked.

"Well, we don't have one at the moment, so I guess you're nominated," Buck proclaimed and then went on, never leaving any room for discussion, as was his usual pattern.

As the meeting was wrapping up, everyone was excited and ready to start the next phase of history at First Covenant Chapel. Buck felt a sense of security with the leadership team he had created. Next Sunday would be momentous. It would be a Sunday of celebration and praise for the rebirth of the tiny white clapboard church in the country. They had new additions to their staff that would be introduced, new ideas and a whole new direction. *God does make all things new,* Buck thought to himself. And he almost forgot—it would be Communion Sunday, too. *Oh bother,* he thought, *maybe we'll just skip Communion this month. There's too much else going on.*

Chapter Twelve

IT WAS A beautiful Sunday morning. You could sense fall was just around the corner. The haze of summer gone from the morning light, Buck walked out onto the front porch of the parsonage, prepared for the Sunday morning service. He was dressed in a finely tailored suit and a stiffly starched, white dress shirt. The tie, he had chosen especially for today. It had a diagonal stripe of black and red that preached "power." He surveyed the landscape around him. There was crispness in the air and an unusual silence; things were oddly still. He looked to the left. Edward's house was still quiet. To the right he surveyed the church and the beautiful property that lay behind it. In the far distance he could see the honeysuckle, which was still blooming, and the fescue was at least knee high. How desperately he wanted that land. Fifteen acres for First Covenant Chapel to grow onto was a gold mine for bringing in new members. He had only just turned sixty-six, but at this age, time flies and he would be sixty-seven before he could blink. He began to pray.

Oh Lord,
My clock is ticking. I so desire to make You proud of this little church. I have brought so many people to You. Lord, I

have heard You calling me. I know, Lord, that You want to build a new sanctuary at First Covenant Chapel and then fill it with Your people. You have given me the gift of Ashley March and Ben Montague, and I thank You most graciously. But, Lord, I need that property. If You give me that property of Edward's, then I will know that You truly want me to build a larger building. And if I build it, Lord, Your children will come. I ask Your blessing, Lord, upon the service this morning. Be with Ashley, Ben and me as we lead. I ask all of this for the sake of Your glory and honor. Amen.

He glanced toward the little church. A black E 320 Mercedes pulled up. Ashley stepped out of the car. *He's bright and early,* Buck thought to himself, and then called over to him, "Ashley!"

Ashley turned and put his right hand above his eyes to block the sun. "Brother Bob, blessings to you," he called.

"Hold up a minute, I'll walk in with you," Buck answered back.

The warmth of the morning sun was just beginning to shine away the mist rising from the grass. The morning smelled sweet. Buck breathed in the fresh air as he walked down the front steps of the parsonage. He crossed the front yard to the parking lot. "Like your car," Buck said as he approached.

"It is fabulous," said Ashley as he was slipping on his sport coat of jet black. He was a slick dresser. His pants were tan, and he was wearing another very tight black t-shirt, this one with a fine white pinstripe running horizontally through it, and his black sport coat was the cherry on the top of his ensemble.

"Are you ready for this morning?" Buck asked.

"Brother, I am more than ready," Ashley replied. "I've been commissioned by the big guy Himself. And when He calls, I answer."

"I like your spirit." Buck said.

They walked into the back door of the church. "Follow

me," Buck said. They walked down the hall past the portraits of all the other pastors that had faithfully served First Covenant Chapel. At the end of the hall, they turned right, and Buck flipped on the light switch to the Sunday School room. There was a large cherry wood desk sitting in the middle of the room with two leather chairs sitting in front of it. Behind the desk were two large windows that looked out over the beautiful property that belonged to Edward Tarken. "We don't use this Sunday School room, so I thought it would make a nice office for you. It's a little sparse right now, but we will get it fixed up for you."

Ashley was startled. "Well, Brother Bob, I wasn't expecting anything like this."

"I didn't think you did," Buck responded, "but you are volunteering your time to this church, and I want you to know how much I appreciate you. I thought since you don't have an office for your freelance work, you could use this office to work from for that business, too. It will help make your time more efficient for both of us."

"The Lord is good," Ashley said with an air about him. He walked around to the other side of the desk and sat down behind it. He set his briefcase of fine black leather, which looked rather like a doctor's bag and perfectly matched his attire, on top of the desk and opened it. Taking out a stack of fliers, he said, "I'd like to add this to the bulletin this morning. It's the words to a few of," he paused for a moment, "some more upbeat songs. I called Sandy and told her I could play the piano this week since she didn't have any advance notice on the change of music."

Buck was a little startled at Ashley's boldness and didn't exactly know what to say, but he liked his initiative and knew that Ashley was a very valuable resource to the church. He certainly didn't want to rock the boat this soon. "Awesome," Buck said. "But what about the hymns we have listed?"

"Well, you, yourself, said we'd be winging it today, didn't you?" Ashley said assuredly. "We will do the hymn after the 'Lord's Prayer.' Sandy will play for that and the closing hymn.

That way, we are keeping a blend of traditional with the contemporary."

Buck smiled. He was unsure of this, but what could he say? He just hoped that people didn't get up and start walking out. He only had a few years to develop this church into the mega church of which he dreamed. If he was going to be successful, he was going to have to take chances and let some of the young blood cut the path. What did he have to lose anyway? "You've got my blessing. The bulletins are in the narthex. Well, I've got to put the final polishing on my sermon." Buck turned and headed back down the hall toward his office.

• • •

HE WAS COMFORTABLE behind his desk, with his cup of black coffee, reading over his sermon for the final time. There was a slight tap on the door. Buck looked up from his desk.

"Good morning, Reverend Buck."

"Ben, good morning," he said in his cheerful voice. "Please come on in, and call me Bob."

"Thank you," replied Ben, and he walked into Buck's office.

"How are you this morning?" Buck asked him.

"I am quite well," Ben replied.

Buck stood up and reached his hand across to shake Ben's, who was now standing in front of Buck's desk. "Please, sit down," Buck said as he gestured toward the chair.

Ben sat with a bit of uneasiness. He had an odd feeling that just wasn't right. Something seemed familiar here, but he couldn't place it. He knew Buck's face from somewhere. Certainly, he did not have memory of it from when he was an infant. And by the time Buck moved to Holy Oak United Covenant Church, Ben had already left for college. His mother had spoken of Buck frequently, but talk can't build an image of a face as strong as the image that Ben was sensing today. It was an image that he had not seen the other day when they sat beneath the old oak tree in the front of the church.

"So, are you ready to be officially introduced to the congregation this morning?"

"Yes, sir," Ben responded enthusiastically.

"I'll do the welcome and announcements this morning, to introduce both you and Ashley. Then, Ashley is going to do some praise music. It's a little different from what is listed in the bulletin. I told you all we'd be winging it this morning," Buck said, as if he had made the changes himself. "And God willing, this is going to be a wonderful service."

Ben was holding a copy of the morning bulletin in his hand and scanning through it. "We will say the Apostle's Creed, then sing the 'Gloria Patri,' and then I'll do the Pastoral Prayer and lead the congregation in the Lord's Prayer, correct?" Ben asked, still looking down at the bulletin in his hand. "What about Communion? I don't see it listed in the order of service. It is the first Sunday of the month." Traditionally, the first Sunday of every month is Communion Sunday in the United Covenant Churches of America, so it was odd to Ben that it wasn't listed.

"The service is too packed today, we'll pick it up next month," Buck said, as if it were a usual option. He stood up. "Follow me. I've set up a small work area for you."

The two men headed out of Buck's office. They started back down the same hallway, past the portraits of the previous senior pastors. As they walked, they stood at equal height, and their shoulders had the same muscular structure. Beside the fact that Buck's hair was dusted with gray, the color was the same. They were both very well tailored in dark suits with jackets that were vented in the back. Ben was carrying a garment bag that held his robe and vestments.

They turned the corner into the reception area where Margaret's desk sat. Right beyond the back door to the church was a smaller door. Buck opened the door and flipped on the light switch. It was a small room with one small window that looked out at the parking lot. The carpeting was probably the original. It was a faded red with worn spots where there must have been a regular traffic pattern. Where the traffic was going was not clear, since the small room was obviously a dead end in the church. Along the back wall was a folding table with crayon marks on the top; it had obviously been borrowed from the children's Sunday School room. A hardback chair with an upholstered seat as worn as the carpeting sat in front of the folding table.

"I know it is sparse," Buck said. "We'll work on getting it fixed up for you. But, for the time being, you'll have a landing space."

Ben hung the hanger of his garment bag over the top of the door and laid his Bible, United Covenant Hymnal and Book of Worship on the folding table. "Ah, to quote a man I admire greatly," Ben said, "'I have learned the secret of being content in any and every situation, whether well fed or hungry, whether living in plenty or in want. This space is quite fine, Reverend Buck. Thank you."

Buck looked at Ben with admiration. "Please, call me Bob," he said again. "Well, I'll leave you to get settled."

"Thank you, and oh," Ben said, "my mother will be coming to the service this morning." Ben let out a small chuckle. "Mothers . . . I'm almost thirty years old and she still comes to my first services as if they were an elementary school play."

Buck's whole demeanor suddenly changed, but he didn't want to show it. In a matter-of-fact manner he said, "We'll meet in the narthex at 10:45 to greet people and prepare for the processional," and he turned and walked out the door.

• • •

THE SANCTUARY WAS peaceful. The sun coming through the clear paned windows on the east side of the church created a warmth inside—the kind of warmth only God can create. The light shone through the stained glass window. A small piece of the window had been cracked sometime in the history of the church and never been repaired. But it added character: when the light hit the cracked pane just right, it had a prism effect and spots of rainbow light reflected into the sanctuary.

No one had entered the sanctuary yet. Buck walked through the backdoor that led from the church offices and Sunday School rooms into the pulpit area. He was alone except for the presence of God, which he felt powerfully and abundantly.

Buck walked over to the altar and kneeled at the rail.

Father God,
I sense Your presence in this place today. It is powerful and how I thank You for the many gifts You give. I thank You that You never forsake any of Your children. I ask, Lord, that You anoint me this morning and that You let my words be Your words. I ask Your blessing on each and every person that walks through this door today. There is so much pain and suffering in this world, and if You would allow just a small part of our service today to touch those that are especially in need, giving them a place of refuge and a sense of hope. Amen.

For a few moments longer, Buck kneeled in silence. He felt himself reinforced by God's approval. He lifted his head and looked over his shoulder toward the narthex. People were beginning to arrive and he saw Ben, already robed, greeting each person as they came in. Buck hurriedly walked toward the narthex to join him. As he walked he had a feeling as if this was surreal. There must have been twenty people in the narthex, talking and laughing and greeting one another.

Ashley had come into to the sanctuary and was fiddling with the sound system, primitive as it was. There was a lady dressed in a pretty blue dress with tiny flowers on it, handing out bulletins to everyone as they walked through the door. They had made sixty-five bulletins for the service today, which amazed him, because only eight months ago, they didn't even need a bulletin for the seven members that held the little country church together.

"Reverend Buck," Miss Mary said as she saw Buck enter the narthex.

"Good morning, Miss Mary," he responded. "You look lovely this morning." She was as elegant as ever and donned a blush pink hat with fuchsia flowers around the brim. Her fashion was trying to squeeze the last bit of warm weather out of the month, before she had to switch to felt hats for the winter. It's not uncommon in the South to go straight from summer into winter, which usually happens around the first of November.

"Ben is a charming young man. What a wise decision you made in bringing him on," she said in a very pleased voice.

"I'm glad he meets with your approval," he returned.

With that, she nodded knowingly and said, "I must go get my seat," and she began walking into the sanctuary.

"Good morning, Reverend." Edward Tarken was right behind Miss Mary, and now they were both walking as fast as they could, which wasn't very fast.

"Morning, Edward!" said Buck as Edward breezed past him.

The original elderly members of the church liked to get to their seats early now. Those had been their seats for a lifetime, and now with the new folk coming in, they didn't want to take a chance on losing those favored spots.

For the last couple of Sundays, the pews had been nearly full of mostly younger couples with small children. The time was coming that they were going to have to create another children's Sunday School class.

There was a beautiful hum of voices that sounded through the sanctuary as people were taking their seats. The little country church was no longer quiet. *What a blessing,* Buck thought to himself.

Buck turned to see who was still in the narthex. Peggy was standing off to the side talking to a very professionally dressed woman, about forty years in age, probably from one of the new luxury subdivisions down the street. Julia Matthews and several of the other ladies from the weekday Bible study were gathered and enjoying an animated discussion. It could have been about anything. When Julia was involved there was no limit to the conversation.

He scanned the balance of the room and then did a double take at the woman entering the door. "Katrina," he said to himself. How good it was to see her. She didn't look much different than when he last saw her, more than a year ago. Perhaps a little grayer. Katrina was sixty-one years old. She stood five feet, six inches tall and had a thin frame. Her complexion was beautifully smooth, and her shoulder length hair was a silvery gray which framed her face with soft curls. She had the left side tucked behind her ear. Even from the distance, Buck could see her magnetic green eyes, which lead to her soul and revealed the wonderfully kind person that she was. There was something about seeing people from your past—nostalgia, perhaps. Warmth ran through him. He almost had to shake his head to regain focus on what he was doing. He watched Ben hug his mother and kiss her on the cheek. Her smile was captivating.

Buck headed over to say hello, not even realizing that he had just walked past two new visitors without even acknowledging their existence. Peggy, however, viewed the scenario and headed to the visitors to rectify her husband's faux pas.

"Trina," Buck said, extending his hands out toward her.

She put her hands in his. "Bob, wonderful to see you."

They gave each other a standard welcoming hug, a part of a pastor's job description. But, holding her he was surprised of his awareness of her breasts briefly against his chest. It stirred a sensation that he remembered well.

Quickly, Buck pulled away. "So glad you're here today. Well, if you'll excuse me, I must get my robe on or they might start the service without me." Desperately trying not to let his discomfort show, he grabbed his robe, threw it around his shoulders and quickly zipped the front. From now on, he was going to put on his robe in his office, before he ever headed to the sanctuary.

The prelude began. Sandy was playing the piano, and it was lovely as always. Ben and Buck processed up the aisle, both dressed in their black robes. Buck wore his stole, an ivory moiré with fringe trim and it was crested with the United Covenant Churches of America symbol embroidered in red at each end. Ben and Buck took their seats in a matching pair of heavy wooden chairs with red velvet seats and high backs of intricately carved mahogany wood. They looked like thrones.

Buck surveyed the congregation. It was a glorious sight. The church was nearly full. He enjoyed seeing the faces of his parishioners each Sunday. He could usually read in their faces what their week had held and could surmise who would need to be ministered to during the coming week.

With a well-defined saunter and a little too much sway, Ashley stepped up to the microphone. He took it off the stand with his right hand and moved it up to his mouth. A gold ring with diamonds in the center was blaringly visible.

"How wonderful it is that we can all come together this morning, in God's house, and worship Him!" Ashley shouted, visibly filled with passion. "I hope that each and every one here knows the love of God and the mighty power that love has!" He was well rehearsed. "Please stand and greet your neighbor with a warm Christian 'hello,' then stay standing and take the insert from your bulletin and join me as we lift one up to the Lord!"

People began to turn and shake hands, creating quite a little chatter in the sanctuary.

Julia Matthews, who was next to Miss Mary, leaned over and whispered out the side of her mouth, "If lifting one up to the Lord means we are all going to pass gas, I'm out of here." Julia knew that she wasn't going to like Ashley. Miss Mary giggled.

As the chatter began to dissipate, Ashley made his way over to the piano, taking the microphone with him. He placed it in the stand attached to the faded baby grand piano and began to play and sing. He closed his eyes and swayed, giving the image that the music had taken him into another dimension.

You have taken hold of me
And Your love has set me free
I no longer am alone
When I face the enemy
Singing praises to You my God, forever and ever…
Singing praises to You my God, forever and ever…
Singing praises to You my God, forever and ever…

Over and over Ashley continued to sing:
Singing praises to You my God, forever and ever...
Singing praises to You my God, forever and ever...
Singing praises to You my God, forever and ever...

Julia leaned over to Miss Mary again. "He's not kidding, is he? I think he really is going to sing forever."

Without saying a word, Miss Mary reached down to her side, took Julia's hand and gave it a little squeeze. They both knew they were allies.

After what seemed like an eternity, the music stopped for a moment, but Ashley's eyes still were shut tightly, almost giving the appearance of pain. He began to play a quiet melody on the piano, leaned his mouth to the microphone—which was still in the stand—and began to pray. "Father God, You are so merciful to us. How undeserving we are. Sinners. Everyone of us sinners." His "s" sounded like snake hisses. "You came down to earth, sacrificing Yourself on the cross, for us. This is grace!" His voice was getting louder and each 't' harder. "I ask You, Lord, to come into the hearts of every person sitting here today. Fill them with Your spirit, oh merciful God. Amen."

Then Ashley was still. His head was bowed down to his chest and he didn't move. The prayer seemed to have absorbed every bit of consciousness from him.

Buck was taken totally off guard by the performance and wasn't sure exactly where they were in the order of service. There was stillness in the church for a moment while the new message sank in. He nudged Ben, who was equally taken aback by what had just transpired.

"The pastoral prayer," Buck whispered to Ben. "It's time for the pastoral prayer."

Ben wasn't sure what to pray about now. How could he follow that act? The pastoral prayer, which is supposed to be one of the most important elements of the service, was severely overshadowed and seemed rather insignificant at this point. He prayed anyway and then led into the Lord's Prayer, which certainly brought on a few sighs of relief.

• • •

BUCK WAS NOT sure he wanted to know how the people were going to respond after the service was over, but he remembered what he preached: *you have to be prepared to bear the consequences of your actions.* Following the Benediction, he took a deep breath and began to shake hands with the people as they recessed.

"Great service!"

"Ashley is awesome!"

A first time visitor stopped and said, "I'll be back next week."

"I think it was a success," said Doug Miles.

"Praise God," Buck said. "I was sweating bullets."

Julia Matthews walked up. "Well, Reverend Buck." She paused for a moment, not really sure what to say. And then she confessed, "I don't know what to say. I am thirsty, though. Think I'll go find some grape juice to drink," so to acknowledge the fact that there had been no Communion. And she walked on by, heading out the door to where she saw Ben.

Ben was standing outside the front door of the church, talking with people. Everyone seemed to be uplifted. It was an unconventional service, but it seemed to have been received well. And reaching the people is what it is all about.

Buck glanced over at Ben. Katrina was standing next to him, and she was talking to Peggy. Certainly, there was nothing wrong with that. So why did it make him uneasy? He went to join them in order to say goodbye. He purposefully put his arm around Peggy. Subconsciously, he thought she was protection. But, protection from what?

"Bob, Peggy," Katrina said, "the service was delightful." She smiled and looked straight at Bob. "Bob, thank you for giving Ben this opportunity."

Buck returned a broad smile, but didn't say a word.

Chapter Thirteen

THE FIRST SUNDAY in Advent is a favorite time of the year. Now that First Covenant Chapel had an official altar guild, the church was finely dressed in greenery. In front of each window hung a live wreath with a red velvet bow attached at the bottom, allowing the streamers to move freely. The tiny choir loft was framed with fresh garlands, and the Advent wreath stood to the right of the altar. The smell of pine was prolific. Today, the paraments had been changed from white to purple, signifying the beginning of the season of Advent.

The church membership had grown even more over the last two months and the number of visitors had doubled. Today also marked the day that First Covenant Chapel would be offering two services each Sunday, one at 9:30 and another at 11:00.

Ashley was extremely gifted, and people were coming just to hear the music. Sandy was still playing the piano for the Prelude and Benediction, but all the Praise and Worship music was now canned and played through the loud speakers from a stereo system.

"We haven't sung a hymn in two months," Julia complained as she stood talking to the usual ladies that gathered in the narthex before the service. "I don't get what all the hoopla about Ashley is. The man does karaoke!"

The other ladies laughed. Julia had a way with words.

"Well, look at what he has done," Susan said in response. "I'd say the numbers are the verdict."

"Certainly I can see that," Julia said in an exasperated tone, "but they are coming here for the wrong reason. They are coming to be entertained, not to worship God. If things keep on like this, I bet he'll be serving mimosas before the service!"

"Listen to you, all high and mighty, Julia," said another. "And how do you know why people are coming? I'd have thought you would have enjoyed the music."

"It's not that I dislike it, it's just I feel that it is bringing people in for the wrong reasons." Julia's response was calm, although she was getting a sense that she was being ganged up on.

"But," Susan added, "it does get people here that would have never come to a church in the first place. Isn't that a plus?"

"I guess that depends on your perspective," Julia said in a matter-of-fact tone.

"We better hurry and find our seats, ladies," another interjected. And they began to file into the sanctuary and take whatever seat they could find available.

Miss Mary had saved Julia a seat next to her, as usual. Miss Mary was very fond of Julia. She saw her as the granddaughter she never had. And Julia had never known her own grandmother, so she had adopted Miss Mary.

The Prelude began. Ben and Buck proceeded as usual wearing their black clergy robes. Buck was wearing a purple stole this morning, one with gold fringe at the bottom.

The service was about to begin. *Where is Ashley?* Buck thought to himself as he looked around in a slightly nervous fashion. For the past two months of Sundays, Ashley had been sitting on an old wooden chair to the right side of the piano, halfway behind the altar. This was so that the congregation could only see half of him before he grabbed the microphone and made his way to the front of the altar—what he called center stage—clapping his hands above his head during his procession there.

Buck looked at Ben. Ben returned the look with a shrug of his shoulders and a face that said, "I don't know."

Just then, the door that led into the pulpit from the back of the church opened. Ashley appeared already holding the microphone in his hands and immediately started speaking.

"Everyone stand up and put your hands together for the Lord!" Ashley shouted, and he began to clap as he made his way to the front of the altar.

The congregation followed suit and the soundtrack began to play.

Shout your praise to His Heavenly name.
Give Him your life, you're no longer the same.
His sacrifice was above all compare.
We no longer shall fall into despair.
Wrapped in His love feel the warmth from above.

The singing continued. Buck stared at Ashley, as well as half of the congregation, who was staring at him, too. Aside from his flamboyant entrance, Ashley was also sporting a new outfit. He was dressed in the usual black pants, but today he was wearing a gold silk Nehru jacket with no collar. It had four gold buttons down the front with two flap pockets on either side. Beneath the gold Nehru jacket was a matching waistcoat.

The singing faded, but melodious music continued softly in the background. Ashley began to speak. "I have a story that I want to share with you all today." He bit down on his lip as if he were holding in some overwhelming emotion. "I was visiting with my sister and her family this week. They were unpacking their Christmas decorations. Her three boys, my nephews, were sitting on the floor, each holding a Wise Man . . . the Wise Men who traveled to witness the birth of our Savior!" He cleared his throat for emphasis. "My nephews were playing war with the Wise Men . . . battling each other. One of my nephews brought a few G.I. Joes into the battle." He lifted his left hand to the outer corner of his eye and wiped a finger across it giving the impression that he was drying a tear. "In the battle, one of the Wise Men lost a leg," he paused. "The shepherd boy, who stood on the side of their makeshift battlefield, lost an eye." The congregation was very intent on Ashley and his story. "My sister walked over to the boys. She looked at the scene and she looked at the Wise Man with the broken leg. The nephew that was holding the injured Wise Man looked up at his mother and said, 'I'm sorry Mommy. I'm really sorry!'" The soft melodious music continued in the background. "My sister looked at him and said, 'I forgive you. I can superglue him back together.'" He wiped the corner of the other eye. "I was so moved by what I saw. Because of the revelation it brought me! It was then I realized that is just what we are like—fighting and hurting each other." He was silent for a moment and then shouted, "That's what we do! Hurt the innocent because we are careless!" Then in a whisper voice he said, "But God superglues us back together and makes our lives anew. Whether predator or victim, He loves us all the same!" Ashley's voice was cracking and he had his left hand now resting on his chest, over his heart as if there was a pain there. Ashley continued, his voice now an octave higher, "At this moment I realized too, that is exactly what Jesus is like. He loves us all, whether we are broken and parts of us are missing, or if we are different and don't seem to fit in anywhere . . . Jesus loves us all. Each and every one of us is invited to the manger with the Wise Men! And my prayer this morning is that you live this Advent season knowing Jesus came just for you!"

There was a moment of stillness as the soft melodious music continued, and then it quickly changed back to the chorus of the previous song.

Shout your praise to His Heavenly name.
Give Him your life you're no long the same.
His sacrifice was above all compare.
We no longer shall fall into despair.

Julia was holding her hand against her chest, over her heart, as if it were hurting. Her mouth was slightly open, her eyes wide. She couldn't believe what she just heard. It infuriated her. She had heard a similar story told last year by the comedian Tim Allen, but it was funny when he did it. She looked around the church. People were passionately singing, and there were tears in a few eyes. *This guy is a fake,* she thought to herself, *and people are buying it.*

For the rest of the service, Julia sat. Her only emotion was anger. When it was over she slipped out the back door without being noticed. She didn't want to talk to anyone because she was afraid of what she might say.

Chapter Fourteen

IT WAS WEDNESDAY morning, the day the ladies met at the parsonage with Peggy for their weekly Bible study. Julia arrived early that morning in hope that she might catch Reverend Buck in his office.

The church door was unlocked. She walked down the hall past the portraits of the previous senior pastors that had served First Covenant Chapel. The light was on in Buck's office. She stuck her head in the door. Buck was on the phone, but motioned Julia to come on in and sit down. She sat down in one of the leather chairs that faced Buck's desk and waited. Whomever he was talking to must have been singing his praises, because all Buck kept saying was "Thank you, thank you." He must have said it a dozen times. Finally, he hung up.

"Hello, woman!" Buck said with his usual exuberance. He got up, walked around to the front of the desk and gave Julia one of his dutiful pastoral hugs, then sat down in the chair next to her. "What can I do for you so early in the morning?" Buck asked.

"Well, to be honest, I have some things that are troubling me," Julia said.

"I'm sorry to hear that," Buck responded. "What's the trouble?" He had a compassionate face and gave the appearance of being genuinely concerned.

"Well, you know, I was one of the first people to visit the church after you and Peggy came here," Julia began.

"I remember," Buck said.

"There was something so special here. The presence of God was everywhere, and the peaceful reverence is what brought me back around to a closer walk with God." Julia was choosing her words very carefully.

"So far I don't see a problem," Buck responded with a smile.

"No, that's not a problem." Julia usually didn't mince words, but she was obviously tiptoeing today. "I am concerned that Ashley is making more of a show than he is leading worship."

"Ah," Buck said, "I understand what you are saying. He is a bit dramatic, but I assure you he is genuine."

Genuine? Julia thought. Trying to keep a calm voice she said, "Reverend Buck, I am sorry to tell you that the story he told on Sunday he stole from a similar one Tim Allen told. You know, the comedian."

"Really?" Buck looked surprised. He paused for a moment and then said, "Julia, I wouldn't worry too much about that. Pastors borrow from each other all the time. The idea is to get a message across, and Ashley did that."

Julia was surprised at Buck's lackadaisical attitude, but moved on. "We haven't used the hymnal since he came here," she said. "We haven't said The Apostle's Creed or sung the 'Gloria Patri.'"

"It's a change, I know," said Buck. "Give yourself a chance to adjust. Why don't you talk to Ashley? Stop by his office. Get to know him. I think you'll find him charming."

A little too charming, she thought.

"Contemporary worship is the trend of the new church," Buck continued with what appeared to be a persuasive speech. "Look how many people Ashley has brought into our church.

We were packed on Sunday. Even Edward Tarken said he liked the music, and that surprised me."

"Have you ever considered *why* all the people are coming?" Julia asked.

"I understand what you are trying to say Julia, but for whatever reason they are coming, at least they are coming, and that is the first step."

She disagreed. But now she had an understanding of where Reverend Buck stood. She also recognized that she wasn't going to convince him otherwise.

"Well, my Bible study with your lovely wife awaits me," Julia said as she stood up. "Thank you for your time."

"That's what I'm here for, woman. I hope you feel better. And remember . . . I love you," Buck called after her as she was walking out the door.

Julia walked out of Buck's office very dissatisfied. She walked past the portraits of the previous senior pastors and past Margaret's desk that was still vacant that morning. As she was opening the door to head out to the parking lot, she caught a glimpse of Ben sitting in his office. Julia paused for a moment. Ben turned and looked at her.

"Good Morning, Julia," Ben called out.

She looked at him and her only response was, "If I had wanted to be a Baptist, I would have joined a Baptist church!" And she walked out the door.

Chapter Fifteen

IT WAS MID-DAY and the sun was a welcome relief from the gloom of the previous days. It was cold, bitterly cold. The ambulance was parked outside Miss Mary's house when Buck arrived. A neighbor had called to let him know that Miss Mary had fallen on the ice. The paramedics already had her on a stretcher and were getting ready to load her into the ambulance.

He went up to the stretcher and lifted her hand, which was resting to her side on a very sterile looking, white sheet. He held her hand in his. It was cold. They had been having terrible weather for the last several days. It had rained for several days, and at night the temperatures were dipping below freezing. Many areas were covered with ice, especially the front walk of Miss Mary's house.

"How are you?" Buck asked, getting close to her face.

"Oh dear," she said, "I have been very foolish. I was just going to run down to Porter's Store to get a few items. I'm all out of eggs. It didn't look icy."

"My goodness," Buck said, "I'm going to follow the ambulance to the hospital. You hang in there, woman!" Then he let go of her hand and headed back to his car.

Mary gave a little chuckle and then called out after him, "No hanging on necessary. It's not my time yet. This is just one of those little inconveniences that life deals us."

"I like your spirit, woman!" Buck shouted back to her as he got into his car.

He followed the ambulance into Salem Regional Medical Center. They didn't use their sirens or lights, and they didn't need to drive above the speed limit. Miss Mary was in stable condition. When they reached the hospital, Buck pulled in right behind the ambulance. He walked with Miss Mary and the paramedics into the hospital. The automatic glass doors closed behind them.

"We're going to take her into the ER, you'll need to wait here for now," one of the paramedics said to Buck. And they wheeled her through a set of double doors that flapped back and forth.

He turned and walked to the waiting area, which was cold and sterile. Four rows of connecting seats were covered with royal blue plastic cloth. Two of the rows had their backs to each other, leaving the other two rows to face them. There were televisions hanging high on each wall, both of them running CNN without the sound on. The room was very full. A lady holding a sleeping child in her arms sat staring at one of televisions. An Hispanic man holding a bloody cloth wrapped around one of his hands sat across from her. There were three other people sitting next to each other with their backs against the wall; they all looked very healthy and were obviously waiting for somebody else. At the far end, a man sat with his elbows on his knees, his forehead resting in his hands and a plastic bag between his legs.

Buck hated hospitals, and he had been to enough to know that speed was not the name of the game. It could be hours before there was any word on Miss Mary. He took his cell phone out of his pocket and walked through the automatic glass doors into the chilling weather outside. He dialed his cell phone.

A voice answered, "Reverend Montague."

"Ben, it's Bob. Mary Fletcher fell outside her home."

"Oh, no!" Ben responded with considerable concern.

"She'll be fine. May have broken a hip, we'll see. They brought her into Salem Regional Medical Center. I'm here now and have been waiting, but no word as of yet."

"What can I do?" Ben asked.

"Well, I have a meeting I need to get to. Are you available to come down here and wait for her?"

"No problem, I'll be right over. Have you notified anyone else?" Ben asked.

"Not yet," Buck responded.

"I'll handle it," Ben said. "You go ahead, don't be late for your meeting."

Buck hung up the phone and walked toward his car without going back into the hospital.

He headed home. He was tired and wanted to get a head start on his sermon for next week.

• • •

BEN MONTAGUE WALKED into the emergency room at Salem Regional Medical Center. He carried his cell phone in one hand and the church directory in the other.

He went up to the window where a middle-aged woman with big hair and chewing gum was sitting. "Can I help you?" the lady said.

"Yes, you may," replied Ben. "I'm Reverend Montague and I'm here to check on Mary Fletcher. She was brought in a little while ago."

"Are you family?" the lady asked.

"I'm her minister," Ben said.

"Is any of her family here?" said the lady while smacking her gum.

"No, she doesn't have any family in the area, just her church family, and I'm here," said Ben with a slightly irritated voice. The new privacy laws had made it really difficult to minister to people in the hospital.

The lady looked at Ben for a moment, checking to see if he

looked like a real minister, and in a short tone said, "Just a minute." And the lady got up and disappeared behind a wall.

A few minutes later the lady reappeared and said to Ben, "Take a seat. Someone will be with you shortly."

Ben went over to the rows of connected chairs. He took a seat at the end of one row next to a table with a telephone on it. He put his cell phone in his pocket and opened the church directory to find Julia Matthews' number. He dialed the phone on the table.

On the third ring, Julia answered the phone. "Hello?"

"Julia, Ben Montague here."

"Reverend Montague, how are you?" Julia replied.

"Well, I'm doing just fine, thank you," Ben said, "but Miss Mary took a little fall outside her house today and may have broken a hip."

"Oh, no!" Julia said with shock.

"I'm down at the hospital now waiting to hear some information," Ben said, as he was looking around the waiting room at all the other people waiting, too.

"Is she alright?" Julia asked.

"Don't know any information yet, I'll call you back as soon as I hear," he said.

"That's alright," Julia said, "I'm coming down there." And she hung up the phone.

Ben took a deep breath and leaned back in his chair. He looked up at the television that was hanging on the wall: CNN without sound. He surveyed the waiting area of the emergency room. He saw an Hispanic man with his hand wrapped in a bloody cloth. At the far end of the room a man sat with his elbows on his knees, his forehead resting in his hands and a plastic bag between his legs. There was also a lady holding a sleeping child in her arms, who sat staring at one of televisions.

He looked at the lady and the child. Her face told a sad story, but he had no idea what it was, only that it hurt. Ben bowed his head for a moment of silent prayer for the lady and then got up and walked over to her.

"Excuse me," Ben said, "I'm Reverend Montague."

The lady looked over at him and put what seemed to be all that she had into a partial smile.

Ben continued, "I just wanted to let you know if there is anything I can do for you, I would be happy to help."

The lady stared at Ben blankly, almost as if she were looking straight through him. Then, in a very weak voice, she said, "Just tell me why."

Ben, of course, did not even know the problem, but that didn't really matter. He knew exactly what the "why" meant, and he also knew that he didn't have the answer. And he said, "I don't know why, but I do know where to find strength."

The lady looked down at the child in her arms, kissed her on the top of the head and began to stroke the child's hair. A single tear rolled down the lady's cheek. "She's only nine months old," the lady said. "Her name is Mary."

Ben didn't know if Mary was sick or if both the lady and Mary were waiting for someone else. "Your Mary is beautiful," Ben said. "For such is the Kingdom of Heaven." He paused for a moment. "I am waiting for a lady named Mary, too," he said. "Is your Mary alright?"

"She is fine," the lady said. "It's her father . . . my husband."

Ben was relieved that it was not the baby. Suffering is hard under any circumstance, but when it is that of a child, there is no other heartache comparable.

"Would you like to tell me about it?" Ben said.

The lady was silent and so was Ben. She just sat and stared, and Ben sat with her. They both stared at CNN and watched it in silence.

"An accident," the lady said after awhile. "A car accident."

Ben listened.

"His spine is broken, a lung collapsed." The lady spoke in monotone and never blinked an eye. "We've been married four years. We bought our first house two months ago." She was rambling. "Mary has his eyes. Aren't they beautiful?"

"Very beautiful," Ben said, even though the child's eyes were closed while sleeping. He couldn't see them, but he knew they were beautiful.

"He was going to the hardware store to buy paint. We were painting the kitchen. Yellow. I love yellow in a kitchen; it is so sunny." The lady paused and then said, "We were happy." She took a deep breath and released the air slowly, and then she turned and looked Ben straight in the eyes.

Her tone changed completely. Her voice became low but strong and she said in an angry tone, "The girl that hit him is nineteen years old. It was two o'clock in the afternoon and she was drunk. She wasn't even scratched." Her voice began to get louder and it broke with pain. "You tell me why, Reverend," she said. "Why?" And she began to sob, "it's not fair . . . it's just not fair."

Ben took a deep breath. Every pastor wishes there were magical words they could say that would take people's pain away, but there aren't any. However, he had always remembered the words his mother said to him when he was a little boy, at a time when he was so angry that his father had abandoned them. He was mad about it. Crying, he yelled at his mother, saying the same words the lady had just said: "It's not fair . . . it's not fair." And his mother said these words to him: "Son, there is nothing fair on this side of Heaven."

Remembering this, Ben looked at the lady and said, "I don't know why, and I know that it seems unfair, but there is nothing that is fair on this side of Heaven."

The lady looked at him again. "If that's the case, Reverend, then tell me, why did Jesus come if we are just to have this kind of pain?"

Ben smiled at her tenderly and said, "Jesus did not come to take away our pain, He came to give us the strength to endure it."

The lady closed her eyes, and although she didn't make a sound, tears poured from beneath her eyelids.

Ben very softly said, "May I pray?"

She slowly nodded her head without looking up.

Ben place one hand on the lady's shoulder and the other he placed over the sleeping child's hand. He prayed for the presence of the Holy Spirit and for peace. Then they sat in silence.

• • •

THE DOUBLE DOORS that led to the emergency room flapped open and a young girl in a peach colored striped dress appeared. "Is there a Reverend Montague here?" she said in a sweet voice.

Ben got up and walked over to the young lady. "I'm Reverend Montague," he said.

"Please follow me," she said.

They walked back through the double doors that flapped back and forth.

"Ms. Fletcher is in the third room on the left," the young girl said as she pointed down the corridor.

Although the door was standing open, Ben lightly tapped on the doorframe and said very softly, "Miss Mary?"

There was no response. He walked on in and went over to the side of the bed where Miss Mary lay already with an IV in her right arm and oxygen in her nose. The room glowed with fluorescent lighting and smelled of rubbing alcohol. He gently touched Miss Mary's hand. She opened her eyes.

"Reverend Montague," she said in a soft, but very sweet voice, "looks like I've gotten myself in a pickle." She smiled.

"You are definitely a sweet pickle," replied Ben.

Miss Mary smiled a little more. "Any word on what they're going to do to me?" she asked in a very tired voice.

"Not yet, I've been waiting," Ben said.

"Where's Reverend Buck? Is he still here?" Miss Mary asked.

"He had a meeting he needed to go to, so I guess you're stuck with me," Ben said with a chuckle.

"How blessed I am," Miss Mary replied in a tired voice, but still with the shadow of a smile on her face.

A petite woman in a white medical coat walked through the door. She was looking down, reading a medical chart. She stood at the foot of the bed as she flipped the pages, still not looking up and not saying a word.

Ben was caught totally off guard when she entered the

room. There was a quiver in his stomach and a heat that ran across his chest. He stared at her. She was the most beautiful woman he had ever seen. She had long brunette hair that was pulled back at the nape of her neck. A few locks of her ponytail draped over her right shoulder. The only skin he could see was her face and hands, and they were smooth and of the softest peach color. Embroidered in dark blue on the left chest panel of her medical coat was "Sylvia DiLeo, M.D." He had to take a deep breath.

The petite woman, still reading the chart, moved close to the side of Miss Mary's bed. She lifted her head and looked Miss Mary straight in the eyes and smiled. Ben's heart was beating rapidly. Her lips were soft and her smile . . . Ben felt weak in the knees.

"Ms. Fletcher, I'm Dr. DiLeo, the orthopedic surgeon," the woman said. She didn't even seem to notice that Ben was in the room. "Well, it looks like you've broken your hip."

"Oh dear," Miss Mary said with a slight shake in her voice. "And I guess the fact that you're a surgeon means I'm in for surgery."

"I'm afraid you've guessed right," said the petite doctor.

Then, Dr. DiLeo looked up and for the first time and noticed Ben, who hadn't taken his eyes off of her. Their eyes met over Miss Mary, who, even with the pain medication making her a little loopy, could see that they both had forgotten that she was even in the room.

Ben was holding the side rail of Miss Mary's bed, petrified to let go because he feared it was the only thing holding him up. Their eyes locked on each other for what seemed like hours. Sylvia smiled at Ben and extended her hand over the bed to shake his.

In a very soft voice she said, "Hi, I'm Sylvi—" She stopped herself to maintain her professionalism. "I'm Dr. DiLeo," she continued.

Ben knew he had to let go of the rail with at least his right hand in order to shake Sylvia's hand that was extended toward him.

You can do it, Ben, he thought to himself. *Slow, steady, reach your hand out.* He did it. His hand was clasping hers and he said, "I'm Ben Montague."

Her hand was soft and warm. The electricity that ran through his hand from hers went up his arm, down his body, through his legs and made the bottoms of his feet tingle. Now, he didn't want to let go of her hand. But he knew he had to. *Come on, Ben, you've got to let go,* he thought to himself. And he did.

"Reverend. Reverend Ben Montague," came a soft voice from beneath them.

Both of them tried to snap back into the moment. Dr. DiLeo looked down at Mary and said, "I'm sorry, Ms. Fletcher, did you say something?"

"He is *Reverend* Ben Montague," Miss Mary said, again placing the emphasis on "Reverend."

"Oh!" Sylvia said, almost as if she were embarrassed. She quickly looked up at Ben and said, "I am so sorry, Reverend Montague. I didn't know. It's a pleasure to meet you." And she nodded her head toward him as if she were bowing. Her peach cheeks were now flushed.

Why was it that everyone seemed to think that ministers weren't real people, with real thoughts and real feelings? "Please, just call me Ben," he said and smiled.

Sylvia smiled back and slightly shook her head as if to clear it. She looked back down at Miss Mary and forced herself to move back into doctor mode.

"I am going to have to put a pin in your hip," Sylvia said, and then continued to explain the rest of the procedure to Miss Mary.

Ben interrupted for a moment and said, "Excuse me, Miss Mary. I'm going to step back out into the waiting area. Julia was on her way over, so I'll check to see if she's here."

Sylvia looked up and smiled at Ben. He smiled back, and then he walked out the door.

He pushed one side of the swinging double doors and walked through it. He looked around the waiting area. He didn't see Julia, and he didn't see the lady with the sleeping child. For a moment he paused to think about what he needed to do next. Then he walked back over the reception window to the woman who was still chewing gum.

"Excuse me," Ben said.

The woman looked up, but didn't say anything.

"The lady with the small child that was here, can you tell me where she might be?" Ben asked.

"Are you family?" she said in a monotone voice.

Ben was resigned. He knew it was the end of the conversation. He turned and stepped to the side. Bowing his head, he offered a silent prayer for the lady with the child, wherever they may be.

He began to walk toward the rows of royal blue chairs when he heard a voice calling him. "Ben . . . Ben."

He looked around. It was Julia. "Julia, how are you?" he answered back.

"I'm fine, but how is Miss Mary?"

"She'll be alright, but they are going to have to put a pin in her hip," Ben replied.

"Oh, no," Julia said in a disappointed voice, "that means surgery. Can I see her?"

"I'll take you back," Ben said and led her through the swinging double doors.

They walked into the little room, which was getting crowded at this point. Sylvia was still in the room making notes in the chart.

"Miss Mary, look who I brought to see you," Ben said, letting Julia pass in front of him to the side of Miss Mary's bed.

Julia reached to pick up Miss Mary's left hand. "Well, what have you gone and done to yourself now?" Julia asked in a stern voice, but with a smile on her face.

Miss Mary smiled at her. "You really are an angel in disguise, aren't you?"

The both laughed.

Ben piped in, "Julia, this is Dr. DiLeo." He gestured toward Sylvia. "Dr. DiLeo, Julia Matthews."

Phew! Different last names, Sylvia thought to herself as she extended her hand toward Julia. "Pleased to meet you. Well, you know what they say: 'two's company, three's a crowd' . . . I'd say we're well over the limit for this little room." She turned to Miss Mary. "I'll be back to see you in a bit."

The room was indeed crowded and tight. Sylvia had to turn sideways to get to the door past Julia and Ben, which put her within inches of Ben's body. He swore he could feel her warmth radiate through him. He watched her as she walked out the door and closed it behind her. He took a deep breath, let it out quietly and then turned back toward Miss Mary and Julia, who were talking intently and totally unaware of any electricity that might have been flowing through the room. *Thank God.*

Chapter Sixteen

BUCK WALKED INTO the sanctuary about quarter past six in the evening. The lights were dimmed; it was solemn and stark. The altar was covered with a burlap cloth. In the far corner of the front pew was a man kneeling in prayer. Buck watched the man in silence and from a distance so as not to invade his time with God. He recognized the back of the man. It was Ben Montague. Ben reminded Buck of himself when he was a young man—devout and yearning to do nothing more than serve the Lord. As a young pastor, Buck sought guidance from God through prayer for every situation. But now, although he prayed, truth be told, he hadn't felt the presence of the Lord in a while. *But that happens,* Buck told himself, *people go through dry spells.* He wasn't going to get hung up on that. He had a job to do.

Ben got up slowly, looked at the cross that hung on the wall behind the altar and then turned and saw Buck standing in the back. Buck tried to act like he was busy. He didn't want Ben to know he had been watching him.

"Bob," Ben called out. "Good evening. Things are ready for the Ash Wednesday service this evening."

"Oh, Ben, I didn't see you there," Buck replied. "Wonderful. You've done a good job."

There was an undefined tension in the room that they both ignored, a tension that always seemed to be in their presence.

Ashley walked into the room with his usual flamboyance, sucking up all the available air. Usually, it grated on Ben's nerves, but at this moment he was thankful because it broke the moment with Buck.

"Good brothers, how are you?" Ashley said as he slapped Ben on the back.

I am a man of God, Ben thought to himself, *but I swear, if he ever hits me on the butt, I'll deck him.* Ben smiled and said, "Good evening, Ashley."

"Got to do a sound check," Ashley continued as he walked on by, his hips swaying.

"And I need to go finish some things in my office," Ben said and headed toward the hall that led back to the church offices.

Ben was tense. There was no denying it. His shoulders hurt and there was a pain that ran up through the back of his neck. That was always where he felt his tension the worst. As a boy, Ben would ask his mother to rub his neck. She always did, and she always used the time to talk with Ben and share her motherly words of wisdom without him realizing what she was doing.

When he reached his office, he sat down in the hardback chair at his desk, which was still the Sunday School table with crayon on it. He picked up the phone and dialed.

"Hello?" said a soft and sweet voice.

"Hello, Miss Mary, it's Reverend Montague. Just wanted to check on you and tell you I would miss you at the Ash Wednesday service tonight."

"Thank you, Reverend," Miss Mary replied. "I will miss all of you too, but I am doing well. Dr. DiLeo said I can start to get about with a walker in about two more weeks."

Just hearing Sylvia DiLeo's name made Ben weak in the knees and his heart skip a beat.

"Wonderful!" he said. "Many blessings to you, Miss Mary."

"Thank you. And Ben, please tell Reverend Buck hello. I know how busy he is, and I miss talking to him."

"I'll tell him," Ben said. And he hung up the phone.

Ben stared into nothingness for a moment. He thought he would like to see Sylvia again, but he passed it off as a ridiculous thought.

• • •

"THE GRACE OF the Lord Jesus Christ be with you!" Buck said to the congregation.

"And also with you," they responded.

Buck continued, "We have gathered in affirmation of Jesus Christ, we have come to celebrate the mercy and forgiveness proclaimed in the gospel and to acknowledge the need we all have to renew our faith. Ash Wednesday marks the beginning of the Lenten season, which is forty days of spiritual preparation by self-examination, repentance, prayer, fasting and self denial."

The room was still and silent, and the presence of the Lord was abundant. Ben sat in his pulpit chair and offered his silent prayer of his sinful nature to God—especially the sin of his edgy attitude recently, his deepening dislike for Ashley March and his disapproval of the way the Buck was leading the church.

"Oh, Lord," came a loud and articulate voice through the speaker next to Ben's ear. Ben jumped in his seat. *"Oh, Lord," is right,* Ben thought.

"You are the creator of all living things! From the dust of the earth you have formed us, and from the dust of death you will raise us up!" Ashley was holding his cordless microphone with his right hand and directing the show with his left. At least for Ash Wednesday, his Nehru Jacket and waistcoat were of gray silk moiré.

"Please stand and join me in singing," Ashley continued. The canned music began and the congregation joined in . . .

You hold the key, precious Jesus.
The key to my heart,
The key that through Your love sets me apart.

And now I see You shining,
And I am singing,
Holy, precious Lord, Holy.

This wasn't the type of music Ben was expecting on Ash Wednesday, and frankly, he wasn't sure how he felt about it.

The service continued with Old and New Testament readings and a touching meditation given by Buck. Then both Buck and Ben moved to the center of the pulpit, each holding their dish of ashes. The congregation was invited to come to the altar and kneel, confess their sins to God and receive the imposition of ashes.

Sandy was playing the piano quietly. The melody of the hymn "Just As I am, Without One Plea" set a reverent tone for the moment. People began to file up the middle aisle of the little church and kneel at the altar rail. Buck and Ben, each on different sides of the pulpit, walked down the altar rail, and for each soul kneeling there, they placed their thumb into the dish of ashes and marked their forehead with a cross, each time saying, "Repent, and believe the gospel."

As Ben walked and imposed ashes, he saw the faces of people with the stories of their lives scrolled across them. The faces spoke of sadness, pain, loneliness, guilt, fear. There were faces with tears running down them and faces that wanted to cry, but couldn't. For each face he offered his own prayer to God for peace for that person.

Buck, too, was looking at the faces as he imposed ashes. He saw sadness, pain, loneliness, guilt, fear. And Buck knew that the deeper the pain of a person, the more that person was in need of the church. He would be able to reach them at their emotional level, and that would keep them coming to the church—and their money would come with them.

Chapter Seventeen

BUCK PULLED OPEN the screen door and knocked on the red front door behind it. It took almost two minutes before the front door began to open . . .very slowly.

"It's Reverend Buck," he called out.

Miss Mary's face finally appeared around the door.

"Well, hello, woman! How are you?" Buck said, almost shouting.

She smiled and got a steady hold on her walker again to make the turn and head back toward her chair. "Reverend Buck," she said with joy in her voice, "come on in. I'll let you handle the door. It's a bit of a challenge for me."

Buck walked into the living room of Miss Mary's house, closing the door behind him. The room was meticulously clean, and bright sunlight shone through the bay window, illuminating the entire room. It was a cheery room. Miss Mary sat back down in her chair, which had an extra bed pillow in the seat and also one at the back. There were two yellow knitted afghans on either arm of the chair. Miss Mary took one of the afghans and covered her legs, although if you had asked anyone else, they would have said it was at least eighty-five degrees in the room already.

"You look fabulous!" Buck said with emphasis.

"Oh, you are a dear, but I do believe my fabulous days are over," replied Miss Mary.

"Nonsense," returned Buck.

Mary changed the subject. "I am so glad to see you, I've missed you," Mary said with great sincerity in her eyes.

Buck had not been to see Miss Mary since the day he went to the emergency room with her. *That was one of the blessings of having a larger church,* he thought. The work can be spread around. Ben and Julia had been visiting Miss Mary on a regular basis, and the ladies' group had been taking meals to her. Her church family had been taking care of her, so Buck didn't feel too badly that he hadn't been over to visit.

"Oh, well you know how busy things have gotten at the church," Buck said. "We had nearly two hundred people last Sunday. The youth group is growing. We've been doing the Sunday Suppers the second Sunday of every month." Then he leaned over, cupped his hand on the side of his mouth and whispered, "They aren't the same without you." He went on, "We had twelve new families join this last month. They are young couples." Buck was rambling.

"I do miss being there," Miss Mary said with a hint of sadness that comes from being secluded for too long.

"So when are you going to be able to make it back?" Buck asked.

"Well, I'm not too mobile, and I certainly can't drive," she said.

"I tell you what," Buck said, "I will come pick you up this Sunday morning and drive you to church. I'll even drive you in your Mercedes; you know how I have always admired that car. That will give me a chance to drive it." Buck let out a little chuckle.

"How wonderful!" Miss Mary said, her face gleaming. "Now remember, I'm a little slow, so you'll have to get me early to give us plenty of time for this old lady to move about." She smiled.

"Not a problem," Buck said.

Buck did love that car. It was sleek and stylish, like it had driven right out of *Town and Country* magazine. He had always dreamed of having a car like that, but that was exactly what it was—a dream. It was never going to happen on a pastor's salary. Maybe Miss Mary would let him drive it some while she was laid up . . . just to keep the engine in shape.

Chapter Eighteen

WHEN SHE WALKED into the restaurant, Ben was already sitting at the table. He was looking at the menu and thankful to just be sitting for a moment. Rarely did he get the opportunity to stop for lunch. He was usually on the run and lunch would consist of something wrapped in paper. Although, it wasn't so bad; he had fond memories of food wrapped "to go." When he was a child, every Saturday he and his mother would go to a park down on the river. They would take a blanket, spread it out in the grass and have a lovely picnic. It was the day of the week they ate "out." She couldn't afford to go to fancy restaurants, but what kid wants to do that anyway? They would pick up hamburgers or fried chicken. Sometimes they would even get a pizza.

Saturday was the day that he and his mother spent time together. When he was young, she would take books and read to him; they would play tag and hide and go seek; she would sing to him—usually hymns, since that was mostly what she knew. As he got older they used their Saturday picnic to catch up with each other on what had gone on with them throughout the week. His teenage years were hard. There was a period in time that he was so angry his father had left them that it spilled into the other areas of his life and hers as well. But, regardless of anything, the blanket was there every Saturday and so was she.

Ben was so blessed to have his mother, and today was her special day. Even though his minister's salary was very small, he would treat her to a lovely lunch at a fine restaurant. His mother pulled out the chair and sat down across from Ben. He looked up.

"Mom, Happy Birthday!" Ben said with excitement.

"Thanks!" she said with a face that said she was pleased just to be with her son.

"You don't look a day over twenty-five," Ben said, trying to sound serious.

"And you never were good at lying," his mother returned. They both laughed.

Ben noticed the necklace that was hanging around his mother's neck.

"You're still wearing that," Ben said as a statement of fact.

"I never take it off," his mother replied. Ben smiled. It was a small heart shaped pendant of gold with tiny diamonds that curved around one side of the heart. Ben had given it to his mother for her birthday the year he was twelve. He remembered how excited he was to give it to her. When she opened the package that he had so carefully wrapped in a pastel floral paper, her face was motionless. He would never forget the look. And before she even had a chance to say anything, he immediately said to his mother, "I know it's not much, but I spent everything I had." As soon as the tears began to trickle down her face, he knew that her motionless face was not out of disappointment but an inability to express the emotion that was deep in her heart.

"So, how are things over at the District Superintendent's office?" Ben asked.

"Well, I stay busy," she replied.

"I guess that's better than the alternative," Ben said.

"I guess you're right," she said, and they both laughed. "A lot of the work is just having to stay on pastors to turn in their paperwork."

"Ah," Ben said, "and I bet First Covenant Chapel is on your list."

"Always," she said with emphasis. Then she paused for a moment before she asked, "How are things at First Covenant Chapel?"

Ben wanted to tell her that everything was great, but he didn't want to lie to his mother. His mother had gone out on a limb to get him this position and he didn't want to complain, but his mother knew him too well. She could always see through him, so he might as well tell her like it is. "It's challenging," he said.

"Challenging? What does that mean?" his mother asked.

"Well, Reverend Buck and I don't really see eye to eye on doctrinal issues. His sons, David and Bobby, both seem to think I am in the way and," he said with a pause in his voice, "I think the music director has the hots for me."

His mother looked at him oddly, with a confused look on her face. "Did you get a new music director?" she asked.

"No" was his only response.

"You're kidding!" his mother said, taken aback. They both laughed.

"Well," she said, "it looks like you do have some challenges."

Ben changed the expression on his face to a serious one. His mother could see in his eyes that there was something deep in his soul that was disturbed. "What is it, Ben?" she asked.

"On a serious note, Mom, I can't figure Reverend Buck out. I have to question what his motives are."

"It's not yours to question, Ben," his mother said.

"I know, Mom, but I'm not sure he is on the up and up. He has an agenda, and my gut tells me it has nothing to do with God."

"And if that's the case, Ben, Reverend Buck will have to answer to God," his mother said in a very authoritative manner.

The waitress came over to the table, interrupting their conversation to take their order. When the waitress had left, Ben purposely did not go back to the conversation they had been having. This was his mother's birthday, and he wasn't going to spend his time with her talking about issues that could only bring them down.

Chapter Nineteen

BEN WAS SITTING at his desk—still the table with crayon on it—working on his sermon for Sunday. He preached once every six weeks and this Sunday was his turn. He loved to preach. There was so much about the Bible and God to impart to others. Ben took his preaching seriously. He wasn't one of those preachers who used the pulpit as a stage to puff up his chest, telling stories about when he was young and how God changed his life. Although it was true—God had changed his life—but the pulpit was not the appropriate arena for a pastor to talk about himself in an egotistical manner.

He was also concerned that his sermons be academically correct. Ben knew he had become sensitized to Buck and was privately looking for fault in him. He felt guilty for feeling this way, but he disapproved of how Buck was removing all the liturgy from the services, how he was allowing the hymnal to become obsolete and, in Ben's opinion, how the reverence in the church had been overshadowed by the three ring circus Ashley had created.

Ben also felt that Buck's sermons had become weak and lacking in accuracy. In the last two months alone, Buck had used the same scripture verse twice, and he had misquoted it each time. In the book of Matthew, when Jesus predicts Peter's denial, he says to Peter, "I tell you the truth, before the rooster crows, you will deny me three times."

In both of Buck's sermons, however, Buck quoted Jesus as saying, "Before the rooster crows three times, you will deny me." Each time, Ben wanted want to stand up and scream, "Reverend Buck, you are getting the story confused with Cinderella, when the clock struck twelve!" Instead, he stayed quiet and cringed. Most of the congregation wouldn't even notice his mistake.

He was still working on his sermon when Julia Matthews walked through the door to the church office. Ben always knew who was coming and going. His office was situated in a place that seemed like he was keeper of the gate. And he hated to close his door unless he was counseling. He felt that a pastor should always give the appearance of being available.

"Hello, Margaret. How are you?" said Julia.

"Hey," Margaret returned.

"I'm here to help you stuff and stamp," Julia said, as if this small task was the highlight of her day.

It was time for the monthly newsletter to go out, and Julia always came in to help. She enjoyed the mundane work, and besides—the church secretary always knew what was going on with everyone in the church. Julia enjoyed the challenge of weaseling the gossip out of Margaret without her knowing it.

Ben got up from his desk and walked into the reception area. It took all of five steps.

"Hi, Julia," Ben said with a smile.

Julia looked up. "Hey, Ben . . . I mean Reverend Montague." She laughed and so did Ben. Julia stared at him with her usual "melt in your mouth" look. Ben's bright blue eyes caught her every time. Ben was the most handsome man she knew, and she had no qualms about letting him know that. She also knew she was ten years too old for him, and in a joking manner, she reminded him not to even try, that she would never fall for a younger man. They both knew he wouldn't have tried and the joking was all in good fun. There was no stress in their relationship; it was a comfortable one.

"Um, um," Julia said as if she were hypnotized, "there must be an unwritten rule in this church somewhere that the pastors all have to be tall, dark and handsome!" Buck was as handsome as Ben. Both had very similar features: tall, muscular frames, well defined facial features, olive complexions, dark hair and of course, the magnetic blue eyes. People had made comments that if Buck were thirty-five years younger they could pass for twins.

Ben and Margaret laughed at Julia's over dramatization.

Julia collected herself and then completely changed her demeanor and the subject. "I'm taking Miss Mary to the doctor tomorrow. This may be her final recheck on her hip. She's hoping for a clean bill of health," Julia said.

"Oh?" Ben said. "That is wonderful. Which doctor, the orthopedist?" he asked very nonchalantly.

"Yep," she replied as she licked a stamp and stuck it to the envelope.

Ben's stomach started doing flip flops, his shoulder got tight and a sudden pool of sweat began to collect under his arms.

"Julia," Ben said calmly, "you have done so much of the driving for Miss Mary. I haven't had a good visit with her recently. Why don't you let me take her?"

"That's not necessary, I really don't mind," Julia replied. "I enjoy being with Miss Mary."

He had to think of something quick, something not too obvious.

"You'd actually be doing me a favor, Julia, if you'd let me take her," Ben said almost too calmly. "I promised her a visit this week and tomorrow's the only day I can really do it."

"Suit yourself," she said.

Yes! he thought to himself. "Well, ladies, I'll leave you to lick and stick. I've got a sermon to finish."

Ben walked back to his office and sat at his desk. He tried to get back to writing his sermon, but he had lost all focus on his sermon for the day.

Chapter Twenty

BEN HAD GOTTEN up early in the morning. Truth be told, he couldn't sleep. The only other time he had felt this way was when he first met Elizabeth in his third year philosophy class in college. It took him two months to even talk to her, and by the time he did, he was already in love with her, even though he knew nothing about her except that she was taking a philosophy class that semester and she was beautiful. They dated for two years and would have gotten married if Ben had not been called by God to go into the ministry.

Elizabeth didn't want to be a minister's wife. The pain of losing her was devastating to Ben, and it was the only time since he had been a teenager that he sat down and cried until his stomach hurt and it was hard to breathe. He had gotten angry with God, too. Why did serving Him mean that he had to give up the woman he loved? Ben even questioned if God was really calling him. But, when someone is called into the ministry by God, somewhere deep inside of them they know it is real. And Ben knew deep down that his calling was real.

For the better part of an hour, Ben walked around his apartment aimlessly. His mind was wandering. Finally, he focused on what he needed to do: shower and get dressed. He picked out his best suit and the tie that he thought was most striking. He wore his best leather lace up shoes and his dress watch.

He needed one final check in the mirror. He smoothed his hair with his hands one final time and then reached for a bottle of cologne and splashed some on. He rarely wore cologne, but today he did.

The drive to Miss Mary's house seemed to take forever. For the entire ride to her house he was tapping his fingers on the steering wheel and changing the radio station. There just didn't seem to be anything worth listening to, although he really didn't have any idea what he had heard.

When Miss Mary came to the door, she was all ready to go. Ben helped her into the car, took her walker, folded it and put it in the backseat.

"I can't tell you how much I appreciate you taking me to the doctor," Miss Mary said.

"My pleasure," Ben replied. "I had promised you a visit this week and I thought this was a perfect opportunity."

They chatted on the way to the doctor's office. She wanted to know what she had been missing at church. Ben caught her up on things. She told Ben how appreciative she was of Reverend Buck for the few times he had picked her up and taken her to the Sunday service. She was, however, ready to get back to normal, whatever that might be.

"Julia has filled me in on a few things," Miss Mary said. "She told me that Ashley broke into tears while singing praise and worship two weeks ago and he claimed it was the power of the Holy Spirit."

"It was interesting," was Ben's only response.

"Julia doesn't believe that Ashley is for real," Miss Mary said, as if it was a question.

"Well, I understand where she is coming from, but it is not ours to pass judgment. A lot of his worship style is not for me either, but that doesn't make it wrong as long as it is truly worshipping God." Ben glanced over at Miss Mary. "I hope I don't sound like I'm preaching," Ben added.

"Not at all," said Miss Mary. "By the way, you look very handsome today. Have you got something important?"

"Why, I'm taking a very special lady to the doctor," Ben replied. "What could be more important than that?"

The waiting room was crowded with people of all ages, and more than half of them had a cast on some part of their body. Miss Mary asked Ben to sign her in so she could go ahead and sit down. He did as she asked and then took the seat next to her.

"Has Reverend Buck been taking care of my car?" she asked Ben.

"Well, he certainly has been spending a lot of time with it," answered Ben, and they both gave a little laugh.

There was a small space behind the receptionist's desk that opened into the back office. There wasn't much to see, but every once in a while a person would walk by. Ben was watching as inconspicuously as possible, hoping to get a glance of Sylvia DiLeo.

What am I doing? he thought to himself. He might not even get to see her. She was a busy doctor and these were her office hours. And it suddenly dawned on him that he was there to drive Miss Mary and wait for her. And waiting meant in the waiting room. He began to tap his foot rapidly.

The door that led to the examination rooms opened and a woman with a deep voice called Miss Mary's name. Ben helped Miss Mary up to her walker. Once she got her footing secure, Ben said, "I'll be here waiting for you when you're finished," and he began to sit back down.

Miss Mary turned her head back sharply and looked at Ben with eyes that meant business. "You're coming with me," Miss Mary said firmly. Then with a smile on her face and in a very soft voice she whispered, "This is what you came for."

Ben felt like he was a thousand shades of red. How did Miss Mary know? He was so embarrassed, but he did as he was told and got up and followed Miss Mary through the door that led to the examination rooms. The palms of his hands began to sweat.

"So, Ms. Fletcher," the nurse said, "we're hoping for some good news today, aren't we?"

"I've been praying," Miss Mary replied.

The nurse finished what looked like scribbling onto a chart and then said, "Dr. DiLeo will be with you shortly," and she walked out the door and closed it behind her.

Ben didn't know if his stomach was reacting to the impending encounter with Sylvia DiLeo or from embarrassment with Miss Mary. Either way, he seriously thought he might be sick right there in the examination room.

"Don't worry," Miss Mary said, "your secret is safe with me." Her smile was comforting to Ben.

"I am so sorry, Miss Mary," Ben said.

"For what?" Miss Mary said in a tone that almost sounded like a bark. "You don't owe me an apology. Who knows, maybe my broken hip was all so you could meet her."

"Miss Mary!" Ben said with a startle in his voice.

"Oh, for Pete sakes, Ben, I knew it the day I was in the emergency room. Why, for a moment I thought I was disturbing the two of you."

They both laughed.

"Nothing gets past you, does it, Miss Mary?"

"I've let a few things get past me I wish I hadn't have, but it's too late now. So, the best advice I can give you," Miss Mary said, "is to learn from my mistakes." With that, the door opened.

Sylvia DiLeo walked in carrying a chart and reading it as she walked, just like she did when she was in the emergency room. But today, she was wearing her hair down. The waves reached to the middle of her back and she had it tucked behind her ear on the right side. And today she was wearing a skirt. Pastor or not, Ben was a carnal man.

It was obvious that Sylvia DiLeo was not expecting Ben to be in the room. When she looked up from the chart, her face immediately turned pale white as if she had seen a ghost and then it promptly turned flush. Sylvia seemed to be speechless.

Ben started the conversation. "Hello, I don't know if you remember me, I met you in the emergency room. I'm Ben Montague."

"Yes, I remember," Sylvia said, "how are you?" She quickly turned to look at Miss Mary without giving Ben a chance to answer. "And how are you, Ms. Fletcher?"

"I was hoping you were going to tell me how I was doing," answered Miss Mary.

"I need to get another x-ray first," Sylvia said. She opened the door and called to a nurse, who came over to the examination room. "This is Libby. She is going to take you back to x-ray. As soon as I get that, I can tell you how you are doing." Sylvia DiLeo smiled sweetly at Miss Mary.

Libby and Miss Mary headed slowly out of the room.

"Where should I wait?" Ben said.

"You can wait here," said Libby. "We won't be a moment."

Sylvia had set the chart down on the counter in the tiny examination room. It looked as though she was writing, but her pen did not appear to be very active. Ben sat back down in the chair. He wasn't sure he had ever before been this uncomfortable in a situation. He knew that when he finally took his jacket off there would be sweat stains down to his waist.

Still looking down at the chart, Sylvia began to speak. "So, Reverend Montague, you haven't told me what type of reverend you are." She now turned around. Leaning against the counter, she was facing him from across the room.

"In the United Covenant Churches of America," he replied. "I'm a Covenant minister." There was silence for a moment, and then he said, "And may I ask what religion you are?"

Sylvia gave a little grin accompanied by a slight chuckle and then said, "Well, outwardly I'm a Presbyterian, inwardly I'm a Buddhist and intellectually I'm agnostic."

He had to admit, that was the first time he had ever received an answer like that, and he wasn't quite sure how to respond. Cleverly, he said, "So, does that have anything to do with the kind of clothes you wear?"

They both laughed.

"You're quick," she said and smiled.

This was the first time he had seen her smile straight on. She had a beautiful smile with stunning white teeth. The left side of her upper lip rose slightly. He couldn't believe he was thinking this, but it was the sexiest smile he had ever seen. He thought he was going to melt right there.

"So where is your church?" she asked.

"I am at First Covenant Chapel over in Wakefield. I started there as a third year seminary student and I've been allowed to stay. Guess they liked me," he said. "So where do you attend church?" he asked.

"I'm sorry to say that I don't really attend. My father was Catholic and my mother was Presbyterian. When we went to church, it was the Presbyterian Church. I guess my parents never came to terms with their religious differences, and neither one was really concerned about it anyway, so most often, we never went."

"DiLeo doesn't sound like a Presbyterian name," Ben said.

"Montague doesn't sound Covenant," she countered.

The room was still for a moment. It was very obvious that there was a lot of chemistry in the room. They both were getting uncomfortable.

"Well," she said, "I'm going to check my next patient so I don't get too behind schedule. I'll be back in a moment, when Ms. Fletcher has finished her x-ray." She smiled and walked out the door.

Ben leaned back in his chair. "Lord, help me," he said out loud.

When Miss Mary returned, Ben was sitting in the room alone flipping through a *Good Housekeeping* magazine; it was the only thing in the room. Before Miss Mary could even get settled, Sylvia DiLeo was entering the room carrying a set of x-rays.

"Things look good, Ms. Fletcher," Dr. DiLeo said as she sat down on the small rolling physician's stool in the corner of the room. She rolled over until she was next to Miss Mary. "Your hip has healed very well, Ms. Fletcher. I am very pleased with your x-ray."

Miss Mary could hear in Dr. DiLeo's voice that there was something else. "I'm no spring chicken," Miss Mary said, "so what's the bad news? No doctor ever speaks to you this way unless there's some bad news."

Sylvia DiLeo smiled. She had compassion in her eyes. She spoke tenderly and soft. "Ms. Fletcher, I think it is time that you consider not driving anymore. Your x-ray looks very good and I am pleased with the results of your surgery, but . . . "

"There's always a but," Miss Mary said with a sad voice.

Dr. DiLeo continued, "Your reflexes aren't what they should be, and I would be wrong not to tell you that I don't think you should drive anymore."

Miss Mary nodded her head very slowly. She understood.

Sylvia patted Miss Mary on the arm and stood up from the rolling stool. She turned and extended her hand toward Ben. "Reverend Montague," she said, "I sincerely hope that you and I will have the chance to see each other again." Their eyes were intent on each other, and it almost felt as if their hands had melted into each other.

"I do, too," Ben replied.

Chapter Twenty-One

BUCK PULLED INTO the parking lot at the Dixie Diner in Miss Mary's dark blue Mercedes. He had been driving it since he had picked her up and driven her to church that Sunday. It was Tuesday and time for his regular lunch with Tom. As usual, Tom was already there waiting. Buck was rarely on time. People just came to accept that fact about him and planned their time accordingly. Buck slipped into their usual booth.

"Brother Tom," he said.

For the first time, that phrase got on Tom's nerves. They had been meeting every Tuesday at the Dixie Diner for the last two and a half years, and the salutation was always the same.

"Bob," was all Tom replied, but he did give Buck a slight nod of recognition.

"What's for lunch today?" Buck asked as he picked up the menu lying on the table in front of him.

A young lady carrying an order pad walked over to the table. She was very pretty, with shoulder length blonde hair and bright blue eyes. She didn't look old enough to even be out of high school, but since it was Tuesday and she was working the lunch shift, she must have been. The Dixie Diner was reminiscent of the 1970s, and the waitresses wore light blue skirts that were hemmed above their knees with a little white apron that accentuated the waist.

"Hi, gentlemen," the girl said, "may I take your order?"

"Where's Sandy?" Buck asked, curious why their usual waitress wasn't serving them.

"Her son got real sick. They don't know what's wrong," the girl began to tell them. "They took him to Children's Hospital two days ago. I don't know much more than that. I'm Michelle. I usually work weekends, but I'm covering for Sandy 'til she gets back."

Michelle dropped her pencil on the floor and leaned over to pick it up. Buck couldn't help but notice that the scoop neck of her shirt allowed him a peak of her cleavage. He took full advantage of the view and then placed his napkin in his lap to hide what might be obvious.

"Well, it must be our lucky day," Buck said. "We couldn't ask for a prettier replacement. I'll have a tuna salad on toast and a sweet tea."

Michelle turned toward Tom for his order. Tom looked at her compassionately.

"I am so sorry to hear about Sandy's son," Tom said. "Is there anything we can do?"

"Just pray, I guess," the young girl replied.

Buck was still fixed on how soft and peachy the skin was that led down Michelle's neck and into the scoop at the bosom of her shirt. He noticed the simple gold cross that hung around her neck. "That's a beautiful necklace," he said. "I'm Bob Buck, Reverend Bob Buck. I am the senior pastor over at First Covenant Chapel in Wakefield."

"Glad to meet you," she said with a shy smile.

Tom, who was becoming uncomfortable, jumped into the conversation. "I'll have the turkey sandwich on whole wheat and a sweet tea."

"It will be right up," she said and turned and walked away. Buck watched every step.

"That's awful about Sandy," Tom said.

"Yeah," Buck said in a murmur. Then with energy, he said, "So how'd we do this week?"

Tom placed the financial report in front of Buck. He watched Buck as he skimmed the paper. Every Tuesday, the same: "What did we make?" Buck would ask. Rarely did they talk about anything else. Buck never asked Tom how he was doing or how his wife, Lisa, was. In fact, Tom felt that Buck was intentionally trying to avoid asking. It had become obvious that all Buck was interested in was the numbers report.

The church had finished their stewardship campaign and the pledge cards were in. They had done well with pledges, but the operating budget of the church had skyrocketed, especially the music department, which was enjoying a new sound system, projectors for visuals and almost weekly guest musicians. The balance sheet no longer balanced. This troubled Tom immensely, but Buck didn't seem to care how much things cost. He always came back and said, "God will provide."

Tom began to speak. "Bob, I know what you want more than anything is to build a new sanctuary, but I have to be honest with you and tell you that I don't think we are in a financial position to even think about it," Tom said with a concerned look on his face.

"Tom, brother," Buck replied with that smile that was beginning to look like the cat that just swallowed the canary, "I've told you, man, you've got to trust me."

Tom trusted Buck. That wasn't in question. Aside from the church not having the financial resources for the building project, Tom also felt that Buck's administrative skills weren't adequate to control a project of this proportion.

The cute young waitress came back over to the table carrying an oval tray with the gentlemen's lunches. She put them down on the table.

"Can I get you anything else?" she asked the men.

Buck looked her right in the eyes and smiled while raising his left eyebrow to her, obviously reading much more into the question then she had intended.

"I think we are fine, thank you," Tom said.

Buck began to eat his lunch. Tom paused for a moment, realizing this was the first Tuesday that Sandy had not served them, as well as the first Tuesday that Buck had not offered or requested a blessing. The men sat in silence while they ate.

Buck began to think about the new sanctuary he was going to build. He had seen an old abandoned barn at a farm as he drove through the back roads of Wakefield the other day. He decided then that he was going to have the floor in his office of his new sanctuary building made of old barn wood. He had seen it in a home he was visiting last week and it was beautiful. It would be expensive, but he would try to get the owner to give the wood to him for free since he was a servant of the Lord, after all.

He hadn't mentioned the property to Edward recently, and Edward hadn't mentioned it to him, either. He needed that land. It was the only way they were going to be able to build anything. He guessed it was time for more Scotch and cigars. He made a note in his mental agenda. Visiting with Edward would be a priority this coming week.

Chapter Twenty-Two

THE SUNSET WAS more lovely than usual. The sky was particularly clear, and the glow of the sun as it dipped beneath the horizon was magnificent with hues of orange and pink. Edward and Buck sat in the room on the backside of Edwards's house, where they always did, to watch the sunset, drink their Scotch and smoke their cigars.

"Can you believe how the church has grown?" Buck said.

"It sure has," replied Edward, "and with so many young folks. Old folks like me are few and far between there now."

"But, it is the people like you who are the pillars of the church," Buck proclaimed. After a slight pause he said, "Have you given any more thought to your land back there?"

"I've thought about it," Edward said with hesitancy.

Buck knew he'd better start some fast talk if he was going to get that property. He needed it, and he needed it now. "I know that your wife would have wanted the church to have it," Buck started. "Just think of the legacy of her which you will carry on. We have so many young people that would grow up in the new church building if we had one. Can't you feel that in your heart, Edward?"

"I do love to see the children at church. Beverly and I were never able to have children and we sure did want them,"

Edward responded. "You're right, it would make Beverly happy to know that we donated the land and children play on it."

"I'm not pushing you, Edward. I know it's a hard decision, but I really need to know soon because we are going to be in a bad mess if we don't do something quickly."

"I know, Reverend. I'll make my decision in the next day or two and let you know."

"You're a good man, Edward. God will bless you for this," Buck said, and they both dropped the subject and turned back toward the sunset. A big white puffy cloud had moved into the picturesque scene, diffusing the usual glow of the setting sun.

Chapter Twenty-Three

BUCK AND PEGGY sat at the dinner table in the parsonage. It was Saturday evening, usually the only day of the week when they ate together unless there was a special occasion happening, like a wedding. During May and June, that seemed to be every Saturday night.

Peggy had made steamed vegetables, roasted chicken and homemade biscuits.

"I went to visit Miss Mary today," Peggy said.

"How is she?" Buck replied.

"She's alright," Peggy said with sadness in her voice. "She has come to a point in her life where she has to deal with the realities of her age."

"Boy, I don't ever want to be there," Buck commented, more concerned about himself than about what Miss Mary was going through. "Did you meet the new folks that were at church last Sunday? The Reeds."

"Yes, I did. They seemed very nice," she said.

"They own Rivers Edge Golf Course and Country Club," Buck said with wide eyes.

"I didn't know that," responded Peggy, thinking to herself that she didn't care in the least what they owned.

"They would be a great resource for the church," he said. "I guess I better dust off my clubs."

His statement made Peggy mad. "I think the church would be a great resource for them," she said.

"Of course it would," Buck replied very matter-of-factly.

Peggy paused for a moment to think and then said, "I think they are seeking spiritual guidance. They lost a son to cancer about a year and a half ago. Laura, the mother, said they haven't been to church since then."

"Oh, wow," Buck said with a shocked tone. "That's too bad," Buck responded, before moving on to talk about growth of the church. "Peggy, can you believe how many people have joined the church in the last three years? I told you I could make this big." Buck was gleaming with pride about his triumph. Peggy was sick of hearing about how much the church had grown and how much more it was going to grow. She knew it was all about a vendetta toward Frank Maddox. Buck was allowing that vendetta to control everything. She also knew that her husband had become cold, shallow and self-centered.

"Miss Mary said she would love to see you. She wanted me to ask you to come by and visit her," Peggy told Buck.

"I'll try to one of these days, but I've been checking with Ben to make sure he's been going to see her regularly." Buck had little interest in the people of the church anymore except for when it came to their checkbooks. But at least he was good at playing the game and the people still loved him.

Buck was serving himself another helping of steamed vegetables when the phone rang. He pushed back his chair from the table and got up to answer. "Hello?"

"Reverend, this is Edward."

"Edward, how are you this evening?"

"I'm quite fine, thank you," Edward replied. "I've made a decision."

Buck stood there frozen. He knew it was about the land, he just didn't know the answer. He crossed his fingers, looked upward and mouthed the words, "Please, God."

"About what?" Buck said in an intentionally curious voice.

"About my property," Edward responded, seemingly startled that Buck had to ask *about what.*

"Oh, that's so far in the back of my mind, I almost forgot," said Buck. "But, now that you mention it, tell me about it."

"I'm going to tithe it to First Covenant Chapel," Edward said and then paused for a moment before he continued, "in loving memory of my wife."

Yes! Buck mouthed, and then said, "Edward, God rewards those who give." He spoke in a very pastoral voice, but inside he could hardly contain himself. He finally had the missing piece for building his dream! "Thanks for calling to tell me. Blessings to you, brother."

When Buck hung up the phone, he went back to the table.

"What was that about?" Peggy asked.

"Oh, just some work the men's group is going to do." And he went back to his steamed vegetables.

Chapter Twenty-Four

TOM SAT AT the kitchen table, alone. He held a glass of wine in his hands and twisted it as he watched the wine slosh from one side to the other. It was nine in the evening and he had not heard from Lisa since three that afternoon. She had called his office to ask him when he would be home. He had told her he would be late, but his real intention was to surprise her by coming home early and taking her out for a romantic dinner at Leo's on the square in downtown Salem. They had not had much private time together recently and he wanted to be with her.

He arrived home at five. The house was dark and the doors were locked. He figured that she was out picking up the boys from ball practice. He decided to clean up for the evening and went to take a shower and put on fresh clothes. While he was shaving his five o'clock shadow, he heard noises in the kitchen. He looked into the mirror and smiled. He was looking forward to this evening. He finished dressing and walked to the kitchen.

"Dad, what are you doing here?" asked his fifteen-year-old son, Kyle, as he was eating something straight out of the container that he had found in the refrigerator.

"I live here," Tom replied.

"I know that," his son said with a "Well, duh" tone of voice, "but Mom said you wouldn't be home until late."

"Where is your mother? Didn't she bring you home?" he asked.

"No, I got a ride home with Ryan's dad. Mom said she had a meeting and would be late herself."

"Oh," Tom said, trying to hide his disappointment from his son. "Well, where's your brother? I guess it's just us men for dinner."

"He's staying over at Spencer's house. They've got some sort of class project due on Monday, and I'm heading to the movies." Kyle gave his dad a look that said, *Don't you remember when you were my age?* "It's Friday night, Dad!" Kyle left the empty container on the counter and said, "See ya, Dad," as he walked past his father.

Meeting? Lisa hadn't said anything to him about a meeting. He wondered where she was. What kind of meeting would she have on a Friday night? He tried her cell phone . . . no answer. *Maybe she won't be too late,* he thought to himself. He sat down in the overstuffed chair in the great room and picked up the television controller. He would watch the news while he waited.

He'd watched the local news and then watched the world news on CNN. He had had all that he could take of the depressing world. He missed Lisa and he was disappointed that his plan had fallen through. He should have told her, and this wouldn't have happened. They would be sitting at Leo's right now, sharing a bottle of Chianti, catching up with what the other one had done that day and anticipating the night to come. He was angry at himself. It's not Lisa's fault. After all, he had told her he wouldn't be home until late. Why shouldn't she go to this meeting on Friday evening?

He paced around the house not really knowing what to do with himself all alone. He tried to remember if he had ever even been in the house all alone before. He called her cell phone again . . . no answer. He decided he would call over at the Buck's to see if there was something going on at the church of which he was unaware.

Peggy answered, "Hello?"

"Hi, Peggy, this is Tom. How are you?"

"I'm well, Tom, how about you?" she responded in a cheerful voice.

"Oh, I'm just fine. I was wondering if there was a meeting that you or Bob knew about that Lisa might be at tonight?"

"I'm sorry, Tom," Peggy replied, "I'm not aware of any meetings and Bob's not here. He said he was going to do visitation at the hospital. You might call Ben and see if he knows about anything."

"Thank you, I'll try that," Tom said with a disappointed tone. "You have a good evening, Peggy."

He hated to bother Ben, but he did have a slight amount of concern that Lisa could have been in an accident. He dialed the phone.

"Hello?"

"Ben, this is Tom. How are you?" He was beginning to feel like a skipping record.

"I'm fine, and you?" Ben replied.

"I'm fine, and I am so sorry to call you on a Friday night, on your cell phone, no less," Tom said with a truly apologetic voice.

"Never a problem," said Ben. "I am always available. And you caught me at a good time. I'm on my way to the hospital to do visitation. In another fifteen minutes you wouldn't have gotten me. What can I do for you?"

"Oh." Tom was a little confused. "I just talked to Peggy, and she said Reverend Buck was doing visitation tonight."

"Well, he was going to, but called me at the last minute and told me he had something come up and asked if I could."

Tom was getting frustrated with the way it had become obvious that Buck had been brushing parishioners off and pawning them onto other people—mostly Ben.

"Really, all I was wondering was if you knew if there was some kind of a meeting that Lisa might be at this evening?"

"I don't," Ben said. "I don't think the church had anything planned for this evening."

"Well, I won't keep you," Tom said. "Enjoy your visitation."

"You have a good evening, Tom." And they hung up the phone.

Tom looked at his watch. It was 7:45. He got himself a glass of red wine and sat down at the kitchen table to wait. How late could she be?

Tom bowed his head and prayed. Even though he didn't want to acknowledge it, there was a tinge of fear that ran through him that maybe she was with another man. He and Lisa had had their problems, but he really believed they had worked them out. Buck had been a good pastoral counselor and had helped Lisa and Tom deal with their problems—problems that Tom felt were probably common to all marriages after twenty years. But Lisa had been different since their counseling. And to a large extent, the difference was good. She had broadened herself and gotten involved in more things. It gave them a new spark to their relationship and more things to talk about. But at the same time, she had become more passive and at times, that concerned Tom. Maybe they should start counseling with Buck again. It had been several years since they had talked with Buck about issues in their marriage.

It was 9:15. Tom's worry had turned into anger. He sat and twisted another glass of wine on the table.

At nine-thirty the side door that led from the garage to the kitchen opened. Tom remained seated, staring straight ahead. Lisa turned the corner and saw Tom sitting at the table. She was startled because she didn't expect him to be home. There was an obvious chill in the air.

"Sweetheart," Lisa said with a cheerful tone, "is everything alright? Why are you sitting there?"

"Where have you been?" Tom said in a monotone voice, letting no emotion show across his face.

"I've been at a meeting. What's wrong? Are the boys okay?"

"The boys are fine," Tom responded. "What meeting?"

"Why are you acting like this?" Lisa's voice was rising in pitch.

"What meeting?" Tom repeated sternly.

"Are you suggesting you don't believe me?" Lisa said with a defensive tone. "You are the one who told me you would be working late . . . as usual," she added at the end for a stab.

"I came home at five-thirty to surprise you. I was going to take you out for a romantic meal at Leo's and then planned to carry that romance into the night. But I guess you had better things to do."

"How was I supposed to know that?" Lisa's tone began to sound angry.

Tom hit his fist against the table. The glass of wine teetered. "Damn it, Lisa, what's going on?"

"I think you are distrusting me, is what's going on, as far as I can tell," Lisa said with a sharp tone in her voice. "Why don't you tell me what's going on?"

Tom was silent for a moment, not knowing what to say. He shouldn't have been suspicious. "I love you, Lisa, that's what's going on."

"Then why are you acting like this?" Lisa asked.

"I guess I'm afraid of losing you," he said in a quiet tone. Tom stood up from the table and walked toward Lisa. He stopped in front of her, looking straight into her eyes, and then put his arm around her shoulder and drew her into him. Her cheek rested against his chest. "I am sorry, Lisa," he said. "I was just worried."

Lisa closed her eyes with relief and slowly and quietly let out her breath, which she had begun to hold the moment she saw Tom's car in the garage.

Chapter Twenty-Five

BUCK BLEW OUT the candles on his birthday cake—all sixty-eight of them. His wish was that in the next two years, before he reached the mandatory retirement age of seventy, he could build First Covenant Chapel to be the size of Uriah Jonah's church. He only had two years in which to do it. Two years wasn't long. He knew he had to work fast.

Since he had been commissioned by the District Superintendent three years ago to close the doors of First Covenant Chapel forever, he had managed to increase his membership from seven to 237. The usual attendance on any given Sunday was at least 350, and on holidays it was greater. They now held three services each Sunday and it was always standing room only. There was no question about it: Buck thought they needed a bigger sanctuary. And thanks to his smooth work with Edward, they had the land on which to build it. Buck's architect friend, Ken Arnold, had been secretly toying with plans for several months now. Buck had promised Ken that he would be obtaining the property soon, and he wanted everything ready to go once he got it.

As usual, Buck snuck out of the kitchen after his birthday dinner was over, leaving Peggy and the girls to clean up while the grandchildren stretched out in the living room to watch television. As he tiptoed up the steps to his study, he stopped for a moment and turned to survey his family. He loved the sight of all of his children and grandchildren gathered around and enjoying each other.

He closed the door of his study behind him and took a deep breath. For some reason, on this birthday, he was a little weary. He needed rest, but there was no time.

He sat down at his desk and began to open the stack of mail that was beckoning him: bill; bill; advertisement; form letter from Don Russell reminding senior pastors that annual reports were due; and a bright blue envelope. Buck held the blue envelope up and looked at the return address: Mary Fletcher. A smile came across Buck's face. He enjoyed birthday cards. When he opened the card from Miss Mary, it was much more than just a birthday card. An official looking piece of paper, which was folded in the middle, fell out of the card. He set down the card without reading it and picked up the folded paper. It was the title to Miss Mary's dark blue Mercedes, and she had signed it over to him. "Yes!" he said out loud with his usual "scoring" gesture. He opened the top right drawer of his desk and stuck the title in the drawer. He set the bills aside, then scooped up the advertisements and Miss Mary's unread card and tossed them in the wastebasket.

This had been a wonderful birthday. He felt particularly youthful for a man of sixty-eight. He didn't want the celebration to end. Buck took his cell phone off the clip that hung on his belt and pushed the buttons. A voice answered.

"Can you meet me?" Buck said.

Chapter Twenty-Six

THE CHURCH WAS packed for the 9:30 service. They had set up folding chairs in the narthex to accommodate the overflow. This Sunday had been a disaster as far as logistics went. Ashley had put on a particularly long show at the beginning of the service. Ben preached a full twenty-five minutes on Sanctification, and it was Communion Sunday. The 9:30 service didn't let out until 10:50, and the eleven o'clock crowd was waiting at the door.

Buck was out front shaking the hands of people both coming and going. Ben was in the small room behind the pulpit area. Ashley abruptly opened the door.

"Come on, Ben, get out there. We've got to start the service," Ashley said, pronouncing his t's hard, as usual.

"Start?" Ben replied. "The Communion table hasn't even been reset."

"Doesn't matter," Ashley replied. "We've got a schedule to keep. Oh, by the way, I told Sandy not to play the Doxology after the offering; that will save us some time in the service." Ashley quickly walked out the door.

Ben couldn't believe what he had just heard. And who gave Ashley the authority to cut the Doxology out of the service? Ben was preaching today—not Ashley. They were doing the

Doxology, and they were not going to start the service until the Communion table was set and there was at least a semblance of reverence in the Church. He was sick of Ashley running the service like it was the "Sunday Morning Follies."

The tension running up Ben's neck had given him a splitting headache. His shoulders were hovering around his ears. He sat down in the wooden straight back chair in the corner of the room, folded his hands and lowered his head. God knew what he needed. He sat in silence for a moment.

As he entered the pulpit, he straightened his stole. Buck was already sitting in his chair to the left of the altar and gave Ben a look of, "Where have you been?" Ben walked past Ashley, who was obviously irritated, and over to Sandy. He leaned down and whispered something into her ear, then crossed in front of Ashley again and sat down in his chair next to Buck. The music started.

Buck looked around the congregation. The sanctuary was packed for a second service that morning. As he looked around, there were two things that became very obvious. Edward Tarken was not there. He had not been at the earlier service, either. *That's strange,* Buck thought to himself. Edward had always said, "If I'm not at church one Sunday, you better come looking for me in the hospital." Buck always thought he was joking, but just to be sure, he would check on Edward after the service.

The second thing that was very obvious was the third row. Katrina was there. Whenever Ben preached, she was always there. And Buck liked seeing her.

Ben looked at his watch. Ashley had been leading praise and worship for a full twenty minutes at this point with no end in sight. *Something has to give here,* Ben thought to himself. This had become the "Ashley March Show" and today, Ben would be his sidekick. Ashley had made a mockery out of worship and, as senior pastor, Buck was allowing it.

The music finally faded into a quiet background melody a full twenty-eight minutes into the service. Ben stood and started to move toward the lectern for the Pastoral Prayer when

Ashley suddenly dropped his head and threw his right hand up into the air.

"Lord!!!" Ashley cried out in a voice that brought everyone to attention in their seats. He continued, "Have mercy on us, Oh Mighty and Sovereign God. We give ourselves up to You!" Ashley was practically screaming. Ben stood frozen at the lectern, not knowing what to do.

"Take us! Mold us! We want nothing more than to be Your servants!" His tone quieted. "Oh, Gracious and Loving Father, we are so unworthy." Then loud again, "We are sinners!" The "s" went on for what seemed like an eternity. "Make us new again in You." Ashley's hand lowered down to his chest and he grabbed the cloth of his Nehru jacket right above his heart and clinched it. "Amen," he said, and sat with a dramatic flair as if he were completely drained of all emotion.

Ben was furious and his heart hurt. He wanted to pray for Ashley and ask forgiveness for making a stage out of God's house. He tried to collect himself for a moment. A pastoral prayer would seem redundant, although there was nothing pastoral about the prayer that Ashley just offered.

Ben was silent for a moment, and then in a very calming tone said, "Please bow your heads and join me in the prayer that our Lord taught us.

Our Father
Who art in Heaven
Hallowed be Thy Name . . .

When they had finished the Lord's Prayer, Ben asked the ushers to come forward for the morning offering. As the plate began to go around, Ben moved back to his seat. He glanced over at Ashley, who was now leading the choir in the anthem. Ashley caught Ben out of the corner of his eye, turned his head and gave Ben a cocky little smile that said, "I'm in charge, don't mess with me."

While the choir was singing, Buck leaned over to Ben and whispered, "We're running long. You're going to have to cut your sermon a little."

Ben looked at Buck with an extremely disapproving face and whispered back, “What do you mean, cut my sermon?”

“You’ve only got ten minutes left,” Buck replied. “Remember, all you need to do is sell the sizzle, not the steak.”

Sell the sizzle, not the steak. Ben wasn’t sure he had heard correctly. Was that what preaching had come to? And how was he going to cut his sermon now?

At the end of the anthem, Ashley seated the choir and started to seat himself when Sandy started to play the Doxology. Ben was motioning the congregation to stand as the morning offerings were brought back up to the altar and lifted up to God.

Ashley jumped back to his feet, hoping nobody had seen him start to sit. He had told Ben that he cut the Doxology, and now he looked like a fool in front of the entire congregation for not knowing the stage directions.

Chapter Twenty-Seven

BUCK WENT UP to his study early the next morning to prepare for the staff meeting. He dialed the phone, and it rang four times.

"Hello?" said the voice on the other end.

"Brother Tom," Buck said in the usual manner, "how are you this morning?"

"Doing well, Reverend, doing well," Tom replied.

"What's the count?" Buck asked.

"Well, we had 571 in attendance between the two services and we brought in $14,732.28."

"Hallelujah!" Buck shouted. "Listen, print me out a list of what everyone's tithed over the last month and bring it to the staff meeting in a sealed envelope, if you would," said Buck.

"Sure," Tom replied. His voice was quiet.

Buck could sense the tone in Tom's voice. "Is everything okay, brother?" he asked.

"I don't know," Tom said. "Things don't seem to be right between Lisa and me. I can't put my finger on it. To be honest," he paused for a moment, "to be honest, I'm worried she might be seeing someone else."

It took a few seconds for Buck to reply. He had to gather his thoughts to think of exactly what he should say. "Tom, sometimes our hearts can lead us to overactive imaginations. I am sure things are fine between you and Lisa. Just relax and let your relationship be."

"I thought maybe it would do us some good to come in for some more counseling," Tom said.

Buck didn't know how to respond. He couldn't counsel them now. "My schedule is tight right now." Buck knew that was the wrong thing to say as soon as it came out of his mouth, but Tom had caught him totally off guard with his suggestion.

"I understand," Tom said, even though he really didn't. "Back to the numbers then. Bob, the numbers may sound good, but when you start looking at the balance sheets, the picture isn't quite the same. We have some huge expenses, and now that you are starting to plan a new building, I'm not sure I feel real comfortable with the numbers."

"Tom, man, don't worry. A church isn't the same as other businesses. We'll get a building campaign going and that will cover the cost. Don't lose sight of the providence of God."

Tom didn't have a response. This was not the same Bob Buck that he knew several years ago. There was something else driving him.

"See you at nine," Buck said, and they hung up the phone.

Buck noticed the little red light flashing on the answering machine. He pushed the button and the machine began to speak. "Reverend, Edward here." His voice was very weak. "I'm calling you from the hospital. I wasn't feeling too well so I went to my doctor and he sent me right on over here. He wants to do some tests." The machine beeped and then said in its mechanical voice, "Friday, 4:18 P.M."

Damn, he had forgotten to check on Edward. He hadn't checked his machine since Friday morning, and here it was Monday. He'd call Edward later. He had a lot to do for the staff meeting, which was only an hour away.

• • •

MARGARET WAS ALREADY at her desk. She was always there early on Monday mornings.

"You're looking bright and chipper today, woman," Buck said as he walked in the door.

"Feeling chipper, too," she replied. "How are you?"

"You know me," he said, "I'm always great. Is Ashley here yet?"

"He was here before me today."

"I," Buck said, correcting her English.

"I, what do you mean, 'I'?" she asked.

"He was here before I," Buck said as he walked out the door and turned right down the hall.

The door was open to Ashley's office. "Morning, brother," Buck said.

"Brother Buck, come on in," Ashley replied. Ashley stood up from behind his desk, walked around to the front of it and sat in the chair next to Buck. He rested his wrists on the arms of the chair letting his hands dangle. He crossed his right leg over his left and began to shake the clog on his foot.

"I want to let you know that I think you are doing an awesome job," Buck said.

"Thank you, brother," Ashley replied. "Man, did you see it this Sunday? It was standing room only."

"We have got to get moving on this building project," Buck commented in recognition that he did notice it was standing room only the past Sunday. "I've got Bobby working with an architect. Actually, between you and me, I started on the plans about a year ago," Buck said in a whisper.

"A year ago?" Ashley said with a questioning tone in his voice.

"You know, it takes foresight to make good things happen," Buck began. "When I saw that you were drawing in people with your music, I knew that the time was right. Edward had already told me he wanted to give the church his property. It was just a matter of when." Although Ashley was an ally, Buck didn't want him to know he had actually asked Edward for the property. "The plans are almost ready, and if we can secure a loan we can have this thing moving in no time."

"Well, let's do it, brother!" Ashley said with enthusiasm in his voice and a certain sway to his hands.

They could hear the chairs moving and the low hum of voices down the hall. "We better get moving. I hear the others down the hall. We don't want them to start the staff meeting without us," Buck said. They both laughed.

As they were walking down the hall, Ashley said, "Oh, David's going to be here this morning. We're ready to kick the music up a notch. We've been working on a new format we're going to share with you all today."

"Wonderful! I get to see my son, too—a double blessing," Buck replied, cheerful as always as long as the situation was benefiting him.

Margaret was pouring coffee into cups. Tom was sitting at the far end of the table with his head buried in a folder. He was scribbling something with a pen. Ben was sitting two chairs down. He looked solemn.

Buck opened the meeting in prayer, as usual, and then ran through the numbers of yesterday's service, comparing them to the previous week. He went over the congregational care needs, assigning most of them to Ben. Included on the list was Edward Tarken, who had not been contacted by anyone from the church since he was admitted to the hospital the previous Friday. Buck did very little visitation anymore. Most of his time was spent with administration and church development.

Buck motioned toward Ashley and said, "Ashley, tell us what's new in the music department."

Ashley stood with the usual drama, flapping his arms with emotion. "David and I are making some changes to the music starting two weeks from now."

David stood up next to Ashley and said, "We are bringing in some electric instruments. Some of my buddies who play jingle backgrounds have agreed to play for us on Sunday mornings." David was very articulate and firm in his way of speaking. He presented himself well, just like his father. "We've been visiting Uriah Jonah's church. They sell their marketing strategies through workshops to churches who desire to grow like they have. This is part of what we have learned it takes to make a church successful."

"Next thing you know," Tom said under his breath so no one could hear, "they're going to be offering stock options."

"We've been watching their format, seeing what it is they do that draws the people in," David continued, telling the details with excitement. "Dad's even gone with us a few times!" Ashley, David and Buck all smiled.

Ben had not said a word all morning. He was still fuming from his encounter with Ashley the day before, and listening to David now, he wanted to stand up and start turning the tables over, yelling, "You are turning this church into a market!" He had held his tongue as long as he could. He had to speak out.

Margaret was watching Ben. She could tell there was something serious on his mind. Ben was rigid with tension that was very apparent in his shoulders. What she saw more than that, though, was the uncanny resemblance Ben had to David. So much so, it rattled her. And right now it looked like the two were heading for a showdown.

Ben pushed his chair back slightly from the table as if to stand, but didn't. He spoke in a low, controlled voice. "I would like for us to step back just a moment and look at the overall picture of this church."

Ashley, David and Buck stared at him. After a moment of silence, Buck said, as if he had been offended, "What are you getting at, Ben?"

Ben stood and began to speak. "What is our purpose? What is our goal? " There was obvious agitation in his voice. "For goodness sake, what is the mission of this church?"

Tom looked up from his papers for the first time since the meeting had started. Those were his thoughts exactly, he had just never had the courage to say them. He knew how important building this church was to Buck. That's all Buck ever talked about at their weekly Tuesday lunch meetings down at the Dixie Diner. Building a larger sanctuary was the most important thing in existence to Buck, and everything Buck did was in effort to make that happen. Tom couldn't go against

Buck. How could he? Buck had been there for Tom and his wife when they were separated, and Buck had helped him patch his marriage back together. If it hadn't been for Buck, Tom would have lost everything that was important to him: his wife and his children. He owed Buck a lot and because of that, he couldn't go against him. But he knew that the way Buck was doing things was leading the church into destruction.

"That's a good question, Ben," Ashley said, jumping into the conversation as if he were in charge, "and I certainly do appreciate your bringing that up. You are right. We need to form a mission statement. However, I think we are very clear on the direction in which we are going."

The muscles in Ben's face tightened as he looked Ashley square in the eyes, and he said, "Ashley, you may be clear on the direction you are taking this church, but what I am questioning is the reason you are doing it."

"What are you implying?" David snapped back in defense of Ashley.

Margaret and Tom sat and observed quietly. They were not going to get in the middle of this. They looked as though they were watching a tennis match.

Ashley gently patted David on the shoulder. "That's okay, David," Ashley said in a soft but patronizing voice. "Let Ben tell us what's on his mind."

Ben took a deep breath and then calmly spoke. "You have reduced God into being simply another commodity, packaged for mass consumption."

Buck had taken a seat. He'd let Ashley and David battle this one. It was too risky for him to appear to take sides.

"Ben, brother, you aren't seeing the big picture," Ashley said calmly.

Ben's hands were clinched. He wanted to yell, *Don't call me brother!*

"What is the big picture, Ashley?" Ben questioned.

David jumped in to answer. "If we are going to compete in this market, we have to reach the people where they are. We can't expect them to come to us. We have to give them some bang for their buck. Look at Uriah Jonah. He knows what the people want and he is taking it to them. And he is pulling people in by the truckload."

Bang for their buck! Do they really think they're doing this for God? Ben thought to himself. He wanted grab them both and shake them, shake some sense into them.

"Worship is not about focusing on what the people want," Ben said in a firm voice. "You seem to be viewing this from the wrong vantage point."

"Wrong vantage point?" Ashley replied. "I have been called by God to save souls, and the best way to do that is to bring them into the church. How many people have you brought in, Ben?" Ashley said in a voice that offered it as a challenge.

Ben wasn't going to stoop to his level, but he wasn't going to let it go, either.

"Do you really believe that God has empowered you to save souls?" Ben asked Ashley and then continued without giving him a chance to answer. "You," Ben said, his voice now full of sarcasm, "don't see the big picture, Brother Ashley." Then with strong emotion and emphasis, Ben said, "Only God can save a soul. The best I can hope to be is the mirror that reflects the light, and in doing so, I become a servant . . . not a celebrity."

Margaret certainly wasn't taking minutes on this. And at this point, all she wanted to do was slide out of her chair, under the table, and crawl out the door.

David stretched his neck from side to side, obviously a trait he inherited from his father. His face was flushed with anger. "My father did you a favor when he let you come to this church," David said, looking at Ben. "You have a lot of nerve acting as if you are the high and mighty one."

Ben wasn't going to let this conversation go any further. It was heading for a bad ending. He knew he was low man on the totem pole and he was only going to hurt himself with any further comments.

"I think that we have outlived the productivity of this meeting," Ben said, looking at Buck. "Reverend Buck, if it is alright with you I would like to go do visitation now." He hoped Buck would understand that he was referring to visiting Edward Tarken in the hospital, as nobody else had seemed to care that he was there.

"I think that would be a good idea," Buck said. "I think we have just about covered everything we need to anyway." Then he turned toward Margaret and said, "Anything else, Marge?"

She quickly scrambled to find her notes and regain her focus on the task at hand. "No," she said. "No, I think that's about it."

"Meeting adjourned," Buck said.

Chapter Twenty-Eight

BEN KNOCKED LIGHTLY on the door of room 307 at Salem Regional Medical Center and then entered.

"Hello, Edward," Ben said in a soft voice.

"Reverend Montague, how are you?" Edward answered.

"I am fine, and please call me Ben. The question is, how are you?"

Edward filled Ben in on his situation. His blood pressure had gotten extremely low, along with a few other unexplainable symptoms. He was there mostly just to be aggravated by the nurses and serve as a pincushion, as far as he could tell. Ben and Edward visited for a good part of the afternoon. Edward asked about the church. He wanted to know what he had missed on Sunday. Ben really didn't want to talk about the church, so he gave Edward just enough information to make him happy and then changed the subject.

Their visit had run long and Ben needed to leave. They prayed together. Ben asked God for healing and strength, he prayed for the doctors and he prayed for comfort and acceptance for Edward.

Ben stood up, walked over to Edward and placed his hand on Edward's shoulder. "May the peace of the Lord be with you," he said.

Edward was obviously touched. He looked up at Ben and said, "And also with you, my friend."

As Ben headed for the door, Edward called out, "Hey, you tell Reverend Buck to come visit me, would you?"

"I'll do that," Ben replied.

"And Ben," Edward said.

Ben had turned around and was looking at Edward. "Yes?"

"Thank you."

Ben smiled at Edward and gave him a little nod, then turned and walked out the door.

Ben had gone into the hospital in very low spirits, but after visiting with Edward he felt fresh and renewed. It never ceased to amaze Ben that whenever he went to minister to someone, he felt he was always the one who had received the blessing.

He pushed the button for the elevator and looked out the window while he waited. The sky was blue with puffy white clouds floating through it. *Beautiful,* he thought.

Ding. The elevator doors began to open. As Ben turned his attention to the elevator, he was confronted with the presence of Sylvia DiLeo, engrossed in a medical chart as she stepped out of the elevator.

Ben's heart immediately started beating rapidly. *Say something, say something!* he was telling himself. *Don't let her walk away.* Why did she make him weak in the knees—and mute, of all things?

She was now completely out of the elevator and about to head on her way. She had never looked up from the chart. If he was going to get the opportunity to speak to her, it was up to him. Did he even want to talk to her? Of course he did! *Say something, Ben. Say something!* He was talking to himself. Why couldn't he just say something to her?

He was now looking at Sylvia's back as she started to walk away. He closed his eyes tightly and took a deep breath, and with every ounce of effort he could muster, he opened his mouth and said the only thing he could. "Hello?"

Sylvia stopped walking, raised her head slowly from the chart and turned to look over her right shoulder. A smile slowly broke across her face. “Reverend Montague,” she said, and then turned around to face him. “Hello.”

They stood there for a moment, an uncomfortable but pleasurable moment. Their eyes had met each other, and for the time it was as if everyone and everything else around them had disappeared. The noises in the background became muffled, and the people walking by were just shadows.

“Please, call me Ben. How are you?” he said.

“I am well,” she said, pausing, “Ben. So what brings you here today?”

“Visitation. One of our parishioners is here. Pastors probably spend as much time at the hospitals as they do anywhere else.”

“How’s Ms. Fletcher?” she asked while fidgeting with a paperclip on the file.

“She’s alright,” Ben replied. “Still having some difficulty getting around, but she is a lady of great spirit.”

Sylvia nodded slightly and smiled. “I hope I didn’t upset her by suggesting that she not drive anymore.”

“You did what was right. I’m sure it is a difficult thing to face, but she seems to have accepted it. She even gave her car to Reverend Buck, our senior pastor!” Ben said, as if he was still having a hard time believing it.

“That’s a pretty good perk for being a pastor,” she said.

“Don’t let that fool you, it’s a rare occasion,” replied Ben.

Ben and Sylvia were so absorbed in their conversation that they had been totally unaware that people getting off the elevator had to walk around them. The elevator door opened again, and a nurse pushing a patient in a wheelchair and rolling an IV pole tried to exit.

“Excuse me,” the nurse said.

There was no response from Ben and Sylvia; they hadn’t heard her.

“Excuse me,” the nurse said in a louder tone.

Sylvia look around and, very embarrassed, said, “Oh, I am so sorry!” She moved to the side and helped the nurse off the elevator. “Please forgive me!” Sylvia said again.

Sylvia's face was bright red with embarrassment. She turned to Ben and said, "I need to get back to work. It was a pleasure seeing you again."

As she walked away, Ben called back, "Yes, a pleasure."

He watched her walk around the corner. He had wanted to ask her if she would like to get coffee or something. He took a deep breath and pushed the elevator button again.

Chapter Twenty-Nine

JULIA AND MARGARET were sitting in the front office of the church, stuffing and stamping envelopes—it was a monthly ritual. They made small talk about this and that and discussed what the weather was going to be like for the rest of the week. They were waiting for Buck to leave the church. When he finally did, there was a shift in the conversation.

Leaning in closer to Margaret, Julia said, "So, tell me what happened."

"In all my years, I have never seen anything like it," Margaret replied. "I thought there was going to be bloodshed right here in the church."

"Between who?" Julia asked. "Reverend Buck and Reverend Montague?"

"No, Reverend Buck sat down and didn't say anything," Margaret said with shock in her voice. "It was Reverend Montague, Ashley and David."

"David?" Julia said. "Why was David at the staff meeting?"

"He and Ashley are starting a new music format. They're bringing in electric instruments, like guitars and bass." Margaret was speaking in a hushed voice, just in case someone was lurking around the corner.

"Oh, no!" Julia said. Then with her usual sarcasm, she commented, "If David wasn't married, I'd think that he and Ashley were an item."

"You think being married matters?" Margaret said.

Julia looked at Margaret with shock. "What are you saying?"

"I'm not saying a thing," Margaret replied, "but I will tell you this. When Ben and David were both standing there facing each other, and they were both mad as hornets, they were a mirror image of each other." Margaret's eyes opened wide and she spoke softly. "It was spooky."

"There must be a disclaimer on the application form when you want to join this church: 'Only men over six feet tall with dark hair and blue eyes need apply,'" Julia said, continuing the sarcasm.

Margaret laughed.

"You think that's a joke," Julia said, "but that's the way this church is going. It's becoming more like an exclusive club than a place of worship."

"That's what Ben was getting at in the staff meeting," Margaret replied. "He feels that Ashley is turning the pulpit into a stage."

"I bet if Ashley had his way," Julia said, "he'd have scantly-clad backup singers."

Margaret laughed. "He is an odd character, but he is a people magnet. This church has more than doubled in the last year because of him."

"That may be so," Julia said, "but I think there is more to this than meets the eye."

Chapter Thirty

ANNUAL REPORTS WERE due to the district office again. Buck didn't see the point. It was all red tape as far as he was concerned, so he never put much thought into them. He had been late to turn them in for the last two years, and Don Russell frowned on that. With Buck's new building project coming up, he didn't need to get on anyone's bad side, especially the District Superintendent. It was time to call in some favors. He picked up the telephone and dialed.

"District office, this is Katrina, how may I help you?"

"Trina, woman, how are you?"

She recognized Buck's voice right away. "Bob, to what do I owe this pleasure?"

"After all these years I'm glad to know I'm still a pleasure to you," Buck said with an underlying tone in his voice that she well understood.

"I thought we were way past all that, Bob," she responded to what she thought was an inappropriate statement.

"You're right," he said. "I need a favor."

"I'll try," she replied. "What can I do?"

"You know, with the church growing as fast as it is, having hardly any staff to help me, except Ben—and by the way, what a blessing he has been—I have been spending all my time on the 'people' side of ministering and have gotten a little behind on the 'paperwork' side." Buck sounded like a wounded puppy dog.

"I bet I can guess where this is going," Katrina said.

"Trina, I really need you to buy me some time on my annual report," Buck told her.

"Bob, you have been late the last two years," she reminded him.

"I know, I know. Forgive me, sister, for I have sinned," he said in a very sarcastic voice.

Katrina giggled. "I can give you a week. But it's got to be complete, no gaps in the report."

"You have always been an angel," he said, "an angel, who for all of these years has never lost her space in my heart!"

"I already gave you the extra time, Bob," she said. "You can cut out the trying to butter me up."

"You could always see through me," he responded. "But, very seriously, Triny, in spite of anything that ever happened, you always have been very special to me."

Katrina was silent for a moment. She was thirty years older and thirty years wiser. "Can you get me your report by next Thursday?"

"I'll have it on your desk," he said.

Chapter Thirty-One

PEGGY ROSE EARLY in the morning. The sun had not yet begun to meet the day. Bob was gone, as usual. She collected the dirty clothes to take to the laundry room before she headed out of the bedroom. She lifted Bob's white button down shirt and brought it to her face. The frequent smell of perfume was not unusual; ministers were always hugging and being hugged. It was part of the job and she knew it. She pressed his shirt to her nose and breathed in. The floral fragrance filled her senses. It was a delicate and distinct fragrance, one that she had come to know well from doing Bob's laundry.

Peggy walked into the kitchen, took the teakettle off the stove and went to the sink to fill it with water to make her favorite Earl Grey tea. As the water filled the kettle, she looked out the window over the sink, which faced the church. There was a single light glowing in the tiny country clapboard church, the light in Bob Buck's office. A pain of emptiness and loneliness ran through Peggy's heart. She took the teakettle to the stove and turned it on.

While the water heated, Peggy stood motionless and thought about her marriage to Bob. She knew he wasn't perfect, but she loved him. She knew that he sometimes lied to her, but she had looked past that. She believed in "For better or for worse." *What God joins together, let no man tear asunder.* It wasn't easy, though.

The teakettle whistled. Peggy poured the boiling water into the teapot. While the tea steeped she turned and looked out the window again. The glow of the sun was beginning to cast its first spray of light above the horizon and lift behind the church. It cast an eerie vision that sent a chill down Peggy's spine. She pulled her bathrobe around her tighter to comfort herself. In the sky were gray clouds that were floating past the steeple, visible only by the faintness of the morning light. The clouds were moving quickly, as if they were being pushed by an evil wind.

Peggy poured a cup of tea and walked to the living room. She sat down in her usual chair. It was the chair where she so frequently sat alone and cried. When Bob would leave and tell her he was going someplace he wasn't really going, she sat in the chair and cried. When dinner was ready and Bob didn't come home, she sat in the chair and cried. Over the years she had watched Bob go from being a godly man to a self-serving one.

The tears welled up in her eyes. *What happened?* she thought to herself. Her sadness turned to anger. She looked at the chair that had been her prison for most of her forty-five year marriage to Bob Buck. She hated that chair. All the chair had to offer her was sadness. She wanted to get rid of the chair. She stood up and walked over to the window that looked over the pond behind the parsonage. The sun was now just visible above the horizon, and it threw magnificent splashes of orange and pink into the blue sky. She watched until the sun was full and above the horizon. Then she dried her cheeks and whispered out loud, "And I, in awesome wonder." Peggy turned and looked at her chair again and realized it was not her enemy. If she got rid of the chair, she would be getting rid of the only thing that gave her comfort in her home.

Chapter Thirty-Two

BEN HAD PICKED up Miss Mary and brought her to the church. It was an overcast day. The gray clouds hung low in the sky and felt like a weight sitting on your shoulders, heavy enough to make you slow down. It was a fitting scene under the circumstances. Ben helped Miss Mary out of his car, which was no longer an easy task—but she never complained. She was as elegant as ever, dressed in a finely tailored black suit with a yellow silk rose pinned to the left lapel and, as usual, she donned a hat. This time, a wide brimmed black hat trimmed in a black grosgrain ribbon. She still gave the appearance of being a vibrant woman, except for the walker she used to help her get around. Miss Mary was definitely one of those people that had chosen to grow old gracefully, and graceful she was.

They walked into the church that was already becoming quite full of people both young and old. They were friends that had known Edward Tarken all of his life and new ones that had come to know him over the last couple of years as the church had been growing. Ben helped Miss Mary to her usual seat next to Julia Matthews, who was already seated and waiting for Miss Mary to arrive.

"You look lovely," Julia whispered to Miss Mary. She patted the pew seat next to her, gesturing Miss Mary to come and sit next to her.

"What a dismal day," Miss Mary responded and then turned to Ben and said, "Thank you, Ben, you are such a dear."

Ben smiled then sat down in the pew behind Miss Mary and Julia.

In front of the altar rail were dozens of beautiful sprays of flowers, along with several potted plants in pretty baskets with ribbons of mostly yellow tied around them. The church was quiet and solemn. It reminded Mary of the days when there were only seven members and they would come together on Sunday mornings to pray. In those days the church was always silent and reverence was never in question. Only once a month did they have a sermon when the District Superintendent would send around a circuit rider. Sometimes it was the same preacher, sometimes a different one; but no matter, the message was usually good. On the other three Sundays a month, stillness in the tiny white clapboard church brought peace, and one could feel the presence of God as if He were sitting right next to you with His arm around your shoulder.

Directly in front of the altar was a shiny black casket with gold handles on the side. The casket was covered with beautiful white roses. If only the walls of the little church could talk. Over its 150-year history, how many white roses had they seen covering a casket? How many tears had they seen fall? These were the walls that had cradled generations of joy through births, baptisms and weddings. These walls had comforted generations that gathered together to mourn death and grieve losses. How many people had knelt at this altar seeking shelter from the pain of the world that existed outside the doors?

Bob Buck sat in the pulpit in his black clergy robe. He, too, was mourning. Edward Tarken had been a faithful member of the little white country church, even long before Buck arrived as chaplain for its demise. Edward was one of the few who tithed regularly, which was important to Buck. Edward's younger brother, who was close to eighty himself, was sitting in the front pew. He would give the eulogy today. He would also be handling Edward's estate. Buck was thankful that the transaction for the acreage that Edward had tithed to the church was already complete. Buck was still sad, though, not only about losing a faithful member. He was losing a friend as well.

The memorial service was a simple but beautiful remembrance of Edward Tarken and his life, most of which was spent in the tiny town of Wakefield with his wife Beverly. Edward's brother spoke eloquently, and tears came to almost every eye when he said that Edward had often talked about the time when he would be reunited with his beloved Beverly in their eternal home with God. With his words, he painted a beautiful picture of Edward and Beverly joined together again, hand in hand, dancing through Heaven, free from pain and fear. Edward's brother said that this was a celebration indeed.

By the time everyone returned to Edward's home after the graveside service, the gray clouds had given way to the beautiful sunshine which had dried up the dew on the grass. There was a light breeze in the air, which was always welcomed at this time of the summer. It brought the scent of honeysuckle strong enough that you could taste it on your tongue. Peggy and a few of the other ladies had prepared a beautiful luncheon for everyone to enjoy. The front door was wide open in order to welcome everyone. The dining room table was set with a buffet of ham and cheeses, fruit and fresh vegetables. There were at least ten different types of breads, and others brought casseroles of all kinds. And desserts! There were desserts of every kind: pound cakes and pineapple upside down cakes, cookies and lemon bars. Julia brought her double fudge brownies, which, Edward had been sure to tell her at every Sunday Supper at the church, were his favorites. Peggy had made her prized Angel Food cake. It was the lightest and fluffiest you'd ever taste.

After serving their plates, most people moved to the front porch of Edward's house and gathered around to talk. It was obvious that Edward had been a very special man. Edward's brother and Ben sat on the front porch swing and gently swayed back and forth, not saying a word. Ben knew that words were not necessary; it was his presence that was important. They sat there and swayed and listened to the others share stories about Edward's life.

An older gentleman, who appeared to have known Edward for most of his life, was telling stories about how Edward loved baseball. He said that years ago the church had a baseball team for the young boys, and Edward was their coach. He had set up a baseball diamond on the property that he owned, which sat behind the church. The gentleman pointed in the direction of the property that the church now owned, thanks to Buck. He said every once in a while, the men of the church would form teams on Sunday after church to play ball, but the competition seemed to be about who was really the fittest among them, each trying to outdo the other. It was certain that none of the men would be able to move a muscle the next day. However, Edward always was the one who hit the ball so far into the outfield that it sent all the other men chasing it. Then he tore around the bases like nobody's business, usually scoring a home run.

Edward's brother and Ben smiled at hearing the story and continued to slowly swing in silence. The gentleman went on to tell another story about one time when he had stopped by to see if Edward wanted to go fishing. Nobody answered the door, so he headed out to the back property where Edward was certain to always be found working on something. The gentleman chuckled a little and his face turned flush. He said he came upon Edward and Beverly. They were lying on their backs out in the middle of the green grass. Beverly's head was cradled in Edward's shoulder and he had his arm wrapped around her. They were evidently watching the clouds go by. "I was just thankful they had their clothes on!" the gentleman said.

Julia had been working in the kitchen and decided to step out onto the front porch for some fresh air and a survey of the goings on. She quickly noticed that Buck was neither inside nor out; he was nowhere to be seen. She thought that was curious. Why wasn't Buck with his congregation and the family of his close friend during their time of grieving? She walked over to Margaret, who was thoroughly enjoying a piece of strawberry pie as she sat in a white wicker rocker on the front porch. Julia leaned over and whispered, "Where's Reverend Buck?"

"He said he had to run to a meeting, some banking issue," Margaret replied.

"And it couldn't wait 'til later?" Julia asked, as if Margaret was supposed to have stopped him.

"Hey, I'm his secretary, not his keeper," Margaret came back.

"You know," Julia said with disgust, "if it weren't for Ben, I don't know where this church would be."

Margaret understood how Julia felt. Increasingly, there were more and more members who felt the same. Over the last several months, tension among members had become noticeable. The plan to build a new sanctuary was creating a division in the church. There was the "inner circle" that consisted of Buck, his sons, son-in-laws, Ashley, Doug Miles and of course, Tom. Tom had kept to himself recently, though, and that was concerning Buck. Buck didn't need any obstacles right now.

The "inner circle" was pushing as hard and as fast as possible for the building of the new sanctuary on Edward's property. The "inner circle" were the leaders of a large group of members who attended First Covenant Chapel, but who were not really committed to the church as a whole. This group represented numbers, and they were easily swayed and didn't really care how much the church was going to spend—even if it was millions of dollars—on a new sanctuary. It wasn't their money anyway. They just showed up on Sunday mornings for the entertainment and the ability to say they had been to church. For the most part, this group didn't really understand that there was a real relationship with God that comes through sanctification. All they knew was that they believed Jesus was Lord, and according to all the songs they sang in church, that was enough. To Buck, though, this group represented the masses, and that was important him.

The other group, which the "inner circle" privately referred to as the "obstacles," was comprised of only a handful of members of the congregation who were very committed to the church and its structure, both physical and spiritual. They felt that First Covenant Chapel was getting ready to head down a path of complete demise if the church were to take on a building project of the magnitude that was being suggested. This group of people had grown up in families that were faithful to a church. They grew up learning what it took to make a church succeed by watching their parents and grandparents be leaders in a church. They understood the function of the church and its commitment to the greater good. They understood that evangelism was a key function of the church. They understood evangelism brought in new people, oftentimes new Christians. But they also knew that a church could not build a new sanctuary—one that was going to cost millions of dollars—on the tithing of new Christians, because for the most part, they didn't understand tithing. That comes with the maturing Christian.

Margaret went back to her strawberry pie and Julia headed back inside to the kitchen.

Chapter Thirty-Three

"HAPPY BIRTHDAY TO you . . ." Buck blew out the candles on his birthday cake, all sixty-nine of them. He had one year left before he had to retire. In the four years he had been there, he had worked hard. He had Edward Tarken's property, a building committee that his son, Bobby, chaired, a congregation that was rapidly approaching 500, a music director the people loved and an associate pastor he had between a rock and a hard place—not to mention the dark blue Mercedes that Miss Mary gave to him. All he needed now was a bank loan.

It was the usual birthday dinner. Peggy was by far the best cook he had ever known. This birthday, she had made her famous sausage lasagna for the adults and macaroni and cheese for the grandchildren.

"Bobby," Buck said to his son after dinner, "come on up to the study and catch me up on things."

Buck and Bobby excused themselves and climbed the steps to the study. Buck sat down in the chair behind his desk and Bobby in the old armchair in the corner of the room. These were the only two places to sit in the room, besides the floor.

"How are the plans coming?" Buck asked.

"Ken said they would be ready next week," Bobby replied. "Oh, he also asked me to give you this." Bobby pulled a folded envelope out of his back pocket and handed it to his dad. Ken Arnold was a longtime friend of Bob Buck. He was also the architect that was drawing up the plans for the church.

"Thanks," Buck said, and took the sealed envelope and slid it under some papers on his desk. "We need to get the capital campaign rolling, start getting pledges in for a building fund. I'm going to start the loan application process, and a bank will require those."

Buck leaned back in his chair, feeling proud of himself. Proud of where he was and what he had accomplished, proud that he was finally proving Frank Maddox wrong about him. As he looked at Bobby, he thought about how proud he was of his son and the relationship that they had. They were close and his son respected him. Buck had hated his own father. He was a self-serving man who never had time for his family. Buck supposed his father probably loved them, but it was obvious that his father had loved his work more. Not only that, Buck's father was a dishonest man. He cheated in business, and when Buck was in his early twenties, he learned that his father had cheated on his mother . . . more than once. While he was growing up, Buck did everything he could to avoid his father. He could never remember sitting and talking to his father the way he talked with his own sons. Buck couldn't understand what a man was made of who placed a son so low on the priority list. Buck would never allow that kind of relationship with his sons.

He smiled at Bobby and said, "Thanks for sharing my birthday with me, son. I love you."

Bobby returned the smile. "I love you too, Dad."

Chapter Thirty-Four

IT WAS LATE in the afternoon and it wasn't a pretty day. The forecast was for rain, but it hadn't started yet. The gray clouds hung in the sky. Ben had been doing most of the visitation, as had become the norm over the last year. Buck was always busy with "more important" things, like paperwork. Three of their church members were in the hospital for this and that, which meant he would be at the hospital for at least two hours, maybe longer. Either way, it would put him leaving after dinnertime.

Ben pulled into the parking lot of Salem Regional Medical Center and parked in a space designated for "Ministers only." He got out of his Toyota Camry, closed the door and then clicked the remote on his key chain to lock it as he walked toward the doors of the hospital. He stepped up to the information desk and got the room numbers of the people he was there to see. They were all on the third floor.

Ben walked to the elevator and pushed the button. The lights over the elevator door indicated it was currently at the basement level, where the cafeteria, vending machines and gift shop were. He waited for it to come up one floor to the main level. The elevator "dinged" and then the doors opened. He got in and didn't need to push anything; the number three on the panel had already been pushed. The only other person on the elevator had obviously come from the basement and was standing in the back corner with her head down, reading what appeared to be a medical chart. He recognized her immediately.

"Hello, Dr. DiLeo," Ben said in a soft voice.

She looked up and smiled. "Well, hello, Reverend Montague."

He smiled, too. "I asked you to call me Ben the last time we saw each other."

"Then you should call me Sylvia," she replied.

"It looks like we're going to the same floor, Sylvia," he said.

"Visitation, right?" she said.

"And you're doing rounds, right?" he came back.

The elevator "dinged" and the doors opened. They both stepped out. Neither one knew what to say, but certainly something needed to be said. They just stood there for a moment. It was awkward.

"Good to see you, Ben," Sylvia finally said and turned to walk off.

"Good to see you," he responded and began to walk in the other direction.

He stood outside the door of Henry Blakeworth's hospital room for a few moments. He needed to collect himself. There were butterflies fluttering around in his stomach, and he needed to move his thoughts of the beautiful Sylvia DiLeo out of his mind so he could focus on his purpose for being at the hospital in the first place.

• • •

BEN WALKED OUT of Barbara Almand's hospital room and looked at his watch; it was 6:35 in the evening. He had spent over two hours at the hospital. He really did like visitation. Usually, it was a blessing to him. At times it was very hard work as well, but whatever the circumstance, he felt called to it.

He started down the hall to the elevator, which was on the other side of the nurse's station. As he passed by the station, he saw Sylvia DiLeo sitting on a small stool making notes on a chart. He took a deep breath and walked over to her.

"Excuse me," he said in a whisper.

Sylvia looked up and smiled. "Hey," she said.

"You're working late," he said.

"I have just finally finished."

"Me, too," he replied, "and I'm starving."

"I know the feeling," she said.

He was going to do it. He could do it. He wanted to have an opportunity to get to know her better, to talk with her in more length than just their encounters at the elevator.

"Would you like to join me for dinner?" he asked.

She look at him with a smile that he could feel right in the middle of his chest. "I'd love to," she said.

"Fine," he responded very calmly, but inside he felt like jumping up and down.

"If you give me about ten minutes," she said, "I'll meet you down at the front entrance."

"I'll see you there," he replied and turned to head to the familiar elevator.

He stopped in the restroom on his way to the front entrance. He checked his hair, straightened his collar and took a deep breath. He had been out with friends and people over the last years, but since Elizabeth, he had not had this feeling. He let the breath out, raised his eyebrows and gave himself a look of "You can do it" in the mirror.

There was a waiting area next to the front entrance of the hospital with the same type of royal blue plastic chairs that the emergency room had. He sat in the one that was closest to the door and he waited. Ben tapped his foot rapidly on the ground, unaware that he was doing it. Then he stood up and walked down the hall a little ways and turned around and came back. He looked at his watch. He sat back down and began to tap his foot again. It felt like he had been waiting for two hours. He looked at his watch again; it had only been six minutes. *Where were they going to go eat?* He hadn't thought about that. All he had thought about was being with her. He knew he had to have a place already chosen before she got there, but just as he started to think about where that would be, he saw Sylvia walk around the corner and head down the hall toward him. He stood up and waited for her to reach him.

"Thanks for inviting me," she said. "Too often I eat in the cafeteria or go home and end up having a bowl of cereal for dinner."

"Sounds like a typical pastor's dinner." He smiled at her. "Anything in particular you're hungry for?" Ben asked.

"I always like a good Italian meal," she said. "It's in my blood!"

Thank goodness, he thought. She had an opinion, and better than that, she expressed it. He disliked the kind of conversation that went, "Whatever you want . . . no, whatever you want."

"Have you ever been to Leo's on the old square in Salem?" he asked.

"Once for lunch," she said, "but never dinner. That's perfect. We'll go there!"

And they headed out the doors of the hospital together.

He hadn't really thought about the driving situation. He would drive, of course. He was the gentleman. "I'll drive," he said. "My car is right over here." He pointed to his car, which was parked just outside the door to the hospital in the "Ministers only" space.

"Well, how do you like that?" she said. "Clergy get better parking than doctors." She smiled and they laughed as they walked to his car.

• • •

THEY WALKED UP to the front of Leo's. Ben reached to pull the door open for Sylvia. She passed in front of him and walked in. He followed her.

Leo's Italian Restaurant sits on the corner of Main Street and Maple Street in the old section of Salem. The shops along the street are quaint, and as you walk down the sidewalk of red brick, you have a feeling of stepping back in time.

Leo's was a cozy little restaurant with a black and white tiled floor and lace café curtains across the front. Aligned along the windows were tables for two. Each table was covered with a red and white-checkered tablecloth, and a small candle illuminated each table, creating a romantic glow.

Leo's was comfortably crowded, but there was still a table at the window available for Ben and Sylvia. Ben reached for Sylvia's chair to pull it out for her and then again helped her slide it under the table. The hostess placed menus on the table in front of each of them and said, "Enjoy your meal," and walked away.

Ben and Sylvia didn't even hear the hostess. They had already begun talking, and as far as they knew, they were the only ones in the restaurant.

"So how long have you lived in Salem?" Ben asked.

Sylvia began to tell her story about going to Medical School at Georgetown University and doing her residency there as well. She had grown up in Maryland, in a suburb outside of Baltimore. She went to the University of Maryland for her undergraduate work, majoring in Biology.

A voice from the side said, "May I get your drink order?"

Sylvia and Ben were in such deep conversation that they didn't even notice there was someone standing next to their table speaking to them.

"Excuse me," the voice came a little louder.

Ben and Sylvia both looked up and simultaneously said, "I'm sorry." They looked at each other and laughed.

"I'm sorry to interrupt you," the waitress said. "What can I get you to drink?"

Sylvia secretly wanted to order a glass of Chianti, but didn't think she should in front of a minister. "I'll have iced tea," she said.

"I'll have the same," Ben followed.

The waitress smiled and turned and walked away.

It took no time for Ben and Sylvia to get back to their conversation.

"So how did you end up in Salem?" Ben questioned.

"My little brother, Anthony," she replied. "He's been married now for two years. His wife grew up in Salem." Sylvia went on to explain that their father had died of colon cancer when she was twenty and Anthony was seventeen. They both stayed near home to be close to their mother. Five years after their father's death, her mother was diagnosed with stage-four breast cancer. Unfortunately, the cancer had already begun to spread and there was not a whole lot they could do but watch her life diminish. She died two years later.

Sylvia told Ben that her brother had met a girl of which he was "very fond." She laughed about her brother's terminology. "It was more like he was head over heels for her," she said. Sylvia continued to tell Ben that the girl lived in Salem and her brother wanted to move to Salem to be near this girl. "And Anthony was the only thing I had left," Sylvia said. She explained that there was nothing to keep her in Maryland. Her father was dead, her mother was dead, her residency was over and her little brother was moving to Salem. So she decided to start a new life "down south."

"How about you?" Sylvia asked.

As he was about to share his story, the waitress returned with their iced tea and took their dinner orders. When the waitress had retreated again, Ben took a sip of his iced tea and began to speak.

Ben told Sylvia that he had grown up in a little town to the south of Charleston and never left it except to go to Columbia to attend the University of South Carolina, where he earned his undergraduate degree in Communication Arts with a minor in Philosophy. After graduation he worked for a couple of years as a speechwriter for a small communications firm, which, he emphasized, was akin to being a meatloaf. Early in his college years he felt that he was being called by God to go into the ministry, but it took him several years to fully submit before he decided to go to seminary. "The rest, they say, is history," he said with a smile.

The waitress arrived with their food and placed a large plate of spaghetti with Bolognese sauce in front of Sylvia and a dish of baked ziti in front of Ben.

"May I bless the food?" Ben asked.

Sylvia was a little uncomfortable. She had never prayed in a restaurant before. In fact, she really hadn't prayed very much at all before. *What kind of question is that?* she thought to herself. What was she supposed to say, "no"? She looked at him, smiled and said, "Of course, please do." And they both bowed their heads.

"So, what about your parents?" Sylvia asked Ben.

He smiled at her. Ben told Sylvia he was raised only by his mother, that he never knew his father. His father had left before he was born, while his mother was pregnant with him. He shared with Sylvia that one of the hardest things he had ever done was find the strength to forgive his father for leaving him and his mother. Ben told her how wonderful his mother was and that they were very close. He talked about how she worked as a church secretary.

"So you grew up in the church?" Sylvia asked.

"I guess you could say I did," he replied. Then he smiled. What Sylvia said about growing up in the church made him realize that he really did grow up in his Father's house after all.

Long after the waitress had cleared their table, they sat and talked. When they finally returned to the hospital for Sylvia to get her car, it was 10:45 at night. They had spent three hours talking, and it had seemed like only ten minutes.

He pulled up behind her car, a silver Lexus, and put the gearshift of his Toyota in park. She turned and looked at him. "Thank you very much, Reverend Ben Montague," she said. "I've had a wonderful evening!" Her eyes were glowing and her smile was hypnotizing.

"It was wonderful," he replied. "I'll see you to your car."

They both got out of his car. He left the engine running while he walked around to hers. She pushed the remote button on her key chain to unlock her door. Ben pulled the handle and opened it for Sylvia. She moved to the inside of the open door and stood there for a moment.

"I hope we can do this again sometime," she said.

He looked at her. His heart was beating rapidly and his shoulders were rigid with tension. More than anything, he wanted to kiss her right then. He smiled back at her and said, "You can count on it. Drive home safely." And he turned and walked back to his car.

Chapter Thirty-Five

THE SUNDAY SCHOOL room was lined down both sides with small, army type cots, each with a disposable pillow covered with a disposable paper covering. Outside in the hallway two folding tables and half a dozen folding chairs were set up. They hosted the cookies and juice that were payment for each pint of donated blood. First Covenant Chapel had been advertising in the community for three weeks: "Give Life at First Covenant Chapel!" Their goal was to collect 800 pints of blood in two days for the American Red Cross. By the looks of the number of people, both lying on the cots with tubing connected to their arms and those nourishing themselves with cookies in the hallway, it was going to be a success.

Julia Matthews walked into the Sunday School room. "I'm ready to be drained," she said in a loud voice.

David Buck had just taken the prone position on his cot and was waiting for the nurse to come around for his turn. He didn't really like needles, but the combination of needles and Julia Matthews in the same room, at the same time, would turn this act of service into a time of sheer torture.

"David," Julia said as she walked to his cot. "Just the man I wanted to see."

What on earth could she want with me? he thought to himself. "Hi, Julia, how are you?" he said in a reserved voice.

"I'm surprised to see you here," she said. "I heard you had a phobia about puncture wounds."

He couldn't believe she actually wanted to talk to him about his "phobia." *And how did she hear that anyway?* David thought to himself. *A puncture wound sounds a little drastic,* he thought.

"Well, I'd rather be fishing," he said, "but I'm AB negative and also a CMV Hero, which is the rarest. So if this is a gift I'm called to give, then I thank the Lord I am able."

"CMV Hero?" Julia said with a questioning tone. "What's that?"

"It means my blood is negative of cytomegalovirus," he replied nonchalantly, as if that was common information that everyone knew.

"Right!" Julia said with exaggerated sarcasm. "What's that?"

"It's a common virus found in blood, which, for many recipients, is not an issue. However, for infants and people with compromised immunity, they need blood that is CMV negative. So, they call donors with this type of blood CMV Heroes. Plus, my blood type is AB negative."

"Well, my, my," Julia said, "I always knew there had to be something special about you." She was teasing him, of course . . . sort of.

"Well, now you know what it is, Julia," David responded. He wasn't going to let her suck him under. "Did you want to ask me something?"

"Oh, yes," she replied. The cot next to David was empty and Julia sat on the edge of it. "Ashley is doing a wonderful job with the music." She had to start on a positive note, whether she meant it or not. "And, he certainly has drawn in a crowd, but I miss doing some of the old hymns."

David looked at Julia with a questioning eye. He wasn't quite sure where this was going.

"You and Ashley seem pretty close," she continued. "I've

asked Ashley several times if he would do some hymns, and he always says he will. He is so nice about it, but," she paused for a moment, "he never does it." Her voice was in a higher pitch now and she was emphasizing with her hands. "I thought maybe you might ask him."

"If he said he will do it, I'm sure he will," David responded. "It's probably just a matter of scheduling. He has things planned out pretty well in advance."

Julia took a pen out of her black patent leather purse, reached to her right side and tore a corner off the little white disposable paper sheet that covered the pillow. She scratched something out on it. "Here," she said as she handed it to him, "I've written it down. This is my favorite: 'Blessed Assurance.' It's number 274 in the United Covenant Hymnal. Please ask him."

She looked at him with pleading eyes—not a look he had ever seen on Julia Matthews' face before. *She was serious,* he thought to himself. And maybe it wasn't so bad having Julia in the same room with the needles. She had completely distracted him. He had given a pint of blood and wasn't even aware of it.

"Sit up slowly," the nurse said to David, "and be sure to get some juice and cookies before you leave. Don't drive 'til you feel ready."

"Thank you," David responded. He turned to Julia, who was now lying down preparing for her "puncture wound."

"I'll give this to Ashley." He held up the little white torn piece of paper.

"Thanks," she said, "enjoy the rest of your day. Ouch!" Julia said in a soft voice as the nurse stuck the needle into her arm.

"Oh, now, now, it's not that bad." A deep voice came from her other side.

Julia turned her head. "Reverend Montague, how are you today, sir?"

"I'm quite well," he said, "and you?"

"Well, aside from the fact that I am lying flat on my back having all the blood sucked out of me, and I just spent the last ten minutes trying to convince David Buck that it really is okay to sing hymns in church," she took a deep breath, "I am quite well, too."

Ben smiled at her. "Well, let me be company for you. I think this nurse is getting ready to drain my veins, too. And between you and me, my soul is thirsting for the hymns in the service again as well."

"Then why don't you do something about it, Ben?" Julia asked.

Ben laughed. "I'm the low man on the totem pole, you know. I've tried to bring it up in staff meetings, but it just doesn't seem to be the way that Reverend Buck, Ashley and David want the direction of the church to go."

"Reverend Montague," the nurse interrupted as she was looking at the clipboard in her lap, "do you know your blood type?"

"Oh yes, I'm sorry, let me give you my card," he said as he reached for his wallet. "I'm a CMV Hero, AB negative."

Julia, who had turned away to glance how full her bag was, whipped her head back around and stared at Ben Montague like she had seen a ghost. "That's very rare, you know," she said.

"You know what that is?" he said. "Most people have never heard of it."

"I know all about it," she said in a very slow voice.

Ben smiled and said, "Tell me, Julia, are you pleased with the changes in the services? There has certainly been a dramatic change over a very short period of time. I have been concerned about how some of the more long-term members are adjusting."

"Uhhhhh." Julia was a little lost for words at the moment. She shook her head slightly, feeling a little dizzy.

"Are you alright?" the nurse asked.

"I'm fine," Julia said. The nurse put a piece of cotton and a Band-Aid in the bend of Julia's arm. Julia sat up on the edge of her cot. "You're a pretty traditional minister, aren't you, Ben?"

"I am," he said. "That is my personal worship style, but when you're leading a church, it's not about you. It's about servanthood." He paused for a moment and a slight smile came across his face. "Servanthood puts others first."

"That's got to be tough," Julia said.

"It is. Especially when you have half a congregation that's traditional and half that's contemporary, and you only have one style of worship to offer."

"Do you really think that half of our congregation is contemporary?" Julia asked.

"Well, of our members, no. But we have more visitors than members now, and those visitors are a young generation. The contemporary style is what brings them in," Ben replied.

Julia stood up. "Thanks for the conversation, Ben. I've got to run, but it makes me feel good to know that I can talk to somebody who seems to care." She smiled at him and walked out of the room.

Chapter Thirty-Six

BEN WAS SITTING in his office trying to prepare his sermon. For many different reasons, this Sunday was going to be the first Sunday he had preached since his encounter with Ashley. Buck had become very possessive of the pulpit, and he catered to Ashley. For the last several months, Ben and Ashley had managed to work together, be in worship together, attend staff meetings together and hardly say a word to each other. David had managed to avoid Ben, too.

Being associate pastor at First Covenant Chapel had become very difficult and he didn't like being there. But he still had one more year left in his appointment, and Bob Buck had complete control over him. It was Buck's review of Ben that would determine where his career as a United Covenant minister would go. Buck had the power to make or break him. And in all honesty, Ben resented it, because he felt like he was living a lie to some extent. Ben knew that if he dared to disagree with Buck, he would be slitting his own throat. And if that wasn't enough, he had been instructed to write sermons that "sell the sizzle, not the steak." *This is all so corrupt,* Ben thought to himself. "Sell the sizzle, not the steak," he whispered out loud and shook his head. How contrary that was to the very essence of being a pastor. Ben leaned back in his chair to think. *Buck wants me to be nothing more than a marketer for Jesus. Does Buck really believe that Jesus needs a marketing agency?*

While he was sitting there stewing, his cell phone rang.

"Hello?" Ben answered.

"Ben, this is Tom. I hope you don't mind that I'm calling your cell phone, but I didn't want to have to go through Margaret to reach you."

Ben was very curious. "No, that's quite alright. Is everything okay?"

"I want to know if you and I could meet," Tom asked.

"Well, sure," Ben said. "When? And, I feel I should ask where?"

"Would you be able to come to my office in Salem around lunchtime? I'll have my secretary order some sandwiches."

"I can do that. Tell me exactly where your office is," Ben said.

Ben jotted down the directions and they hung up the phone.

This is odd, Ben thought. He and Tom had never met about any personal issues, and certainly with his close relationship to Buck, he would have gone to him on any spiritual issues. Time would tell. In two hours, to be exact. He went back to writing his sermon.

• • •

BEN RODE THE elevator up to the third floor and stepped out. The sign on the wall had an arrow pointing to the right for suite 301. When he entered the office, there was a middle- aged lady with a sweet face sitting behind the desk. He walked up to her. "I am here to see Tom," Ben said without telling her who he was.

"Yes, he told me he was expecting someone for lunch. Right this way," she said and got up from her desk and began walking down a hall. Ben followed her.

She stuck her head in the door at the end of the hall and said, "Tom, your visitor is here."

Tom stood up from his desk. "Ben, come on in," he said.

"Thank you," Ben said, with obvious curiosity in his voice.

"Let's sit over here. Lunch has already been delivered." Tom pointed to a small round table in the corner of the office. Before Tom began to move toward the table, he walked over and closed the door.

Tom's office was very nice. Two walls were floor-to-ceiling windows that overlooked a pond in which two white swans floated gracefully and carefree. The furniture was very "executive" and on the far wall were several diplomas framed in rosewood. Ben sat and Tom joined him.

"As you can imagine," Ben started, "I am very curious. I pray that everything is alright with your family."

"My family is fine," Tom said. "I want to talk with you about some church matters. And frankly, I haven't known what to do."

Ben was still confused. "What church matters?"

Tom took a deep breath and blew it out. "Well, bare with me," he said. "Let me start back a little ways."

Ben nodded slowly.

Tom began to tell Ben about how Buck had saved his marriage through his counseling and that he felt truly indebted to Buck. He recounted how when Buck was moved to First Covenant Chapel, Tom and his family moved there because Buck had personally asked them to come to his new church, and they were happy to. They loved Buck.

"I would never do anything in this world to hurt Bob Buck," Tom said, "but I am in turmoil."

Ben unwrapped his sandwich and began to eat while he listened to Tom.

"Bob brought me on to handle the church finances, which I am happy to do. It gives me a sense of service. But, finance is what I do for a living. I know what works and what doesn't work, and I know when a company is setting itself up for a financial crisis."

Tom paused for a moment and unwrapped his sandwich, and then he looked at Ben and asked, "Are you following me?"

"I'm listening," was all that Ben said.

Tom continued, "I know that building a new church sanctuary is more important than anything to Bob. But, Ben . . . the numbers aren't there. Bob is talking about building an $8.5 million structure. Bob keeps telling everyone that we have 500 members, but we don't. We have 221 members and about 200 visitors. Even if we do have a successful capital campaign, and all 221 members returned a pledge card—which would never happen—that will still not be sufficient for a bank to approve a loan."

"I wasn't aware of that, and I understand your concern, Tom," Ben replied, "but I think the cart is really getting ahead of the horse. There are guidelines set out by *The Book of Rules* on how a church is allowed to build. I know that when Edward gifted his property to the church, a lot of people began to start mentally building on that property, but there are a lot of steps that have to be gone through before we would even think about drawing up plans."

Tom was quiet for a moment. Looking down at his sandwich, he began to speak as if he were in confession. "I have been writing checks to an architect for over eight months now. My understanding is that the plans will be finished next week."

Ben looked at Tom dumbfounded. "What?" he said. "Plans for what?"

"A new sanctuary building," Tom replied.

Ben was totally lost and almost speechless. He opened his mouth as if to ask a question, but didn't even know what to ask.

"Maybe I shouldn't have told you this," Tom said. "It's just that at the staff meeting several months ago—you know, the one that was a little tense? You started talking about the direction of the church and what the purpose and mission of the church really was. Those have been my thoughts exactly, but I could never express them for fear of hurting Bob."

"What committee approved this building project, and who chose the architect? When was the Member Conference for the congregation to vote, and am I the only one that doesn't know anything about this?" Ben asked, noticeably disturbed.

"The only people that know about this are Reverend Buck, David, Bobby, Bob's son- in-law Michael, Ashley and me. Bob asked us to keep it confidential until everything was in order, and we would present it to the congregation as a whole package," Tom said. The lines in his face looked like he was carrying the weight of the world.

"Ashley?" Ben said. "Ashley knows?"

"That is another issue, Ben," Tom said. "When Ashley came on, he was volunteering his time. Shortly thereafter, Bob told me to start giving him $500 a month in cash out of the offering plate. He said that was common practice and called it a "love offering." I didn't really think anything about it because Ashley has done so much for this church. But, slowly, the amount kept increasing."

Tom was silent for a moment. "Then about a year ago, Bob told me to put Ashley on the payroll. This church pays Ashley $65,000 in salary plus another $20,000 in expenses. I'm not saying it's not legit, but I hardly ever get a receipt for the expenses. It just doesn't make good business sense, and it makes it nearly impossible to keep accurate books."

Ben couldn't believe what he was hearing and wasn't sure how to respond, but he knew this had to be handled carefully. "Well, Tom, I admire you for sharing this. To be honest, I'm going to need to think on this for a little while. Certainly, there are some issues of real concern, but maybe since the church is growing so fast, Reverend Buck just hasn't realized that all the appropriate steps haven't been taken." Ben felt fairly certain, however, that Buck knew very well what he was doing. "And, I would suggest in the future that cash never be taken directly from the offering plate, although I'm certain that Reverend Buck didn't mean any harm."

"I would appreciate it if you didn't let Reverend Buck know that I spoke with you," Tom said. "He is constantly telling us how important it is for the growth of the church that administration issues be kept confidential."

"I certainly will respect your request," Ben answered.

The two men sat in silence while they finished their lunch.

Tom had something else on his mind that he wanted to talk about.

"Ben?" Tom said in a quiet voice. "May I talk to you about something else?"

Ben looked at him with compassionate eyes. "Anything," he said.

"It's about Lisa and me." Tom spoke with his eyes down, as if he were ashamed.

Ben was silent, giving Tom the opportunity to just talk.

"Before we came to First Covenant, we had some real problems with our marriage. A lot was my fault." Tom lifted his head and began to talk straight to Ben. "I put so much into my work. I made that the priority in my life. Lisa was calling out to me and I guess I just never heard her; I was too busy." Tom fiddled with the corner of his napkin, which was now lying to the side of his plate. "She finally had enough and asked for a separation. I convinced her to go to counseling and she agreed. We went and saw Reverend Buck. I am so thankful to him. He really helped us pull our marriage back together."

Ben nodded, but still remained silent.

"I love Lisa and never want to lose her," Tom continued, and then took a deep breath and blew the air out—a sign that let Ben know this was deeply troubling Tom. "Things got better. I focused more on the family and her, and she developed a new self-confidence. But she's become distant. I didn't really notice it at first. Her sister lives over in Springdale, in the Sheridan Towers. She's single and a flight attendant, so she's gone a lot." Tom thought he might be rambling, but Ben just listened. "Lisa goes over to check on her place and waters her plants." Tom looked at Ben and asked, "Am I making sense?"

Ben smiled and just nodded.

"Anyway," Tom continued, "something doesn't feel right. I can't place it. Nothing is really wrong between Lisa and me, but there is a gap." Tom stopped.

Ben waited a few moments before speaking, giving Tom the chance to go on if he wanted to. When it was apparent that Tom was finished, Ben asked, "What are you worried about,

Tom?" He could tell that Tom was having a hard time trying to get the words out, but Ben knew what he was afraid of. He'd seen this scenario too many times before—sometimes the husband, sometimes the wife.

Tom took several deep breaths. Then he finally said it. "I worry she is seeing another man." Tom stared down at his plate, not lifting his head.

"I am sorry this is troubling you," Ben said with a very steady voice. "But remember, everything is not always as it seems. Have you told Lisa about this concern?"

"Yeah, but of course she says I'm being ridiculous," Tom said, as if it were a confession.

"Since you have counseled with Reverend Buck in the past, have you considered doing it again?"

"I have," Tom replied. "I talked with him a little about it one Tuesday at our lunch meeting. I actually was a little disturbed by his response. He just brushed over it as if it were insignificant, and pretty much told me he didn't have time for counseling right now. He said it in a nice way, of course."

Ben felt a surge of anger. It didn't surprise him that Buck had responded that way. It seemed to have become Buck's usual response recently.

"Well, Tom," Ben replied, showing no emotion of his anger toward Buck, "my door is open anytime. If you and Lisa would like, I'd be happy to counsel with you."

Tom gave a small smile. "Thanks, Ben. I'll talk with Lisa."

The two men had finished their lunch and the conversation had drained them both.

"Let's have a prayer before I leave," Ben said. The men bowed their heads.

Chapter Thirty-Seven

FOR SEVERAL DAYS Ben prayed about what to do with the information that Tom had given him. He was in a very precarious position. He was already treading on thin ice with Buck because he had confronted him with other issues that he thought were being handled incorrectly. Ashley, David and Bobby were just waiting for the moment when they could put his head on the chopping block. If he brought any of this up now, all hell would surely break loose, and that might possibly be the end of his career as a United Covenant minister. On the other hand, if he swept something like this under the rug for his own purposes, then he would be harming the Body of Christ, and that would mean that he was not serving the church to the potential to which he was called. Tomorrow was the usual Monday morning staff meeting. He really didn't know how he was going to approach it.

He decided he would wait a few days before deciding what to do. Right now he needed a change of pace. Since the night they had dinner together, he had not been able to keep his mind off Sylvia DiLeo. The very thought of her sent a warm tingling through his body, which meant that for the last week, he had tingled almost constantly.

He had kept the card on which she had written her home telephone number in his wallet. Every day he took it out, at least once, and held it in his hands. Some days he took it out even more. It had been over a week since they had gone to dinner, and every day since, his hunger had gotten stronger. Today was the day he was going to call her, and he was going to call her now. He looked at his watch. It was 7:00 P.M. He hoped she'd be home.

• • •

"Hello?" Sylvia's voice sent butterflies to his stomach.

"Sylvia, this is Ben Montague."

"Reverend Montague, how are you?" Sylvia had a playful tone in her voice, which set him at ease.

"I'm well," he replied.

"I was beginning to worry that Italian food didn't agree with you," she said jokingly.

"Oh, no," he replied. "That was the best Italian food I've ever had." He could hear her smiling through the phone. Ben paced the floor of his tiny apartment, carrying his cordless phone as they made small talk. Finally, he was going to get the nerve to ask her out.

"The real reason I was calling," he said, "was that I have two tickets to see *Joseph and the Amazing Technicolor Dream Coat* this Friday, and I was wondering if you would like to join me."

"Is that allowed?" she said. He could still hear her smile.

"Is what allowed?" he asked with the same type of coyness in his voice.

"A minister taking a date to see *Joseph and the Amazing Technicolor Dream Coat?*" she said.

"Which one are you concerned about," he asked, "the minister having a date or the minister going to see *Joseph and the Amazing Technicolor Dream Coat*?" They were both aware they were flirting at this point.

"Well," Sylvia said, "I guess both."

"Let me set your mind at ease," Ben said. "I'm not a Catholic priest; therefore a date is permitted. And just for the record, we're," he said with emphasis, "allowed to go see movies, too."

She laughed. "Well, now that's been clarified, I would be delighted to join you."

"Wonderful," he replied. "May I pick you up?"

"Is that allowed?" she said, obviously trying to get at him. Which she was . . . and he liked it.

"What? Driving a car?" he came back. "Only on every third Friday, and you're in luck. This just happens to be the third Friday."

"Well, then, I better take advantage of it while I can," she said quickly. "I live in Springdale in The Sheridan Towers. Do you need directions?"

The Sheridan Towers was a very well known and popular high-rise condominium full of wealthy, young, single professionals.

"I think I can find it," he said. "How is five-thirty? We'll have dinner beforehand."

"Perfect," she said. "I'll meet you in the lobby of my building."

When they hung up the phone, a smile came across his face. He couldn't wait until Friday.

Chapter Thirty-Eight

ASHLEY AND DAVID were already in the Sunday School room. David had become a regular at the staff meeting. It had crossed Ben's mind more than once that maybe Buck was sneaking him a salary under the table, as well.

Ben walked in and sat down across the table from Ashley and David. "Good morning, gentlemen," Ben offered graciously.

"Brother Ben!" Ashley declared with his usual flare. "Wonderful to see you this morning!"

Ben knew he was lying, but would accept it at surface level. "Thank you."

David didn't say a word. Ben wasn't exactly sure what the chip on David's shoulder was, but it was there . . . as plain as day.

Margaret and Buck walked in, claiming their usual places around the table. Buck was carrying his coffee mug and set in on the table in front of him. He nodded at Ben with a half smile. The air between them was getting thicker every day. Ben nodded back.

"Tom called. He's running a little late," Buck said. "So, we'll go ahead and get started without him." Buck turned to look at Margaret. "What's first on the agenda, Marge?"

Buck had not offered an opening prayer. Ben didn't know whether it was an oversight or if that was what this had all been reduced to. It wasn't his place to challenge it, so Ben quietly bowed his head and offered a private prayer.

Marge went over the basic housekeeping items: deadline for the newsletter, results of the blood drive, events coming up in the next couple of weeks and of course Sunday Supper this coming Sunday.

Ashley stood. It was his time to report. "Hallelujah! God is good!" he shouted as he lifted his hands upward. He always had an attention-getter, and it usually worked. Small perspiration spots were noticeable in the pits of his lime green shirt.

Ben remembered when he was a teenager, one evening he was flipping through the television channels. He came upon one of the TV preachers that was healing people in an auditorium that held thousands. Even as a kid, he wondered what it was that drew all those people there. The auditorium was packed, and people of all sorts were coming forward.

One man who hadn't walked in ten years came to the front in a wheelchair. The preacher looked at him and yelled, "Brother! Do you believe?" Quietly, the man answered, "I believe." The preacher yelled again, "Say it louder, brother! Do you believe? Do you believe in the Power of Almighty God?" This time, louder, the man said, "I believe!" Evidently that wasn't loud enough for God to hear because the preacher yelled again, "Louder, brother, louder!" And the man began to yell as loud as the preacher, "I believe! I believe!"

Then, quietly, the preacher spoke into his microphone so his words sounded like a whisper to the audience. "Because you believe, God has healed you." Then he yelled again, "Stand up, my friend, and walk!" The man stood and began to take small and very shaky steps, and he began to cry. Then other people gathered around him and they began crying with him.

Ben remembered that what struck him most about this show was a lady that later came to the front. She had been diagnosed with a cancerous tumor and she wanted to be healed. She went through a similar routine with the preacher yelling and telling her to say it louder. Then he told her she was healed, that the cancer was gone from her body. The lady began to tremble with emotion. Then, quietly into the microphone, the preacher said, "So that you will believe this is true, God is telling me the name of your doctor." He looked at the lady and asked her, "Have you ever told me the name of your doctor?" She said, "No."

And he yelled at her again, "Tell all these people that I do not have any knowledge of the name of your doctor." And the lady did. The preacher got quiet again and whispered into his microphone; his eyes were shut tightly. "God's talking to me . . . God's telling me . . . God's giving me the name . . . Steven . . . Steven . . . Steven Wash . . . Steven Washburn." He opened his eyes and looked at the lady. "Tell me, what is the name of your doctor?" Through tears the lady sobbed, "Steven Washburn," and she fell to her knees on the floor. Then the preacher threw his hands up into the air and shouted, "Hallelujah, God is good!"

That show had stayed with Ben all these years. He often thought about the lady and wondered what ever happened to her. He prayed for her frequently and vowed never to play on people's emotions by offering them things he was not empowered to give. Ben's thoughts returned to the meeting.

"David and I have met with selective groups of our members," Ashley said.

While Ashley was talking, Tom came in and sat down quietly next to Ben. "Have I missed much?" he whispered. Ben shook his head, no.

"It is obvious that a large extent of what draws people to First Covenant Chapel is our music," Ashley continued. "This focus group has concluded that we need to completely move away from the horizontal songs and only sing vertical songs. They are more powerful in helping people to connect with Jesus."

Tom, who had a look on his face that said "I am totally lost here," leaned back over to Ben and whispered out the corner of his mouth, "What the heck's a vertical song?"

Ben let out a small sound of exasperation and whispered back, "Got me."

Obviously, Ben and Tom weren't the only ones who didn't know what a vertical song was. "What's a vertical song?" Margaret asked.

With exaggerated flowing motions Ashley swung his hand in an up and down motion and said, "They are songs that are sung directly to God. They go vertical, from a person's mouth straight up to God's ears."

With a noticeable bit of sarcasm in her voice, Margaret said, "Okay . . . then what's a horizontal song?"

Now Ashley's arms began to swing from side to side. "Those are songs like the ones in the hymnal. They don't go any place, they just lie flat."

This topped it all. Ben was having a hard time not breaking into hysteria. Wouldn't all those composers be surprised to know they were horizontal? But, he composed himself, realizing this was a serious issue that was not just common to this church alone. "I'm not sure I understand what you are saying, Ashley," Ben said. "Does this mean that we are not going to use the hymnal anymore?"

"Exactly," Ashley said with a matter-of-fact tone.

"I'm not sure that's a wise decision," Ben replied. "There are still a lot of our members that cleave to God through those 'horizontal' songs in the hymnal."

"If there are," Ashley answered, "then it is only a handful, and we can't afford to cater to only a handful."

"What do you mean, 'we can't cater to only a handful'?" Ben was becoming defensive.

Margaret looked around the room. *Here we go again,* she thought.

Ben continued before Ashley could reply. "Do you realize that there is a large group of people that call those 'vertical' songs, '7-11 songs?'"

What the heck's a 7-11 song? Tom thought to himself.

"What's a 7-11 song?" Ashley asked.

"It's a song that only has seven words that you repeat eleven times." Ben's sarcasm was very evident.

David stood up and began to add his two cents. "You know, Ben, it amazes me that you are only in your thirties and you have no concept of the modern world."

Ben wasn't going to respond. He looked over at Buck, who was just sitting there, not saying a word. Ben collected his thoughts and then in a very controlled manner said, "I am not opposed to the contemporary music. In fact, I, myself, enjoy a lot of it and I also believe that it has a place and serves a purpose in the church. However, I have a concern that we are raising a generation of children who have no idea what a hymnal is. The hymnal is full of theology and is certainly a place where one can abundantly find comfort. I am not advocating that we do away with the contemporary music, but I feel strongly that we can't do away with the hymnal, either."

Ben was trying hard to change the tone of the conversation and bring it back to a place of common discussion. "David," Ben said looking straight at him, "you and I are roughly the same age. In fact, I'm told that your brother and I used to play together when we were little. Tell me, who of our generation that has had any sort of religious training doesn't know 'The Old Rugged Cross' or 'Amazing Grace?'"

"I'm sure you're right, Ben," David replied, "but you don't build a church on nostalgia."

"Okay," Buck finally said, "I think we need to move on."

Ben was fuming, but he wasn't going to let it show. He leaned back in his chair and turned his attention toward Buck. Ben wanted to stand up and start questioning Buck about all the things that Tom had told him, but he had promised Tom he wouldn't.

When they had finished covering the agenda, Buck closed the staff meeting with a simple "Praise God!" He was the first to leave the room.

Chapter Thirty-Nine

BEN WAS NERVOUS and excited at the same time. He felt like he was seventeen and going on his first date, and in a way, he was. Ben had not been on an official date since he had broken up with Elizabeth. Springdale was a good thirty-minute drive from Wakefield, all the way on the opposite side of Salem. This evening, the drive felt like a good hour and thirty minutes instead.

He pulled into the parking lot of the Sheridan Towers at exactly 5:15. The Sheridan was well known for its exclusivity. It had become known as place for the young, single, wealthy—certainly not a place one could afford on a pastor's salary.

He had fifteen minutes before he was to meet Sylvia in the lobby. He sat for a moment in his car, collecting himself. He looked around as people walked by. Friday night was busy with people coming and going. He watched as men and women got in and out of cars. Mercedes, BMW's and a few Porsches went by. The Sheridan was certainly true to its reputation.

Across the parking lot, he watched at a distance as a champagne colored Lexus pulled in and parked. An attractive middle-aged woman stepped out. Ben immediately recognized her: it was Lisa Werner. Then Ben remembered that the Sheridan was the complex in which Tom said Lisa's sister lived. He watched as Lisa walked through the front doors of the Sheridan. Seeing her there gave Ben a sense of relief for Tom's sake. At least she wasn't lying to Tom about going to her sister's apartment.

Ben looked at his watch again . . . 5:25. It was time to go in. He took a quick peek in the rear view mirror and then opened his car door and stepped out. Entering the lobby of the Sheridan was like walking into the Park Place Hotel. The floors and walls were of marble, and in the center of the ceiling was an enormous chandelier that sparkled and reflected light that made patterns on the ceiling. To the right of the front door was a sitting area with dark brown leather chairs and an oriental rug. At the far side of the sitting area was a stone fireplace with a blazing fire, which he certainly welcomed. It was already into late March and the temperatures still hovered in the mid-forties, which was unusual, but not unheard of. During springtime in the South, one day you could be mowing your grass in shorts and the next be shivering next to a fire.

Ben sat down in one of the leather chairs next to the fireplace and waited. A young woman, who couldn't have been more than twenty-one or twenty-two years old, walked through the front and sat in one of the leather chairs on the opposite side of the sitting room. She was tall, had long legs and was extremely pretty. She gave the appearance of being well-polished and refined. She wore a black leather skirt that hovered at the tops of her thighs and a blouse that allowed you to see the entire curve and flesh of her breasts. Her long blonde hair was wavy and swept over her right shoulder. She wore black heels, which where at least five inches tall and tied with black leather straps at the ankles. Both her fingernails and lips were decorated in a deep red. The young woman was a portrait of a corrupt world, and it broke Ben's heart.

A man who appeared to be in his mid-fifties or so walked out of the elevator. He was balding and wore a dress shirt that was open to his mid-chest, exposing his chest hair. He walked over to the young woman and said to her, "Are you Carrie?" The young woman smiled and nodded. He then extended his hand and said, "Hi, I'm Larry." The young woman shook his hand and stood up, and they both walked to the elevator. When it opened, they both stepped inside and the doors closed behind them.

Ben wanted to run after the young woman and grab her by the arms and say, "Don't . . . don't do this. Don't you know there's another way?" The scenario he had just watched made him sick to his stomach, and all he could do was to pray for Carrie. And he did.

Sylvia walked off the elevator. The moment he saw her, his eyes lighted up. She was wearing a black skirt that reached to just above her ankles, a white long sleeve cashmere sweater with pearl buttons down the front and black leather pumps. Her brunette hair was wavy and framed her face, which was soft and natural. Quite a contrast to what he had just seen in Carrie. Sylvia had far more beauty and appeal than the younger woman. He was thankful, too, that she had asked him to meet her in the lobby and not at her front door. He respected that.

He stood and walked over to meet her.

"Good evening, Reverend," she said with the playful smile he was beginning to like.

"Good evening, Doctor," he returned with a similar smile.

They both laughed.

Ben offered her a bended arm for her to hold and said, "Shall we?" And they walked out the front door of the Sheridan.

• • •

AT THE END of the evening, when Ben and Sylvia pulled back into the parking lot at the Sheridan, it was almost eleven-thirty. The evening seemed to have flown by for both of them. They had a tremendous amount in common, and the only time during the evening when they were not in deep conversation was during *Joseph and the Amazing Technicolor Dream Coat,* which led to a rather intense conversation about religion on their drive home.

Ben walked Sylvia into the lobby of the Sheridan and over to the elevators. She turned and told him she enjoyed the evening, and he responded, "Yes, I did, too." They looked at each other for a moment—a very uncomfortable moment. They both knew they wanted more, but neither one would acknowledge it. She got into the elevator and the doors closed. Ben took a deep breath of satisfaction and walked back out the front door.

When Ben was walking through the parking lot back to his car, he noticed that Lisa Werner's car was still in the same spot. *That's over five hours,* he thought to himself.

Chapter Forty

BUCK HAD BEEN meticulously planning every detail of how to present his building project to the congregation for over a year. The time was now or never. Buck had already missed the timing on being able to see the new sanctuary finished as senior pastor of First Covenant Chapel. He only had eleven months until he would be seventy years old, and he had to retire—hardly enough time to build a new church sanctuary. But, if he could get the bricks and sticks started by his retirement, he would get the recognition for building it. He was even certain that the congregation would dedicate the building in honor of him. He had never told anyone he had promised Edward Tarken that they would dedicate the building in memory of his wife, Beverly. And now that Edward was no longer around, no one would ever know. Buck could envision the plaque that would be built into the stone wall at the front of the new sanctuary: "This building is dedicated to the Reverend Bob Buck for his faithful service to First Covenant Chapel."

The first of several Member Conferences was this evening at seven. The church body would be voting on the plans that the architect, Ken Arnold, had now completed. They had been displayed in the narthex for the last two weeks so that everyone in the congregation had the opportunity to thoroughly study them. They would also vote on the commitment to proceed with a capital campaign to raise the $8.5 million necessary to build the structure.

If it were up to Buck, he would have canned the Member Conference meeting. It was a bunch of hogwash red tape, as far as he was concerned. But he couldn't let this one slip past. They were getting into big business and high finance, which would eventually come to rest on the District Superintendent's shoulders if something went wrong. Buck had known Don Russell for a long time and knew that he was a man who would bend the rules as long as he could cover himself. And for Don, this Member Conference was what covered him.

Buck intentionally planned the meeting for the evening instead of the morning after the Sunday service, because it would eliminate some of the people from being there. The fewer the people at the Member Conference, the better. Fewer people lessened the chances of controversy. Buck just wanted this motion to pass so he could move on his way. Edward's death having come right before this meeting was probably a blessing. His death had drawn people together in a real sense of community, and the thought of building the new sanctuary on Edward's property was nostalgic right now. *Timing is everything*, Buck thought to himself.

Buck had appointed Doug Miles the new chairman of the Church Council since Edward had passed away. Doug was a good old boy and a "yes man" to Buck. He was the only one, outside of the Buck family, that he thought would never question him or his decisions.

Doug would run the meeting this evening. Ken Arnold would be there to present the architectural drawings and his son-in-law, Michael, would make the motion to approve a capital campaign. Bobby and David knew to make quick seconds on the motions. Buck was praying for no discussion and *Wham, bam, thank you ma'am, I'll be out the door,* Buck thought to himself. Still, the tension of just having to go through this evening was killing Buck's shoulders and neck. As soon as he was over tonight's hurdle, he'd be almost home free.

Only one more Member Conference to approve the loan, and he could start moving dirt. Timing was the only issue. A capital campaign takes time, and he had loan applications almost ready to go to the banks. He needed pledge cards now!

• • •

AT SIX-THIRTY Ken Arnold arrived at First Covenant Chapel with several easels and elaborate boards of floor plans and renditions of the new sanctuary. Ashley came through the back door into the pulpit and walked up to Buck, who was talking to Ken Arnold.

"Well, gentleman," Ashley said, "this is the big moment."

"Hope you said your prayers today," Ken said with a jovial tone.

"This is cut and dry this evening," Buck replied and then added, "not to suggest that praying isn't necessary."

"Good, then I should get home early," Ken said as he turned back to the drawings in order to finish some last minute arranging. "Gentlemen, if you will excuse me."

Buck and Ashley stepped over to the second pew, where David and Bobby were already sitting and in deep discussion. "Everyone ready?" Buck interrupted them.

"Don't worry, Dad," Bobby said, "this will be a piece of cake. You've worked hard for this and everyone knows it."

"I'm worried about Ben, though," David said. "He seems to be marching a little too much to the tune of his own drum."

"Not to worry," Buck responded. "Ben's not a voting member anyway, so I asked him to go the hospital to do visitation." Truth be told, Buck didn't want Ben anywhere around the church this evening. He had become a thorn in Buck's side and he frankly just didn't want to have to worry about him.

There was a handful of people that had begun to arrive. Buck identified them as the "obstacles." Yet nevertheless, he still put on his politician smile and went to say hello. "Friends!" he said with his usual enthusiasm. "This is an exciting night for the church!"

"The plans are beautiful," one of them said.

"Glad you like them," Buck replied. "It is so incredible what God has in store. Can't you just see it?"

"But don't you think God still has use for this little church?" another asked.

"Sure He does! And the little church isn't going anywhere." Buck lifted his hand and motioned around the church as if he were waving blessings into the air. "We'll use it as a chapel for smaller events, but with the number of members we have now, we need a bigger building." Buck was blowing hot air worse than any con artist. "I am so thankful that everyone is pulling together for this." Buck wasn't giving them any choice. "If you'll excuse me, I'm going to step back here and say hello to some other folks."

Buck made the rounds, shaking hands and smiling as if campaigning. He also gave the appearance that he didn't have a worry in the world. At 7:00 on the nose, he gave Doug Miles the signal to start the meeting; he had no intention of waiting for latecomers. Doug opened with a prayer and then turned it over to Ken Arnold, who began to explain the details of the plan as if he were describing the dissection of a frog. Because of the tedium of detail with which he was lecturing, much of the congregation began to lose attention, which was just as they planned. Buck watched the congregation begin to fidget and doodle on prayer request cards. Buck sighed in partial relief. *So far, so good,* he thought to himself. But the inevitable question and answer session was nearing.

Buck was jittery. He hadn't been this nervous since the first time he lied to Peggy after they were married. He remembered how nervous he was when he pulled his car into the driveway of their very first parsonage. He was so afraid that when he walked through the front door and Peggy saw him, she would immediately know what he had done. It took him fifteen minutes to collect himself enough to get out of the car and face his destiny. But, he also reminded himself that Peggy had run to the door on that day and kissed him hello, never knowing otherwise. Lying became easier from then on.

Forty-five minutes had passed, and Ken was about to open the floor for questions. Buck had seen several people slip out the back door. Boredom had either overcome them or they had not allotted that much time in their Sunday evening. Buck wished more people would leave.

Questions were asked about the total number of square footage, length of time to build, seating capacity in the sanctuary, and if there were multiple uses for the fellowship hall. The answers smoothly rattled off of Ken Arnold's tongue, and people seemed impressed with him and his professionalism. Then the question came of how much. And without batting an eye, Ken Arnold stated $8.5 million. He said this in a tone which was convincing that it was a normal and reasonable price for a church of this size, with the number of members that First Covenant Chapel had. *He's good!* Buck thought. When Ken finished his answer, he immediately turned the floor back over to Doug, not giving any further opportunity for discussion.

Doug made a motion to accept the building plans, David quickly jumped in with a second and the vote hit the floor. Buck watched. "All those in favor, please signify by raising your hand," Doug commanded. Hands started to go up—lots of hands! So many, in fact, it wasn't even worth a count. Buck glanced around. Almost every hand was up except for the few "obstacles" sitting on the left-hand side of the church. "It's a landslide!" Buck whispered out loud, and he let out the breath he had been holding since the meeting first began almost an hour ago. As usual, he looked upward and mouthed the words, *Thank you.*

Chapter Forty-One

THERE WAS BUZZ in the church that there was a rift between Ben and Ashley. It was no secret to most people—including Ben—that Ashley, David and Bobby wanted Ben out of the church. Buck played it close to the vest. Although Ben was a thorn in his side, Buck still saw Ben as an asset because his mother was the secretary to the District Superintendent, and that was powerful when you needed a favor called in. Buck also knew that he had control of Ben, because it was his annual review of Ben that would determine where Ben's career in the ministry would end up.

Ben had driven to Miss Mary's house to pick her up and drive her to church. Miss Mary had not been to church in several months, and Ben and Julia seemed to be the only ones that cared whether or not she was becoming a shut-in.

Ben got Miss Mary settled in the car, put her walker in the back seat and walked around to the driver's side. As soon as Ben closed his door, the first thing Miss Mary said was, "How's Sylvia?"

Ben smiled and gave a chuckle. "That walker's just a cover, isn't it?" he said. "You're really a private investigator, aren't you, Miss Mary?"

She smiled. "Well, are you going to answer my question?" she replied.

"She's wonderful," Ben said with a smile. "We went to dinner and the theater last week."

"Well, if you want my opinion," Miss Mary said, "I think she is just lovely."

"I value your opinion," Ben replied, "and I agree. In fact, just between you and me, Sylvia and I are going to have dinner again this evening."

Miss Mary gave Ben a suspicious smile and said, "I remember what it was like to be young and in love."

"Miss Mary! Shame on you!" Ben said. "And who said anything about love?"

"You may not know it yet," she said, "but just you wait."

When they arrived at the church, the parking lot was already packed. People were milling about outside. The air was still particularly cool, but the willow trees were starting to bud, which is always a sign that spring is not too far away.

Ben helped Miss Mary and her walker down the sidewalk and into the narthex of the church. Buck was there, meeting and greeting, and at the sight of Miss Mary and her royal blue hat, he immediately broke into a warm smile and went to her.

"What a sight for sore eyes!" Buck exclaimed.

"It's mighty good to see you too, Reverend," Miss Mary replied.

"How have you been, woman?" he asked.

"I've been dandy, just a little house bound," Miss Mary said. "I am sorry that I haven't been here."

"Well, as long as you keep sending your checks, we'll excuse you," Buck said with a tone that was meant to be joking, but Miss Mary wasn't really sure anymore. She had not heard hide nor hair from Buck since she had given him her Mercedes. And in all honesty, she was a little miffed.

"Miss Mary!" Julia Matthews' voice came from the other side of the narthex. Miss Mary turned to see one of her dearest friends coming toward her.

"Hello, angel," Miss Mary returned and then turned back to Buck and said, "If you'll excuse me, Reverend."

Julia walked with Miss Mary down the aisle to the seats where they usually sat together when she was able to make it to church on a regular basis, not too long ago.

Julia whispered to Miss Mary, "I've been telling you this is a different place. Now you can see firsthand."

Looking around, Miss Mary could certainly see that the crowd was different. She hardly recognized anyone. The sanctuary was full of young couples and small children. In the back two pews were lines of teenagers squished together like sardines. Three of the young men were wearing baseball caps. One had his on backwards.

"Well, I am pleased to see all the young people here, but where are the folks my age?" Miss Mary asked.

"Oh, Mary," Julia said with a sad face and pain in her voice, "things have gotten really tense around here. Many of the older members have left. Ashley has done away with the hymnal, and the piano is only used as backup for the electric guitars and bass."

"Oh, goodness," Miss Mary replied with a look on her face as if she had just eaten a lemon.

"Tempers are flying high. Ashley, David, Bobby and Reverend Buck are like the four musketeers, and they treat Ben like he's the villain. But Ben's the only one around here that seems to realize that this is a church, you know . . . God's house," Julia said with a slight bit of sarcasm in her voice. "It's all over building this stupid new sanctuary! Reverend Buck seems to be on a mission for something. The whole thing doesn't really make sense, and there are a lot of people that are upset. But Reverend Buck only brushes them off, and then the next thing you know, we never see them at church again."

The band began to play the prelude, which was loud and indistinct. Miss Mary's heart was broken as she sat and watched what had happened to the tiny, white clapboard country church in which she had grown up.

Chapter Forty-Two

BEN WALKED INTO the lobby of The Sheridan at five minutes until six. He was less nervous and more comfortable this time, wearing blue jeans and a white polo shirt. He and Sylvia were going to have pizza. While he waited in the lobby for her to come down, he thought about what Miss Mary had said to him about falling in love and wondered if she really knew something that he didn't.

Sylvia walked off the elevator wearing blue jeans, a pink long sleeved t-shirt and Nikes. Her long brunette hair was pulled back in a ponytail.

"Wow!" she said when she saw Ben. "Is that allowed?"

Ben laughed, even though he didn't know to what she was referring. "Is what allowed?" Ben played along.

"Blue jeans. Are preachers allowed to wear blue jeans?" she asked with the little crooked smile that sent a tingle running through him.

"Only on every fourth Sunday," he said coyly. "So you're in luck; today's the fourth Sunday." They both laughed and headed out the door.

• • •

THEY WENT TO a popular pizza place on the south side of Springdale. Ben really didn't want to go out anywhere near Salem. For the time being, he didn't want any of the congregation knowing that he was seeing someone. He would never hear the end of it from them.

They were seated in a booth in the back corner of the restaurant. The table was covered with a red plastic tablecloth, and a small white candle was lighted in the center. The hostess handed them each a menu and said, "Enjoy your meal," before she turned and walked away.

"So what do you like?" Ben asked. "Anchovies, pickles?"

"I usually get my pizza chocolate covered," she came back.

Ben felt very comfortable with Sylvia. He enjoyed her company and they seemed to have a lot in common. Talking with her was easy and natural, and it appeared that she felt the same. They sat in the corner booth of the little pizza restaurant eating and talking, never noticing the other people in the restaurant. It was only when it got very quiet that they noticed the absence of other customers. They were obviously the last customers there.

"You think we ought to leave?" Sylvia said.

• • •

THE CAR RIDE back to The Sheridan was no less interesting than the conversation at the restaurant. "So how long have you lived at The Sheridan?" Ben asked.

"For about four years now," she replied.

"It certainly is an impressive place," he said.

"Well, you know how humble we doctors are," she smiled. "Did you hear about when St. Peter was showing a new soul around Heaven?"

"I don't think I have," Ben answered.

"Well, St. Peter was showing this new guy around Heaven, and they went into the cafeteria. There was this really big man in a white jacket in the food line, carrying a tray and getting his lunch. Well, the man asked St. Peter who it was. St. Peter replied, 'Oh, don't worry about him, that's just God. Sometimes he thinks he's a doctor.'"

Ben laughed. "I like it," he said.

They pulled into the parking lot of the Sheridan. "The sister of one of our church members lives at the Sheridan," Ben commented.

"Oh? Who's that?" Sylvia asked.

"Well," Ben replied, "I don't know the sister's name, but the lady who is a member of our church is Lisa Werner."

"I've met Lisa!" Sylvia said with enthusiasm. "Her sister Marie lives across the hall from me."

"It's a small world," Ben replied.

"I don't see her very often, but . . . " She paused for a moment. "I probably shouldn't say this to you, but she seems to meet her lover there."

"Lover?" Ben said in a shocked tone of voice.

"Marie's a flight attendant and not there very much. The only time I've ever talked to Lisa, she said she watches her sister's apartment for her."

Ben sat silent.

"But, I've seen a man coming and going, too. He seems to be a lot older than she is, probably by twenty years or more," she said.

She noticed that Ben suddenly seemed uncomfortable. "Are you alright?" she asked.

"Yes, I'm sorry. I'm fine," Ben replied. "That just caught me a little off guard. I didn't know she was seeing anybody."

He parked the car. Ben walked Sylvia into the lobby of The Sheridan. They stood and talked by the elevator for a few more minutes. Their eyes would meet and then one would look away. It was awkward, and it was obvious that both of them were feeling something. All of a sudden they seemed to have nothing to talk about, which was odd because throughout the rest of the evening, the conversation hadn't stopped.

"So, how's Miss Mary?" Sylvia asked.

"She's doing well," Ben responded. "Do you enjoy going to baseball games?"

"I haven't been to one in a while, but yes, I do," she replied.

The conversation was choppy. Neither one really had anything more to say, but they knew they didn't want the evening to end. Ben's heart started beating rapidly and he was beginning to perspire. He had not felt these things for so long. He truly did want to kiss her, and it really took every ounce of strength he had not to. The time wasn't right, not now . . . not here.

"I had a wonderful evening," he said and smiled gently at her, looking directly into her eyes.

"I did, too," she answered.

"I guess I better go," he said.

"I suppose I should, too," she said.

"Goodnight," they both said simultaneously in soft whispered voices. Then they each turned and went their separate ways.

Chapter Forty-Three

BEN ROSE EARLY. He couldn't sleep. There were too many things on his mind. His apartment was small, certainly nothing like what he imagined Sylvia's to be. But, his apartment suited him fine. In the corner of his living room was an old comfortable armchair that his mother had given him when he first moved out on his own. It had been his grandparents' and always sat in the corner of the living room in the house where his mother grew up. It was covered in a beige fabric with a small pattern like a *fleur-de-lis*, and the arm rests were well worn. It was the chair where Ben sat and read the Bible, studied Scripture, did devotions, prayed and sometimes just sat there and thought. Today was one of those days.

The window next to his chair looked out over a wooded area. The window faced east, so when the sun rose in the morning, its radiant beams would break through the curtain of trees in its foreground, creating a twinkling effect that reflected on the window in Ben's apartment. The result was a mesmerizing light show like only God could have provided.

His mind was running wild this morning. He had been entrusted with too much information—information that could hurt other people. He sat and prayed, asking God to show him how he was to handle all that he now knew. He knew he had an obligation to confront Buck with some of the issues that Tom had brought to his attention. He also knew that Buck didn't like to be questioned. And he knew that Buck wasn't dealing with a conscience, so Ben wasn't sure what kind of outcome to expect if he brought these issues out in the open.

He now knew that Tom's wife was indeed having an affair, and that was an even more difficult thing to face. Ben knew that it was not his place to tell Tom, but he did have an obligation to lead him spiritually through the trials that were inevitably ahead of Tom. And then, to make it more difficult, Ben felt anger that Buck had chosen not to counsel with Tom. Buck already had a relationship with Tom and Lisa, and he was certainly the natural one to help. But it had become more than evident that Buck was only focused on the building of the new sanctuary.

And as much as he enjoyed Sylvia DiLeo, that was adding stress to Ben as well. She was seeping into every waking and sleeping thought he had, and he wasn't sure he was ready for that.

Ben kneeled down on the floor in front of the old beige chair with the *fleur-de-lis* pattern. He placed his elbows on the seat cushion, folded his hands and bowed his head.

"Father . . ."

Chapter Forty-Four

THE WEATHER WAS gloomy. It had been overcast for five days and the temperature hadn't risen above forty-five degrees. That was nearly a deep freeze for the South, and not only that, it was the middle of March. Peggy got out of her car—which she had parked outside the hospital—bundled her coat around her and walked hurriedly through the cold drizzle into the hospital. She went through the automatic glass doors and shivered when she got to the other side. The lobby of the hospital had become too familiar. She knew it almost as well as she knew her own home.

This winter had been hard on the congregation of First Covenant Chapel, especially the elderly. The words "his cold has turned into pneumonia" seemed commonplace now. She had taken it upon herself to try to spend at least a small amount of time each day with every member that had fallen ill and been admitted to the hospital. Many of them were lonely and she knew that feeling all too well. If she could do something to make a difference in one person's life, then a difference she would make.

Ben had been overwhelmed with visiting families with troubled teenagers and broken marriages, Peggy was helping out with hospital visits and Buck was busy with trying to run the business of the church and obtain the financing for the building of his new sanctuary.

This particular day was hard for Peggy. She was more exhausted than she had ever been. Each step seemed to take unmerited effort. She was depressed by the number of their members that were fighting for their lives in the hospital, and it seemed that the newspapers, radio and television were covering nothing but bad news about the war in the Middle East and other disasters that had killed thousands. The media seemed to delight in announcing the current death toll. She was sick to her stomach. *Has the world ever seemed darker?* she thought to herself. *Have we ever before been so overwhelmed by dreadful natural and human-caused disasters? Have we ever before been in such crying need, globally, for the comforting Light? Why is it so difficult for us to see it? The Light is there, is here, where it has always been,* she thought, *but it is hard to see when we have our back to it.* Even Buck had confided in her that he hadn't been able to see the Light recently. "If the Light seems dim, let us realize that the dimness is of our own eyes and not of the Light." She hadn't realized that she had spoken out loud when she said that.

A young lady in a pink uniform gently touched her arm. "Are you alright, ma'am?"

Startled, Peggy turned around. "Yes, thank you. I am just tired," Peggy responded and began to walk toward the elevator. She realized that she was drained—not only physically, but also spiritually.

Chapter Forty-Five

IT FINALLY APPEARED that perhaps spring had truly arrived. It was Tuesday morning and today was the first day of the year that Buck would to head out to his yard for his grass cutting ritual. He threw on his old work clothes, grabbed his grass stained tennis shoes and head toward the door.

He heard Peggy in the kitchen. She had a bad cough that she had not been able to shake for months, and she looked tired. He turned and walked to the kitchen. "Peggy," Buck said, "I'm worried about you. Don't you think you should see a doctor?"

"Oh, no, I'm fine. It's just the pollen now. Nothing a doctor can do." She smiled.

Buck walked over to her and kissed her on the cheek. "Okay then," he said. "If you need me, I'll be cutting the grass."

He walked across the side yard of the parsonage and to the shed where he stored the lawn mower and garden tools. He dragged out his old push mower and pulled the cord to start it up. It took several tries to get the engine going, but it finally roared like a lion. He loved the sound of the lawn mower engine. It was like an alarm clock saying, "Spring is here!" Mowing Buck's lawn was one of the ways he stayed in shape. However, the fifteen acres of land which Edward Tarken had given the church was a different story. It was going to need a bush hog. But Buck was not going to worry about that right now because he had total confidence that within weeks, there would be large equipment out there moving dirt, and that would handle the need for cutting the grass.

He began cutting in his usual criss-cross pattern, which he had perfected over the years. As he pushed along, he heard a loud vibrating noise that was easily heard over the roar of the lawn mower. Buck cut the engine and walked from the side yard to the front of the parsonage. Pulling into the drive of Edward Tarken's house—which had sat empty since his death—was a large moving van. An SUV and a sedan pulled in behind it and parked on the street. He watched as a woman in her thirties and two pre-teen children hopped out of the SUV. From the sedan stepped a man who appeared to be about the same age as the woman. The man walked over to the SUV, opened the back hatch and a large fluffy white dog popped out. Buck turned and went back to his mowing.

Chapter Forty-Six

EACH TABLE WAS decorated with balloons as a centerpiece. The balloons were purple and gold to symbolize the royalty of Jesus and signify that God, indeed, had ordained this day. It was the first Sunday Supper of the year. First Covenant Chapel was celebrating the arrival of spring, and this was also the day of their commitment to the building fund for the new sanctuary. For weeks, Buck had asked during the Sunday service that everyone, members and visitors alike, be in thoughtful prayer about their commitment in giving financial support for the building of the new sanctuary. Buck gently reminded the congregation that, "God rewards those who give freely." Once he even said, in a joking tone, "Remember, it's your ticket to Heaven!"

The building committee had set a goal of raising $2 million in pledges on this Commitment Sunday. "And if we do," they said, "this would be proof that God truly blesses this project." It was a manipulation of words that Ben saw as deceptive.

The churchyard was packed. Buck stood under the old oak tree alone for a moment and surveyed the grounds. It was incredible to him to see the number of people stirring about, serving dinner plates with fried chicken and chocolate brownies. There were close to 400 people there. They had gone from only needing to set up six tables to setting up fifty. *Eat this, Frank Maddox,* he thought to himself as he looked around.

The band had set up on a small stage that had been assembled in the parking lot, and the property that had been Edward Tarken's was being used to accommodate the overflow of cars. People spilled into the front yard of the parsonage, some sitting in the white rocking chairs on the front porch. Children made up at least half the people. A game of kickball was being played on one side of the field and baseball was being played on the other. Buck wondered if they were playing baseball in the same place that Edward Tarken had played so many years ago. All signs of the original baseball diamond were long gone, but that was not of any concern to Buck. He did not concern himself with yesterday. *For whatever I did, yesterday is gone,* was what he always told himself. It was really a way that Buck insulated himself from the destruction and hurt that he left in his wake for other people to deal with. It kept him from having to deal with guilt.

After everyone had appeared to finish their supper, Buck took center stage surrounded by Ashley, Bobby, David, Michael and Doug. Neither Tom nor Ben had been asked to join them.

"This is the moment we have all been waiting for," Buck announced through the microphone. "We have been in deep prayer over the last several weeks, asking God to speak to our hearts about this little church and our need to build a bigger sanctuary in order to serve Him better. Several of our good brothers and sisters in the Lord are out there with baskets, which have a pledge card and envelope. Please take one of those and fill it out, put it in the envelope, seal it and bring it up to this box and drop it in." Buck pointed to a large box covered in gold foil paper with a large purple bow on the top and a slit to place the envelope inside. The box was decorated to represent this tithing as a gift to God.

Ben was a part of this, he knew, but he couldn't get the bitter taste of it out of his mouth. These folks were being brainwashed and being sold a bill of goods that Buck didn't own.

People began walking forward, placing their envelopes in the box, which Ben knew was really a gift to Buck. One after another, as they walked up to the box, dropping in their envelopes, Ashley was singing:

You are the God of my heart and my soul
You are the One where I place all control
God walks with me and He abides
God my creator stays by my side.

Ashley then made a theatrical shift and the electric bass took over. He continued with a chorus of:

All to Jesus I surrender
All to Him I freely give
I will ever love and trust Him
In His presence daily live.
I surrender all
I surrender all
All to Thee my blessed Savior
I surrender all.

Ben stood and watched, shaking his head. He was sick to his stomach. What a beautiful hymn, so rich in meaning, and this was not what it meant.

Chapter Forty-Seven

BEN WAS DRAINED physically and emotionally. He had only briefly talked to Sylvia in the last couple of days. They had both been so busy. And even though he didn't want to acknowledge it, he missed her. He wished that he could see her that evening, but she was on call at the hospital. He wouldn't even be able to talk to her on the telephone.

He enjoyed their conversations. They talked about a variety of things, but Sylvia seemed most interested in talking about things of a spiritual nature. Of course, that pleased Ben. Although Sylvia seemed to be a well-rounded person, Ben had discovered that she was empty on the spiritual side and also had gotten the feeling that she was seeking. He wanted to guide her as a minister, but he also knew that he didn't just want to be a minister to her.

He had bought a copy of *God's Joyful Surprise* by Sue Monk Kidd and was going to give it to Sylvia the next time he saw her. But since he wasn't sure when that might be, he decided that he would drive down to The Sheridan and leave it for her at her mailbox with a note just to say "hi."

• • •

WHEN HE PULLED into the parking lot at the Sheridan, one of the first things he saw was Lisa Werner's champagne Lexus parked there. He wished he knew what to do. He prayed; that was the only power he really had. But it saddened his heart to think about how people got lost in their own lives. Even so, this was surely more painful for Lisa than it was for Tom. Tom didn't know the sin. She did.

He pulled in and parked, wondering what he would say if he ran into Lisa. He got out of his car carrying the book and the note in his hand. He wandered through the maze of parked cars, and as he did he saw another car that he recognized. He stopped in his tracks. His heart sank. He did not know what to think, what to do, what to say. Chills ran through him and he felt as if his blood had just run cold. "Oh, Lord!" he said out loud, truly crying out to God for help. He didn't know whether to go on in and take the book or turn around and go back to his car and leave as quickly as he could.

He stood there a few moments and collected himself. He had come to leave a book for Sylvia, and that's what he was going to do. He was not the one who would have to explain or scramble around for a cover-up story.

It was all beginning to make sense to him now. Lisa Werner, an older man . . . Miss Mary's dark blue Mercedes in the parking lot of The Sheridan explained it all. It especially explained why Buck did not want to counsel with Tom any longer.

Chapter Forty-Eight

BEN WOULD HAVE to face Buck today. He didn't really want to see his face. He wasn't quite sure how he was going to react or what he was going to say. Would Buck be able to tell that he knew? Ben did not really feel that he could handle being at the staff meeting this morning. He had not missed a staff meeting in the three years that he had been there. One wasn't going to hurt. He would go into the church office a little early and tell Buck, face to face, that he wouldn't be there. And he would just pray that God would lead his words in whatever else he might say.

When he arrived at the church, there were already several cars in the parking lot. It seemed that he was not the only one that had decided to arrive early.

Margaret was already at her desk typing away at her computer when he walked in.

"Good morning, Margaret," he said.

"Morning, Reverend Montague," she replied in a cheerful voice.

It seemed that no matter how many times he had told her to call him Ben, she still called him Reverend Montague.

"You can call me Ben," he said.

Without looking up from the computer she said, "Okay, Reverend Montague."

Ben let out a little chuckle. He needed that this morning.

"Oh, Reverend Montague," she said, "Tom is waiting for you in your office."

Oh no, Ben thought to himself. He wasn't prepared to see Tom this morning.

Ben took a deep breath, looked upward with a quick request for guidance and walked into his office. "Tom, good morning, how are you?" Ben said.

"I've been better," he said. "Look, I am not going to make it to the staff meeting today and I wanted to bring you my report. At least what there is of it. The finances of this church have become such a mess that it's really hard to report anything, and I'm not sure anybody really cares anyway." Tom looked tired and exhausted. His face was pale and his hair was disheveled.

"Okay." Ben took the papers from Tom and didn't tell him that he was not going to the staff meeting, either.

"The big thing that Reverend Buck is going to want to know is how much we raised in pledges for the building fund on Commitment Sunday. Here's the number." Tom pointed to one of the pages he had handed Ben.

Ben looked at the number: $1,232,564.00. "It's not $2 million, is it?" Ben said.

"No, it's not." Tom spoke as if every word was a chore.

"Does Reverend Buck know this yet?" Ben asked.

"He doesn't know the exact figure, but I did leave a message for him last night that it wasn't the $2 million they were sure they were going to raise," Tom said. "I had hoped to speak directly to him last night, but Peggy said he wasn't home, and she didn't know when he might be."

"I'll let him know," Ben said. "I hope everything is alright with you."

"Well, whatever will be, will be, right?" Tom said.

"Would you like to talk about it?" Ben asked.

"I don't know," Tom said. "I'm not sure there's a whole lot to talk about." Tom paused, rubbed his hand across his forehead and down his face, and then went on to tell Ben what was on his mind. "Lisa didn't come home until late again last night. I could tell she had been with another man. Aside from the fact that the writing has been on the wall for a long time, I could smell his cologne on her."

"I am sorry, Tom," Ben said, truly feeling every bit of pain that was going through Tom.

"She starting out denying it, telling me I was just jealous." Tom paused and took a deep breath. "But I didn't believe her; although believe me, I wanted to. She finally broke down into tears and confessed. It was like I had been hit in the stomach with a baseball bat."

Ben just nodded and listened.

Tom was quiet for a moment and then let out a small laugh, obviously trying to cover the pain. "She sat there and kept saying over and over again she was sorry, like that would make it all go away. She kept saying she loves me over and over."

"What did you say?" Ben asked.

"I didn't say anything. I couldn't," he said. "I just sat there and watched her cry and listen to her babble lies about her loving me and wanting me. I wonder if that was what she was thinking when she was with him."

Ben wanted to ask if Tom knew who the other man was, but he knew that was not an appropriate question.

"I eventually just got up and walked out," Tom said. "And she was calling after me, 'Don't go, don't go,' as if she thought I would actually stay."

"Where did you go?" Ben asked.

"I went to my office. That's the only place I had to go. I lay awake on the sofa most the night. Then I came here. I was hoping Reverend Buck would be here early."

"I see," Ben said. He wondered why he wanted to talk to Buck.

Tom continued, "I was hoping that Reverend Buck could tell me what to do. I know that he has been wrapped up with this building project, but he was so helpful when Lisa and I had problems before. I thought maybe he could help again."

Ben realized Tom had no idea that Buck was the other man.

"What are you going to do now?" Ben asked.

"I've got to end this thing quickly. The pain is unreal," Tom said. "I'm going to meet her this morning, tell her I want a divorce and get my things and leave."

Ben was quiet for a moment, then rubbed his hand across his chin and said, "Is that what you want, Tom? A divorce?"

"What do you mean, is that what I want?" Tom said in an aggravated voice. "Of course not, but what other choice do I have?"

"Do you love her?" Ben asked.

"I love her more than anything in this world. And even as much as I hate her right now, I still love her," Tom said, obviously struggling to hold back tears.

"Do you think she loves you?" Ben asked.

"I have no idea anymore," Tom replied.

"Don't you think you ought to find out before you make any decisions?"

"She had an affair, Ben!" Tom said with certain anger.

"I understand," Ben said very matter-of-factly. Ben looked Tom straight in the face and said in a firm voice, "Listen to me, Tom. An affair is not cause for divorce, it is a symptom of a problem."

Tom didn't say anything, he just stared.

"When you married her," Ben said, "did you promise her for better or for worse?"

"Yeah," Tom said with exasperation, as if it had been a stupid thing to promise.

"Well," said Ben, "this is the worse. Think about it, would you?" Ben knew that Tom needed to be left alone with his thoughts now. "Let's pray, or if you can't right now, let me pray."

Tom bowed his head. Ben was certain that he was hiding tears. He prayed for Tom and Lisa, and then out of respect for

Tom, Ben got up, opened the door and walked out, closing the door behind him.

The location of Ben's office was difficult. When walking out of his office he would walk right into Margaret and whoever else might be there. Frequently, it was Julia Matthews, as it was today. He certainly had to put up a front, because he did not want there to be any suspicion. With Julia, the news would be around the church within an hour.

Ben put on the cheeriest face possible. "Good morning, Julia. How are you?" he said.

"Fabulous," she said, "and you?"

"I'm well, thank you," was his simple reply. Then he turned his attention toward Margaret. "Has Bob come in yet?"

"He just did," she said. "He headed back to his office."

"Great," Ben said and walked on past the two women, leaving no time for further conversation. All he wanted to do was give Buck whatever information he needed to—even though he wasn't sure what that was—and get out of there.

He headed down the hall that led to Buck's office. When he approached the wall with the portraits of the previous pastors that had served First Covenant Chapel, he stopped for a moment. He wondered what their appointments had been like. He wished that he could somehow speak into the portraits and ask them for their advice. As he continued to walk toward the door to Buck's office, he began to repeat, "Thy will be done, Thy will be done."

Buck was sitting behind his desk, poring over papers that he quickly tried to hide when he saw Ben at the door. Before Ben had a chance to say anything, Buck said, "Good Morning, Ben. Come on in." His voice was cheerful, as if he had enjoyed a peaceful night's sleep and was well rested.

Ben walked into the room, intentionally not sitting down. He wasn't staying.

"I'm sorry," Ben said, "but I am not going to be able to be at the staff meeting today."

"Oh, well I hope everything is okay," Buck replied.

"I have a personal matter that needs to be attended to

today," he said. Then, lifting the papers in his hand, Ben said, "Tom wanted me to tell you that he could not be there, either, but wanted me to give you these reports." Ben handed Buck the papers across his desk. It was obvious that Buck appeared a little uncomfortable, certainly wondering why neither Ben nor Tom would be there, but he didn't ask.

Buck looked at the numbers on the report. "Man," he said out loud with obvious distress in his voice. "We didn't make the mark. I really thought we would." He mulled over the papers a little further and then said, "Well, I guess we'll have to do a little extra fundraising."

"But I thought the idea was that if we raised $2 million, we would know this was blessed by God," Ben reminded him.

"That was the idea, but I guess it didn't work." Buck was fidgeting with a paperclip as he stared at the numbers. Then he look up at Ben with a confident smile and said, "Remember, Ben, God will provide."

Ben was tired. He was drained by many things, but he was especially tired of Buck's denial about the situation. Ben's face had become like stone. Staring straight at Buck with eyes that could burn through brick, Ben said, "With all due respect, sir, have you ever considered that God is saying 'no' to your building project?"

Buck's eyes locked on Ben's. If eyes are truly the window to one's soul, then this was a history that neither one of them wanted to see; and in an odd way, it was as if there was no distinction between the two pairs of eyes. The blueness of both sets of eyes met in the middle of the room and turned into darkness. There was a sense of familiarity that was chilling, and a rage of anger welled in both.

Ben had opened the gate. His statement to Buck was a confession that they were opponents in this race for the end. But what Buck was missing in Ben's eyes was the statement that said, "I'm not running."

"Ben," Buck said with an emphatic and controlled voice, "you walk a fine line here, son." He paused, but Ben made no response, not even a gesture that could be identified. Buck continued, "You seem to be forgetting that the church is a business as well."

"I am not forgetting anything," Ben said with an undertone that had a double meaning. "I just think we need to start focusing more on the souls that sit in the pews rather than the building in which the pews sit."

"You're a young boy, Ben," Buck said with the obvious intention of insult. "You haven't yet learned that you can't ignore the administration side of the church."

"I am not ignoring the administration side of the church, but the purpose of the administration is to support the spiritual development of its people." Ben's tone was increasing in obvious anger.

"The church is in the business of selling spirituality," Buck said.

"Maybe," Ben replied, "but when the church starts to sell spirituality as an indulgence, then the church has failed."

The tension in the room was so thick that it could be cut with a knife. Buck didn't need this. First Covenant Chapel was his church and the people would do what he decided. He had a sense of *déjà vu*, like he was dealing with Frank Maddox again.

"Bottom line, Ben, if a church can't pay its bills, then the church can't tend to spirituality." Buck's tone was certain. The two men's eyes had still not unlocked.

"With all due respect, Reverend Buck, that falls back to being faithful stewards of *God's* money. As pastors of this church, we have a responsibility not to let this church get into a financial hole that the members can't handle or don't want."

Buck's glare intensified and his speech became sharper. "Are you forgetting, Ben, that this is my church? These are my people. You were not here when there were only seven people. The doors to First Covenant Chapel were supposed to be closed for good. If it weren't for me, none of this would be here."

"And where is God in all of this, Reverend Buck?" Ben questioned.

"I am proving to God how much I love Him," Buck said. "What are you doing, Ben?"

Ben eyes sharpened and he replied, "I am allowing God to love me and love through me."

"Ben," Buck said in a patronizing voice, "I know that you are a man of character. And, I do not question your integrity at all, but . . . "

Ben interrupted Buck mid-sentence and in a low and steady voice he said, "If your definition of integrity is what is being represented by the leadership team of First Covenant Chapel, then please, do not count me among those with integrity." Ben turned and, with a stiff neck, walked out of Buck's office.

Buck put his left elbow on his desk and dropped his forehead into the palm of his hand. He had to either get control of Ben or find a way to get rid of him. His neck was knotted, his chest was tight and his head was pounding. He had an eerie sense that somehow he had just had a solo encounter with himself. He began to pray. He lifted his head, moved his hand to the back of his neck and began to rub. He let out a deep breath. The buzz of the phone startled him.

"Bob," Margaret's voice came through the speaker, "Victor with the bank is on line one."

Victor? His heart pounded. This would either be good news or bad news. But either way, it was the final news. If he didn't receive approval on this loan, it would be the end of the dream of building a new sanctuary, and in Buck's eyes, Ben would have won. But if he did receive approval, it was just the beginning. There would still be time to get this underway before his seventieth birthday, and his name would be the name that people associated with First Covenant Chapel from then on.

"Brother Victor, how are you today?" His voice was energetic.

"I am very well. How about you, Reverend Buck?"

"I couldn't be better. The sun is shining, and that in itself is a blessing. So, are you bringing me good news of great tidings?"

"Well, Reverend Buck," Victor's voice was quiet and low, and Buck's heart seemed to stop, "actually I do."

A sigh of relief came from Buck. He stood up from his desk and began pacing the floor in the short distance that the telephone cord would allow. A quick prayer silently flashed through his mind. *Please Lord, please Lord, please Lord.*

"And actually, the loan board approved the full $8.5 million loan."

Buck began to dance in his head. *Oh, my God! Oh, my God! God does provide!* He needed to gain composure before he spoke. He sat down in his chair and pushed his shoulders back. In a very calm, business mannered voice he said, "That is good news, Victor. The church council will be pleased. Thank you for calling."

"My pleasure, Reverend. Very rarely do you ever see a church with such sound financials. I will have the paperwork ready by tomorrow, if you would like to come over to sign the documents."

"I'll do it. Blessings to you, brother!" Buck hung up the phone. He stood up out of his chair, stretched his arms to the ceiling, and then made a fist with both hands. With a downward motion, he brought his arms and fists to his side and let out, "Yes!" in a forceful whispered tone.

He immediately sat back down and grabbed the phone again. Over the phone intercom he called to Ashley's office. "Ashley, can you come into my office for a second?"

"I'll be right in."

Ashley gave a slight knock on the door and opened it. Upon seeing Buck, he said, "You look like the cat that just ate the canary!"

"Sit down," Buck said.

Ashley moved over to the burgundy leather chair in front of Buck's desk, sat down and crossed his legs. His hand dangled over the armrest.

"I just had a call from Victor at the bank," Buck said.

"By the sight of your face, I would guess it's good news."

"Good news? It's great news! They approved the loan for the full amount! $8.5 million!"

"That is awesome." Ashley was happy, though he rarely showed emotion in front of such a small audience.

"Don't breathe a word of this to anyone. Not even Montague. I want to make an announcement on Sunday to the entire congregation."

Chapter Forty-Nine

BUCK SHOOK HIS head, trying to clear his mind of all of the events of the past. They didn't matter anymore. The Member Conference tonight was the only thing that mattered. And as soon as the congregation approved this loan, he would be in control of $8.5 million to build his new sanctuary. And with more than half a year still left before his seventieth birthday, he could be in control of the majority of the building process. Whoever the district appointed as new senior pastor of First Covenant Chapel, Buck was certain they would still need his help to complete the project. That would allow him to come in as a retired pastor and see the project through to completion. Although it would be out of the ordinary, he was certain the new senior pastor would cherish his help.

• • •

AT SIX-THIRTY people started filing into the tiny white clapboard church in the country. It was an incredible sight to Buck, who was standing in the room on the back of the pulpit, peering through the slightly ajar door. People were squeezed into the pews like sardines. Ben had brought Miss Mary to the church for the meeting, and she was still in her usual space next to Julia Matthews. Something was different about Miss

Mary, but he couldn't quite put his finger on it. And then he realized she wasn't wearing a hat. In the four and a half years that he had been at First Covenant Chapel, this was the first time he had ever seen Miss Mary in the church without a hat. It gave Buck an uncomfortable feeling. Miss Mary's hat had been a staple. *Why the change*, he wondered?

Don Russell, the District Superintendent, was sitting in the front row. He would be presiding over the meeting tonight. Buck would have no control over how the meeting was run. Sitting next to Don Russell was Katrina, as lovely as ever. He always enjoyed seeing her, and he especially enjoyed the sight of her long slender legs that were visible in the front pew. For a brief moment he wondered what it would have been like had they continued to work together all those years ago. Three pews further back sat Lisa Werner. She hadn't been in church for a couple of weeks. He noticed that Tom was not sitting next to her. *That's odd,* he thought to himself and then dismissed the thought as quickly as it came. If tonight's motion to approve the $8.5 million loan passed, he would certainly feel like celebrating. He looked at Lisa Werner again and wondered if she would be able to meet him later. Then he caught a glimpse of Peggy walking in slowly from the narthex. She sat down in the very back pew. She didn't look well. Buck was worried about her. He could not imagine living without her. As soon as this day was over, he was going to insist that she see a doctor.

Ashley, David and Bobby were all sitting together in the first pew on the opposite side of the aisle from Don Russell and Katrina. They had saved an extra space for Buck to sit after he introduced Don Russell to the congregation. Michael and Doug sat directly behind them. Julia and Miss Mary were sitting three rows further back. Julia was particularly taken by the shirt that Ashley was wearing this evening. "Wouldn't Ashley's shirt make a lovely tablecloth?" she whispered to Miss Mary. His shirt was a paisley pattern with bright yellow, pink, blue and green. "The French country ambience," Julia added. Miss Mary smiled, but didn't say a word.

Buck looked at his watch. 7:00 on the nose. Buck lifted his face upward and said, "This is it, God. Let's see what You can do." He and opened the door that lead to the pulpit and walked out into the sanctuary.

After Buck had introduced Don Russell, he took his seat next to Ashley. Don Russell began the meeting. The meeting was to be a simple one. They only had one item on which to vote. Don Russell explained to the congregation why the meeting was important and how it was in compliance with the United Covenant Churches of America Book of Rules. With that, he asked for a motion from the floor.

Immediately, Bobby stood up and said, "I move that First Covenant Chapel approve the $8.5 million loan for the purpose of building a new sanctuary." David seconded the motion without any hesitation. Buck got a knot in his stomach. He was suddenly consumed with fear. What if it didn't pass? What no one else knew was that Buck had gone to the bank and signed the papers that finalized the loan earlier that day. This had to pass.

"The floor is now open for discussion," announced Don Russell.

The room was still and the air didn't move. It was as if a cloud was hovering in the room that froze every single person where they were. Then it broke. A gentleman in the back stood up.

"After the loan is approved, how long until we break ground?" he asked.

Michael Gillard stood up, stepped out of the pew where his was sitting and walked around to the front, facing the congregation. He was apparently going to be the answer man. "We're ready to start tomorrow. But, realistically it would be about a week before we could get the equipment in and start to move dirt."

"How long do we expect the building process to take?" another asked.

"We're shooting for about eleven months," Michael answered, "but a lot will depend on Mother Nature."

Questions started coming from the left and the right.

"What about the entrance?"

"Where will the building sit on the new property?"

"Who is the contractor?" "Are they reputable?"

"What about the furnishings?"

"What is the color scheme of the interior?"

Buck was holding his breath. So far, no one had mentioned the money.

Tom was listening intently and also noticed that no one was asking about money. He looked around at the number of people that were packed into the tiny church, and not one question about money. As he was looking, he saw his wife, Lisa, sitting on the opposite side of the church. He wanted to go back in time. His heart sank into his stomach again. He continued looking around the room and wondered if the man that she had been sleeping with was sitting in here. Anger surged through him. He looked at Buck. He was as angry at Buck as he was at Lisa. Buck was supposed to be his minister and spiritual leader, yet during the most desperate time of his life, he had abandoned him for a building—a building the church couldn't afford, and it was all Buck's ego. Tom knew all along that this building was merely Buck's means for proving to Frank Maddox that he was a better man. And Tom had been a part of it. *Out of what? Gratitude,* he thought to himself. Tom was angry at himself for participating. Tom was angry at the people that sat in this church. *Were they all blind? Could none of them see what was going on?* Tom stood up in his pew.

"I think we need to evaluate this building project based on the amount of money we are talking about versus the need," Tom said in a very calm voice.

"What do you mean?" someone asked.

"I mean, what is really going on here?" Tom answered. "Why are we building this new building?"

Buck swallowed hard. *How could Tom? How dare Tom do this?* Tom was his own finance man, handpicked by Buck.

"We are building this new building because we need more space," someone stood up and said in a demanding voice.

"Do we really?" Tom asked. "Or are we really building a monument to Bob Buck?" Tom couldn't believe he had just said that. He didn't really mean it the way that it sounded. He had just opened his mouth and it kind of came out.

The church became hushed. The stillness lingered as if time had been moving in slow motion. Heads turned as if the earth had stopped rotating. People watched, anticipating what would come next.

Buck stood up and slowly turned around to face Tom, who was still standing six pews back. "How could you, Tom?" Buck said, as if he had just been ambushed by his most trusted brother.

Tom stood silently, not knowing how to respond.

"I was there for you when your marriage was in crisis," Buck said with a spiteful tone, delivering just enough confidential information to hopefully shut Tom up. He neglected to think that he was stabbing Lisa at the same time.

Tom couldn't believe Buck had just announced that information to the entire congregation, but he remained calm. "This has nothing to do with that, Reverend Buck," Tom replied. "This is about the financial obligation that this church is getting ready to take on."

Buck glanced over at Lisa, giving her an eye that suggested, "Make him stop." Lisa's returned glance implied she was hurt.

For a moment, Tom wondered about the exchange between Buck and his wife.

"It is my opinion that this church is not—" Tom began to say before Bobby stood up and cut him off.

"Are you suggesting that my father does not have the best interests of this church in mind?" Bobby said in an almost threatening tone.

"What I am concerned about is the amount of debt that will be attached to this project," Tom replied.

"Do you think my father hasn't considered that and hasn't been prudent in every step of this process?" Bobby paused only for a second, but not long enough for Tom to respond. "My father has spent his life serving God. He has spent forty-five years sacrificing himself for the church and the people in it."

"Bob Buck is the best pastor I have ever known," said a lady from the other side.

"Yes," confirmed another member, "he has worked hard for this church, to bring it to this point. We owe it to him!"

Point in case, Tom thought to himself.

"How could you question his intention?" a man's voice came from behind him.

Tom felt like he was alone in the flood. Everyone else, including Julia Matthews, was afraid to speak. Ben could see that he was drowning, but he was not a voting member and could not interfere in this discussion, even as much as he wanted to. He thought Tom was right and admired the fact that he had the guts to stand up and say it.

"There has been an unwarranted rush to start this building project. Let's try to find out the reason why." Tom spoke out among all the other comments being thrown at him.

People were beginning to speak over other people. There was a hostile swirl in the air. Finally, Don Russell stepped in and spoke directly to Tom. "Sir, sit down. If you don't stop, I am going to have to call you out of order and ask you to leave the church."

Tom didn't mind if he was called out of order and, in fact, it would be a blessing to leave the church. "I'll respect that request," Tom said, and stepped out of the pew and began to walk down the aisle toward the narthex. Then he heard his wife's voice.

Speaking to the entire congregation, Lisa Werner said, "May I please remind everyone that the motion on the floor is not whether or not we love Bob Buck. The motion is, do we accept the obligation of an $8.5 million loan for the purpose of building the church?"

Tom had never heard Lisa speak up in church before. And her words were accurate. He was proud of what she said. Tom didn't turn back. He walked out the front door of the church.

"I am going to call for a vote now," said Don Russell. "By a show of hands, all those in favor."

A sea of hands went up in the air. This was it! Buck, who had still been standing, lowered himself to the edge of the pew. He had done it!

"All those opposed," said Don Russell. Not one hand went up. "Motion approved!"

Chapter Fifty

IT WAS 2:00 A.M. He sat in his study. He was too excited to sleep. It was storming outside. The rain was beating against the windows, and the wind was blowing so hard that it was brushing a tree limb against the side of the house. Buck leaned back in his chair and listened for a moment. It was like music to him. He smiled and allowed the tension to drain out of his body. It was all downhill from here. They would be grading the land next week, and before long there would be a plaque that read, "In honor of Bob Buck, Senior Pastor." He would be certain to invite Frank Maddox to the consecration.

He leaned back up to the desk and started going through some papers, organizing stacks here and there, throwing some into the trashcan. He opened the bottom draw of his desk and pulled out a manila folder to file another check stub, this one from the church's cleaning company. He flipped through the other stubs in the folder, making a mental note that all together they added up to about $35,000. He didn't feel guilty about it at all. Ministers hardly make anything. Just because he had chosen to serve God as a career didn't mean that he wasn't entitled to some of the finer things in life. And he couldn't afford them on a minister's salary alone. Besides, he was a fair man. He allowed the cost to the church to be inflated so that the money the company was writing back to him wasn't cutting into that company's profit.

Buck could hear noises downstairs. *Was Peggy up?* He thought she had been asleep for hours.

He left his desk and walked downstairs. He could hear Peggy coughing from the bedroom. It was a painful sounding cough. He rushed to the bedroom to check on Peggy. She was sitting on the edge on the bed, one hand propping her up. Her face was pale and she was having a hard time breathing.

"Peggy!" Buck said. "What's wrong?"

She didn't answer. She couldn't speak through the coughing. He went to her and kneeled on the floor in front of her. "Look at me, Peggy." She lifted her eyes toward him. She needed help. He touched her arm, which was very warm. He placed his hand on her forehead and it was hot.

He quickly went over to the chair in the corner of the bedroom and grabbed the throw that was draped across the arm, and then took it over to Peggy and wrapped it around her shoulders.

"We're going to the emergency room," he said. She didn't argue.

He slid her slippers on her feet and helped her to stand. With his arm around her shoulder, they walked to the front door. Buck opened the door. The rain was coming down in sheets. He paused for a moment, trying to figure out how he was going to get her into the car. He ran out to the car and pulled the passenger door slightly ajar so that he could open it with his foot when he carried Peggy through the rain.

• • •

The emergency room was crowded. Buck had not been there for some time. He looked up and down the rows of chairs covered in royal blue plastic and glanced at the television that was tuned to CNN with no sound. Peggy sat in a wheelchair next to him. They were waiting for someone to come out and get Peggy. *Why was it taking so long?* He looked at Peggy. It scared him to see her like this. She looked frail and weak, and for the first time ever, she looked old to him. He wondered if she thought he looked old, too.

Finally, she was taken back. A nurse with a very sweet and calming face came into the room. She took Peggy's blood pressure, pulse and the usual, along with the rest of her medical history. People came and went, bringing machines and charts, taking blood. It was becoming a whirl for Buck. He sat in a chair in the back of the tiny room with his head propped against the wall. He was now exhausted. He looked at his watch: 3:45 A.M. He didn't want to call anyone until morning or when he had more information.

Another man came into the room. He was tall and thick with a flat-top crew cut, and he was wearing green medical scrubs. "Mrs. Buck," he said, "I'm going to take you for a chest x-ray." She gave a little smile to acknowledge him. Then he turned and said, "Mr. Buck, if you wouldn't mind waiting out in the waiting area."

Mr. Buck? He hadn't been called that in a long time. Suddenly it dawned on him that he wasn't Reverend Buck here. He was Mr. Buck, just the husband of a patient. Buck answered, "Sure." He stood up and went to the side of the bed and kissed Peggy on top of the head. "I love you," he said.

"I love you, too," she mouthed, barely even audible.

Buck sat in the chairs covered in royal blue plastic and watched CNN for what seemed like days. Every once in awhile he would look around the room at the faces and wonder what their stories were. But the fact of the matter was, he really didn't care.

"Mr. Buck," a voice called. He looked around. A large lady, who looked like she had once been a linebacker and dressed in a white nurse's uniform, was standing at the doors that were swinging back and forth.

Buck got up and walked over to her. "How's Peggy?" he asked.

"Come with me," she said. They began to walk through the halls of the hospital. "We have admitted her. I'll take you to her room."

"What's wrong?" Buck asked.

"She has pneumonia in both of her lungs. She must have been sick for a while. It's pretty bad. We've started her on antibiotics. We are also concerned about her fever. It has gone up one and a half degrees since she first came into the emergency room." They were at the door of Peggy's room. "She's right here, Mr. Buck." The nurse pointed to the door. Buck looked up. Room 142.

He pushed the door open. Peggy was lying in the hospital bed with the rails pulled up around her. She was connected to monitors and tubes, she had oxygen and IV's and the room was beeping with the rhythm of a heartbeat. He walked over to the side of Peggy's bed and placed his hand on her arm. She turned her head to look at him and smiled. "I'll be okay," she said in a weak voice.

"I know you will," Buck replied.

She closed her eyes and drifted off to sleep. Buck looked at his watch. 6:15 A.M. It was still early, but he could call their daughter, Amy. She would be awake, getting the children ready for school. He didn't want to disturb Peggy, so he went out of the room to use a phone. He walked down the hall to the nurses' station. Moving was an effort; he was drained. "Is there a phone I may use?" he asked a lady sitting behind the counter.

"In the waiting area down the hall," she said, pointing.

The waiting area was small, nothing like the waiting area in the emergency room. It only had two chairs and they were covered in tan cloth and had wooden arms. A small table, where a telephone sat, was between the chairs. He sat down in one of the chairs and took a deep breath, and then placed both his hands on his face and rubbed them back and forth. Then he pushed them through his hair and down to his neck.

He dialed the phone. It rang five times before anyone answered. "Amy?" he said.

"Dad, what's wrong? Why are you calling so early?" She was immediately alarmed.

"Mom's going to be fine," he started out saying so she

wasn't more alarmed, "but, we are at the hospital. They have admitted her with pneumonia."

"Oh, my goodness. I knew she wasn't well," Amy said. "What are they saying?"

"I haven't talked to a doctor yet, but they have started her on antibiotics and some other things." Buck wasn't really sure of anything.

"I will be right down," Amy said.

"Wait, Amy," her father said, "I need you to do a few things for me first. I am going to stay here with Mom. Would you please call David, Bobby and Elaine and let them know? Ask Elaine to go by the house, since she lives the closest. Ask her to go up to my study. Sitting right in the middle of my desk is a stack of reports that has to be turned into the district office today. She needs to take the reports to Ben. He can give them to his mother at the district office. She's the one who handles them."

"Okay," Amy replied, "is there anything else?"

"Yes, would you ask her to get my blue sweater out of my closet? It's cold in here."

Chapter Fifty-One

BEN WAS ALREADY in his office when Elaine arrived with the stack of papers. She tapped lightly on the side of his door, which was already open. Ben turned his head to look.

"Elaine!" he said, startled. "Come on in. How are you?"

"I'm sorry to bother you," she replied. "Mom went to the hospital last night with pneumonia."

"Oh, no," Ben interrupted her.

"I'm just on my way there now, so I really don't know much of anything," Elaine told him. She handed him the stack of papers. "Dad wanted me to give these to you. He said they are reports that have to be turned in to the district office today."

Ben took the papers and set them on his desk. "I'll take care of it. Is there anything else I can do?"

"I don't know at this point. Say a prayer?" Elaine said.

"That's a given," Ben answered.

Ben walked Elaine to the door of the church offices. "Tell your father I will take care of everything here."

"Thanks," Elaine said in a weary voice.

The phone rang before Ben even had the chance to sit down at his desk again. He reached for the phone while he was still standing. "Hello?"

A chipper voice came from the other side. "Ben, good morning, it's Julia Matthews."

He did truly care for Julia, but really didn't want to talk to her right now. "Good morning, Julia. How are you?" he answered.

"I'm dandy, but it came to my attention that Lisa and Tom Werner are having problems with their marriage." Julia was whispering as if she were a private investigator passing on top secret information. Her tone lowered even more. "I even heard that they might be separated. That certainly would explain why they weren't sitting together at the Member Conference last night."

"Thank you for letting me know, so I can keep them in my prayers," Ben replied, cutting to the chase.

"So what did you think about the meeting last night?" she asked.

Ah, the real reason for calling, he thought to himself. He didn't want to be rude, but he certainly wasn't going to get into a gossip session with Julia Matthews. "Peggy Buck was admitted to the hospital with pneumonia last night," he said, trying to change the subject. "I know that Miss Mary would want to know. Would you mind calling her?"

"Oh, my goodness!" Julia replied. "I didn't think she had been looking well recently. Absolutely, I'll call Miss Mary right now."

"Thanks," Ben said, relieved that he had diverted the conversation. They hung up the phone.

He turned his attention to the stack of papers on the desk. He shuffled through them. These were the reports that were due over two weeks ago. Ben wasn't surprised. He was surprised, however, that his mother hadn't been onto him about it. They seemed to be fairly well in order, although he couldn't confirm any of the numbers. That was something Buck always kept to himself.

At the bottom of the stack of report papers was a manila folder. Ben opened the folder and looked through it. *What are these?* he thought. Check stubs from Ken Arnold, the architect, and check stubs from the cleaning company. He thumbed through them. They were all labeled "consulting fees."

"Kickbacks," he said out loud. Buck had been taking kickbacks. He was stealing from the church. Ben dropped his arms to his side and leaned back in his chair. *What more could happen?* He closed his eyes and let himself drift to his favorite Psalm. *Be still and know that I am God.* Knowing this was all that brought him comfort right now.

Chapter Fifty-Two

"BEN!" HIS MOTHER said as he walked through the front door of the district office. "What a pleasure."

"Hi, Mom," Ben replied in a tone that only his mother would know something was wrong.

"What is it?" she asked.

"Peggy Buck was admitted into Salem Regional Medical Center last night with pneumonia," Ben said.

"Oh, my goodness!" she replied. "I am so sorry to hear that."

"Reverend Buck asked me to bring these by to you." He handed his mother the papers.

"Finally!" she said with a tone of exasperation.

"These are over two weeks late, Mom," Ben said. "How come you have allowed that?"

"Bob asked," his mother replied. "He has done some things for me in the past. It didn't hurt for me to do this for him."

Ben just nodded with no real expression. She could tell there was something else on his mind. "Mom, why did you want me to work under Reverend Buck?" Ben asked in a very somber voice.

"Because he has a lot to teach you," she replied in a very matter-of-fact way.

He wondered if his mother really had any clue how much. "Mom, do you have any idea how hard these last couple of years have been?"

"Ben," she replied, "you may not like the way Reverend Buck does things, and in fact, they may be plain wrong, but," she paused for a moment, "you and Reverend Buck have more in common than you think."

"Well, I can't imagine," he said. He wanted to be as opposite of Buck as he possibly could.

Chapter Fifty-Three

IT WAS DUSK when Buck stepped onto the front porch of the parsonage. He was weak and emotionally drained. All he wanted was to take a hot shower and put on some fresh clothes before he headed back to the hospital again. He turned and looked out across the field where he would soon see his new sanctuary building. It all seemed so distant now. He rubbed his eyes and walked through the front door of the parsonage and closed it behind him.

Except for when he went to visit his mother, Ben had spent the entire day in his office at the church. In spite of that, he had been entirely unproductive. Across the parking lot a faint light was barely visible through the fading sky in the window of the parsonage. He felt terribly sorry that Peggy was ill, but Ben knew that he had to confront Buck now. A delay could only make things worse.

Ben picked up the manila file folder, clicked off the lights in the church and walked out the door, locking it behind him. He walked slowly across the parking lot and through the field that led to the parsonage, praying along the way—for courage, for strength, for truth.

There was a breeze blowing warm and then cool, even though it was chilling. Ben was tense and he could feel the pain that ran across his shoulder and shot straight up his neck. "How long, oh Lord, must I endure these trials?" he whispered as he reached the bottom of the steps that led up to the front door of the parsonage. He glanced down at the manila folder one more time. He had no clue what he was going to say or do. The sun had completely disappeared and it was dark now. He put his hand on the rail and walked up the stairs. Standing in front of the door, he pushed the little lighted button to the left of the door. He could hear the chime inside. In a few moments, Buck appeared at the door. Looking through the screen door, Buck was obviously startled to see Ben standing there. "Ben, what are you doing here?" he said with a curious voice.

Buck still had not opened the screen door. "Well, um," Ben started, "how is Peggy?"

"She's alright," Buck replied. "Getting some much needed medicine."

"May I come in?" Ben asked.

Embarrassed that they were still talking through the screen door, Buck said, "Oh! Forgive me. Please come in." Buck pushed on the screen door so that it opened. As Ben walked through, Buck noticed the manila folder in his hand. It looked familiar, but surely it wasn't his folder, Buck thought. "Sit down," Buck said as he pointed to a chair in the living room.

"Thank you," Ben replied as he sat down on the edge of the chair.

There was a fog of tension that covered the room. Both men sat uncomfortably, not knowing the intention of the other. Buck fidgeted with a thread on the arm of his chair.

"I am sorry to hear about Peggy," Ben finally said. "I have got things covered at the church, you just worry about Peggy."

"Thank you," Buck said, not really meaning it. There was no way he was going to let Ben use this as an opportunity to weasel into the work he had done at the church. "But, I am sure that Peggy will be just fine in a day or two. I don't really expect to be away from the church for any real length of time."

There was another expanse of silence that seemed to last an enormous length of time.

"Was there something that you wanted to discuss with me, Ben?" Buck finally asked. The atmosphere had become unbearable for both of them.

Ben thought for a moment, not knowing how or what to say. "I got the reports to the district office today." For some reason, he really didn't want to mention his mother to Buck. Ben lifted the manila folder and held it with both hands. He held it out to Buck, and with absolutely no emotion, said, "I believe this is yours. Elaine must have accidentally picked it up with the report papers that she brought to me."

Buck had a sinking feeling in his stomach and he suddenly felt hot. Sweat began to form under his arms and across his brow. Ben didn't move or flinch a bit. He just stared Buck square in the eyes. Buck pursed his lips together and squinted his eyes as if he was in deep thought. Ben still made no move and showed no emotion. Buck couldn't read Ben. *What does he want?* Buck thought to himself. Then without thinking, he said it out loud. "What do you want?" His words could have cut through steel.

"What do you mean, what do I want?" Ben replied and then quickly continued. "I don't want anything. I was merely returning what belongs to you."

It's time to quit pussyfooting around, Buck thought. "Why don't we get this all out in the open?" Buck said.

"I haven't hidden anything," Ben replied, his face straight as a board and showing no emotion.

If looks could kill, Buck would have been guilty of murder. "Look, I told you once before," Buck said, "this is my church and I run it how I think it should be run. I don't need some young fledgling coming in and trying to tell me how things should be done."

Ben didn't comment, he just listened.

Buck continued. "You have been here three years now, all as a favor to your mother. But, let's call a spade a spade." Buck narrowed his eyes and met directly with Ben's. "I don't like you, and you don't like me."

"So how do you propose we deal with that?" Ben asked, not expecting the answer that he was about to receive.

"I am going to ask Don Russell to transfer you to another church. I will give you an excellent report as long as you keep your mouth shut. Do you understand what I am saying?" Buck was adamant.

"And supposing this is the way things pan out, what do you suggest I tell people?" Ben asked with a tone of voice that suggested Buck was crazy.

"If anyone ever asks you why you left, you just tell them you needed a more liturgical church," Buck said and stood up. Obviously, he was finished with the conversation. "Now, if you don't mind, I would like to take a shower and get back to the hospital to see my wife."

Ben nodded and stood up. He didn't speak as he walked to the front door. Just as he stepped out onto the front porch, Buck said in a tone that was definitely final, "Are we clear on this?"

Ben kept walking.

Chapter Fifty-Four

BEN RAN FROM the parking lot into the hospital as fast as he could. The automatic sliding doors seemed to take forever to open. As they opened, a cold gust of wind hit him in the face. *This can't be happening,* he thought to himself. He went over to the window where a lady sat. He recognized her from times when he had been there before. She was still chewing gum and still looked bored.

"Excuse me," Ben said.

The lady didn't look up but said, "I'll be with you in a minute."

Ben stood there, his heart beating rapidly. He lifted his hands and rubbed them back and forth across his face, wishing it could erase the anxiety and fear. The lady at the window, who appeared not to be doing anything, was annoying him.

"Excuse me," Ben said again.

The lady turned and looked at him. In times past he had not seen the lines on her face that spoke of a life of bitterness. For a moment his heart went out to her. "May I help you?" she said with irritation in her voice.

"Yes, I received a phone call that my mother had been brought in, Katrina Montague," Ben said, trying not to let his panic be obvious in his voice.

The woman turned back toward her computer and typed something. In a moment she turned back toward Ben and said, "Are you family?"

Things like this didn't usually bother Ben. He normally let them roll off his shoulder. But right now he had the incredible urge to yell, "Are you an idiot? I just said that she was my mother!" He was sure she had heard that many times before, though, and restrained himself. "Yes, I am her son," he said calmly.

"Have a seat." The lady pointed to the line of chairs covered in royal blue plastic. "I'll let someone know you're here."

Ben turned and walked back over to the waiting area. He sat on the edge of one of the chairs and looked up at the television. CNN with no sound. He wondered if it ever changed or if it was ever turned off. He looked around the room. It was crowded, just as it had been every other time he had been there. As he surveyed the faces, he saw them differently than he ever had before. This time he truly understood the fear that was written across some of the faces. A sense of isolation comes across a person in the face of trauma, as a means of protection, he supposed. He knew that he felt isolated right now, and not only that, he wanted to be isolated. He suddenly understood the reason there was no sound coming from the television. The picture was only another means of artificial distraction, keeping you from having to deal with yourself and acknowledge your fears as you sat in this waiting room of uncertainty.

What was taking so long? He looked around again. This room was a place of perpetual waiting. The doors may open and close, and the faces that wait may change, but that was the sole purpose of this room: waiting. It was a waiting room that gave an appearance of controlling destiny—the waiting room of life and death. Through all of the time he had spent in this room, he had never felt it from this perspective.

Through a fog that muffled his hearing, a voice came, "Is there someone here for Katrina Montague?"

He leaped to his feet with an unprecedented amount of energy.

"Yes, I'm her son," Ben said as he walked toward the lady.

She gave him a half smile to acknowledge him, but it was a smile that also said, "Brace yourself." They walked through the door that swung back and forth. It was a familiar route to him. The lady did not speak a word as she led Ben to a door that had a number "7" posted on it. They stopped next to the door. "If you'll wait right here, Dr. Tolliver will be over in just a moment to speak with you," she said, and then turned and walked away.

Things seemed to move in slow motion. People were coming and going, there were beeping noises and flashing lights, phones were ringing and there was the sound of wheels clattering as a person on a gurney was pushed by. A loud voice came from his left side. "I need help over here!" Ben took a deep breath. Was his mother behind the door marked with the number "7"?

A man walked up to Ben. He was a tall man with gray hair that was thinning. He appeared to be around fifty, maybe fifty-five, and was wearing a white doctor's coat with a stethoscope stuffed in the right pocket. "Are you Ms. Montague's son?" the man asked.

"Yes, I'm Ben Montague," he replied.

The man extended his hand. "Hi, I'm Dr. Tolliver."

Ben just nodded.

"Your mother has had a massive heart attack. We have her stabilized right now, but she is going to need surgery." Dr. Tolliver was very confident in his manner of speaking.

"May I see her?" Ben asked.

"Yes, but keep in mind, she is very weak, but we are monitoring everything. I will be back shortly," Dr. Tolliver said, then turned and walked in the other direction.

Ben stood outside the door marked with the number "7" for a few moments. He had never seen his mother sick a day in his life. She was the strongest woman he had ever known. *How could she have had a heart attack?* As he pushed down the handle on the door, he allowed his mind to be flooded *. . . The Lord is my Shepherd . . .*

The room was sterile and cold and the smell of alcohol was nauseating. His mother lay pale and lifeless on the gurney. The tubes and monitors that were hooked to her body were clearly a life support system for his mother. He walked to the side of her bed and placed his hand on her arm. "Mom," he said softly. There was no response.

A nurse walked in. She walked over to the monitors, pushed a button and then adjusted one of the turn wheels on the flexible tubing that was feeding his mother something intravenously. The nurse looked at Ben, somehow knowing what to say. She'd seen this scenario before. With a comforting smile she said, "She's asleep. This type of trauma is exhausting to the body. You'll be able to talk to her in a couple of hours." Then, she added as she was walking out the door, "All your worries won't add another day to her life. She's in hands greater than yours or ours," and the nurse walked out the door, letting it silently close behind her.

God gives us what we need, when we need it. Whoever that nurse was, she had been an angel to Ben right then.

• • •

TIME SEEMED TO move so slowly, and with each minute that passed, Ben's chest felt that it was being crushed under the weight of fear. Finally, they moved his mother to a room on the floor, number 103. It was a private room with a sunny window. His mother would like that. Also, it happened to be just down the hall from Peggy Buck.

His mother had been awake off and on, and he had been able to talk with her a little bit. Most importantly, he was able to tell her that he loved her. They would discuss her options later. Right now she needed rest.

Chapter Fifty-Five

BUCK ENTERED ROOM number 103. He walked over to Katrina's bedside and looked at her sweetly. She was weak. Her body was tired. She was still beautiful, even though her face was drawn and there were dark circles under her eyes. The monitors beeped in the background. *Only yesterday,* he thought to himself, w*e were both just starting careers in the ministry.* They were both young. Buck and Katrina had worked side by side for three years. She was the best secretary he had ever had, and perhaps one of the best people he had ever known, aside from Peggy. Katrina was a loyal woman. She had not had an easy life, yet she was such a joy to everyone else. She had a kind way of speaking that rolled off her soft lips, and her eyes were the windows to her sweet seduction that she never intended for harm. They just drew Buck in and took control of his senses. There was never anything he could do to stop the desire.

He shook his head, trying to get these thoughts to leave. He couldn't feel this way. But, maybe he really did love her through all these years. It was wrong of them to have let their professional relationship become intimate. It was only several times, but he probably wouldn't have stopped the affair if it had been up to him. It was Katrina who took the stand to stop it. He still remembered her words: "We'll both lose everything. I'll lose Stuart and you will lose Peggy and your church." She was right, and Peggy was pregnant at that time with Bobby. Looking back, he was so thankful that Katrina had been sensible and strong. He would have destroyed everything. He felt badly for Katrina. Stuart still ended up leaving her. He didn't really know why, but he was thankful their affair had been over for several months before Katrina's marriage started falling apart. What a scandal it would have been.

"Reverend Buck," a voice came from the door. It was a nurse. "Your wife is looking for you."

Buck stood up. His knees were weak. Katrina still lay silently, never having known he was in the room. He turned and walked out the door. Buck had never before felt such mortality as he did now.

He stopped for a moment outside Peggy's door and took a deep breath. He rubbed the back of his neck and stretched it from side to side. *Lord, I am weary. Please give me strength.* It was the only prayer he could muster. He put his hand on the door lever, pushed it down and walked in slowly.

"Hi, darling," Peggy said in a very weak voice.

Buck had now donned a large smile and he forced his eyes to be bright. "Peggy, oh praise God, you are looking so much better! How are you feeling?"

"I think I feel better, but I am so weak."

"Strength will come with time," he said.

He sat down in the chair next to her bed. The room was still. The afternoon sun shone through the window creating a stream of hazy dust. Peggy was pale and fragile looking. He had never seen her like this before. There were so many tubes and monitors connected to her body. Her left arm was deeply bruised from being stuck with so many needles.

"How are you, Bob?" Speaking exhausted her.

"I'm doing just fine," he replied and then changed the subject to the more familiar. "It's so exciting, Peggy. I've been at the church all morning meeting with the builders. The plans are incredible. Ashley was there, too. He's got some wonderful ideas. The stage area where the band will stand is going to rotate and he's made plans for extra spotlighting, in order to emphasize the drummer or the lead guitarist during a solo. It turns out that Uriah Jonah's church really has a good format, and we are going to try to follow that."

Peggy closed her eyes. Tears began to fill them. She used every ounce of strength she had to turn her head so that her husband could not see the teardrop trickle from the corner of her eye. Buck continued to talk about the church, but Peggy let her mind wander, and the music of her favorite hymn filled her head.

I come to the garden alone
While the dew is still on the roses,
And the voice I hear falling on my ear,
The Son of God discloses.
And he walks with me,
And he talks with me,
And he tells me I am his own;
And the joy we share as we tarry there,
None other has ever known.

"Peggy?" Buck's voice was very soft. "Peggy?"

She pretended she was asleep.

Buck softly stood up and crept out of the room. Peggy heard the hushed closing of the door.

Buck wanted to go back to Katrina's room, but he saw the back of Ben Montague at the nurse's station, so he turned and walked toward the exit. He knew that Ben was supposed to be visiting with Miss Mary this evening. He'd come back to the hospital then when Ben was busy.

While walking through the parking lot, Buck released his cell phone from the clip on his belt. He began to push the buttons. He opened his car door and got in. Doug Miles answered at the same time Buck started the car. "Brother Doug!" Buck said with his usual enthusiasm. "Just checking in. I'm leaving the hospital now."

"How is Peggy?" Doug asked.

"She's doing great. I tell you, she is a strong woman. Nothing can beat her. Hey, thanks for picking up the pieces with the finance committee. It's such a shame what happened with Tom. Have you finished counting the money yet? How'd we do last Sunday?"

"Yes, I finished," Doug said with a tone that left some doubt. "I don't know, Bob, we were $4,000 short of the budget. That really concerns me."

"Doug, don't sweat the small stuff. I've been doing this for over thirty years. It is not uncommon for a church to hit some hard times, particularly during a building campaign. Things will turn around. Listen, just borrow the $4,000 from the building fund. We'll pay it back next month."

"Bob, that doesn't seem right to me, but I guess I don't see any other solution." Finance was not Doug's specialty.

"Don't let it bother you. It's the way all churches do it," Buck said with confidence. "Well, I'm going to head home for a bit and try to work on my sermon for Sunday. Holler if you need me."

• • •

BUCK PULLED INTO the driveway at the parsonage. He parked the car and got out. Walking through the door to the kitchen, he remembered what Edward Tarken had told him: "You have no idea what it is like when you've been married to someone for what seems like all of your life, and then you lose them. Even the bad times, you remember as good. It may sound selfish, but you oughta start praying that you go first and not Peggy."

The house was quiet, and there were no smells in the kitchen of soup on the stove or bread in the oven. He walked over to the refrigerator and opened it. He pulled out a Styrofoam box that contained his leftover Chinese food from the night before. He grabbed a fork and stood at the kitchen counter and ate it . . . cold.

He left the remains on the kitchen counter, walked to the stairs and headed up to his study. His head was pounding, and the knots in his neck had doubled. He swiveled back and forth in his chair as he thought about what he should preach on this Sunday. He had not used a lectionary in some time now. There always seemed to be an issue that required more immediate attention, and preaching about it had proved to be a good way of reaching the majority of the people in his congregation.

There was a division in the church. Not everyone was on board with building the new sanctuary. Tension was getting tight. He had to find a way to pull this together. He wasn't going to let this come crashing down at this point. Tomorrow morning they would start grading the land. On Sunday when people showed up, they would actually see the fruits of his labor and he needed everyone to be working on the same side—his side.

The clock on the wall behind him seemed unusually loud. *Tick tock, tick tock.* It was driving him crazy. It must have been over an hour that he had been sitting there and he hadn't written a thing for his sermon; he hadn't even decided on what to preach. Truth be told, he didn't really feel like preaching. He had devoted his life to God, and look at what he had gotten for it. He felt like Job. How could a man as good as he, be faced with such difficult times?

The phone rang. "Hello?" he answered.

It was Amy. "Dad, Mom has taken a turn for the worse. They are moving her into ICU and are going to put her on a respirator." Amy's voice was breaking as she spoke frantically.

"I'll be right there." Buck quickly got up and slipped his loafers back on his feet. He ran down the stairs as quickly as he could, grabbed his keys from the kitchen counter and got into his car. He prayed as he drove.

Oh, loving Father,
Please don't take Peggy from me. I can't bear to live without her. She means everything to me. Please heal her, Lord. Please heal her, Lord. Take me first, God, please take me first. Let me die before Peggy.

Over and over again he said it. *Please take me first, Lord.*

The hospital was in Salem, which now seemed like forever away. It had begun to rain, and the windshield wipers swished back and forth in front of his face. They made a noise like that of the clock in his study. It was taunting him. The moon was nowhere to be seen. It was pitch black; without a doubt, the darkest night he had ever known. The rain was hard enough that when a car approached from the other direction, he was blinded by the oncoming lights. His body was rigid. He was grasping the steering wheel so tightly that his knuckles were white. He was approaching the four way stop at the place known as The Four Corners. He glanced both ways. He didn't see anything coming and he didn't have time to stop. All he heard was the screech of tires and the loud wail of a horn.

He hadn't hit anyone and no one hit him. He did even look back. He didn't care. His heart was beating rapidly. He took deep breaths and blew out the air, trying to calm himself.

When he reached the ICU, all of his children were sitting in the waiting room. His heart sank. "How is she?"

"They are working with her now," David said.

"Have they let you in?"

"Not yet."

"Is Dr. Walsh here?" Buck asked.

"I don't know. They just asked us to wait here."

Buck sat down next to his children in the well-worn chair. It was certain that many pastors had sat here. This time, he was on the other side. The room was still. No one spoke.

"I'll be back," Buck said to his children, with no explanation. He got up and walked out of the ICU waiting room, leaving his children there. He couldn't sit there any longer. His mind was racing. He wanted to check on Katrina, and he wanted to see her before Ben got back. Buck pushed the button on the wall by the elevator, the one with the arrow that pointed down. He stared at the numbers above the doors as they lighted up. 1 . . . 2 . . . 3 . . . the door opened. No one got out; it was empty. *Thank God,* he thought to himself. He was in no mood to be in an elevator with another person that he might have to acknowledge.

The doors opened on the first floor and he stepped out. He walked cautiously, looking to make sure that Ben wasn't around. Ben shouldn't be there yet, but Buck was sure that it wouldn't be long before he showed up. He stopped outside Katrina's door, straightened his shirt collar, smoothed his hair across his forehead and tried to drop his shoulders, which were currently close to level with his ears. He let out a deep breath and lightly tapped on the door. Slowly, he pushed the door open and in a soft voice said, "Trina?" He walked on in, leaving the door slightly ajar. She lay in the hospital bed, which looked so institutional. When she saw him she gave him a small smile, just raising the corners of her mouth.

"I was here earlier. You were asleep," said Buck quietly.

"Thanks for coming, Bob," she said. Her voice was weak and sounded muffled because of the oxygen tube that rested beneath her nose.

"You look wonderful, Trina," Bob said with a smile.

"You were always a good liar, Bob."

"Now that's an interesting quality for a minister," Bob replied.

Ben got off the elevator and headed toward his mother's room. The door was slightly open and he heard voices coming from inside. He put his hand on the door jam and leaned his ear toward the crack. *Buck,* he said to himself. He hoped he wasn't asking her to do favors for the church while she lay in her hospital bed. He wouldn't have put it past him. He listened.

"How's Ben doing?" Katrina asked.

"He's fine," Buck said somberly.

"I'm so glad."

"Listen, Trina, I was thinking." Buck wasn't really sure what he was going to say. He didn't want to hurt Trina. "I was thinking that Ben might learn more from being at a bigger church."

"Bigger church?" Katrina said with a confused tone in her voice. "According to your report, you have 750 members in your church. How much bigger do you think he needs?"

Standing outside the door, Ben mouthed, "Please!" He rolled his eyes and shook his head.

Ben already knew that the true membership count was only 380. Obviously, his mother wasn't aware of the truth.

"We have about that many in attendance each Sunday, but our official membership isn't quite that high," Buck replied to Katrina.

Why was he telling her this, she wondered? "But, your annual reports said—"

Buck cut her off mid-sentence. "I know, Margaret made a mistake while typing it." He had lied so much at this point that he wasn't really sure what the truth even was anymore. "I hope you'll keep that mistake between you and me."

Margaret made the mistake? Ben thought to himself, as he continued to listen at the door.

Katrina looked at Buck with heavy eyes. She was tired of his messes and tired of keeping his secrets. "Bob, I have been keeping your secrets for too long," she said.

"I know, Trina, and I thank God everyday that you have."

"You thank God?" Katrina asked. Her voice was suddenly strong and firm. She said each word clearly. "What kind of god do you have, that you thank him for lies and deception?"

Buck was caught off guard by her statement. He squirmed a bit, trying to figure out what she was talking about, trying to figure out how he should respond.

Katrina continued, "You have made a god out of yourself, Bob. I don't know what happened to the man I met thirty years ago. You used to have a passion for the Lord and your work was service to Him. And I summed our affair up to you just being human—and me, too."

Ben, still listening outside the door, put his hand over his stomach. What was his mother talking about?

"Trina," Buck said in a voice that was slightly pleading, "I will have to answer to God for what I have done in my life, but my servanthood is real. I've never wanted anything more out of life than to serve God. And as for you and me, I know we were a mistake, but Trina, what I felt for you was real."

The room was totally quiet for a moment. Katrina had turned her head away from Buck and was staring at the wall.

They should have dealt with this thirty years ago. She had to tell him. He needed to know. She had sacrificed for him too long. Her voice was quiet and she continued to look away. "Bob, moving Ben to another church is not going to erase him from your life. You and Ben lock horns for a reason. You both have the same drive and determination. It's in the genes."

Buck wasn't quite sure what she was saying, but he suddenly felt like he needed to sit down. He slowly took a few steps backward until he felt the chair at the back of his knees and lowered himself. He didn't say a word.

"Bob," Katrina paused. She had wanted to tell him this for thirty years. "Ben is your son."

She turned and faced Buck, who was extremely pale. "How could you have not seen it, Bob? He looks just like you, he has mannerisms like you and he has the same passion for God that you had thirty years ago."

Outside the door, Ben was using all the strength he had to hold himself up. He couldn't believe what he had just heard. He turned and grabbed the handrail on the wall. He had to get out of there before Buck came out of the room. He was numb; he was angry; he didn't know what he felt. He wanted to hit Buck, he wanted to hit his father has hard as he could. He had never felt so much anger toward a person. He was confused. Holding onto the rail, he made his way around the corner. There was an empty room off the hallway. He went in and closed the door. He made his way over to the chair and sat in the darkness.

Buck was speechless. He stared at Katrina. He didn't know what to feel, how to act. He was numb, but there was a chill that ran through his body that was causing his fingers to freeze. He opened his mouth as if to say something, but nothing came out. He tried several times, and then finally said, "I've got to go check on Peggy." Buck stood up and slowly walked out of the room, closing the door as he left.

Buck walked rapidly to the elevator and pushed the button. His head was spinning. He felt like vomiting. He wanted to run, to hide. His mind was rampant with visions of Ben and

Peggy, David, Bobby, Amy, and Elaine. The elevator doors opened and he jumped in, wishing it could take him somewhere faraway, faraway from everything; but most of all, faraway from himself. *Ben was his son.* And then his head was suddenly filled with painful visions of over thirty years ago when he had been unfaithful to his beloved Peggy. Peggy's face flashed before his eyes. She was the best thing that ever happened to him. She was so sweet and pure. If she ever found out he had been unfaithful to her, she would be crushed. What was he to do? His illegitimate son was a daily part of their lives. Would he be able to continue the lie he had been keeping from Peggy for over thirty years? She couldn't find out. His mind was racing and he felt like he was suffocating. He stepped out the door of the hospital and drew in a deep breath of fresh air. The rain was pounding down harder than when he had first arrived at the hospital.

Sitting in the dark, Ben was so full of anger he felt paralyzed. Unable to move, he was frozen in his stillness. He could hear the noise of people passing by the door, voices of people talking, carts being pushed along and the hospital loud speaker. They were deafening noises that radiated through him and down his spine.

"Code 1, room 103," came over the speaker. "Code 1, room 103."

He wanted to run into the hall and yell, "Silence!"

And he heard it again. "Code 1, room 103."

He lifted his head and felt all the blood drain from his body. The words he heard made him shiver. Room 103 was his mother's room. He jumped out of the chair, threw open the door to the room in which he had been hiding and ran around the corner. He saw people, lots of people dressed in white medical coats, gathered around. They were all calmly frantic. The people separated to allow a large man pushing a crash cart through. Ben joined the crowd, but couldn't see his mother's face through all the people.

"One, two, three," came a voice, followed by a jolting sound. "Again!" the voice yelled.

Ben felt someone touch his elbow. He turned and saw a very sweet-faced older woman. Her white jacket read "Becky Patterson, RN." He recognized her as the nurse who had been in the emergency room when his mother had been brought into the hospital. She smiled softly at Ben and said in a very quiet voice, "They are doing everything they can. Why don't you step back here with me?"

Ben felt so distant, as if he were floating above all of this watching someone else. His shoulders were tense and limp at the same time. He took several steps backward and stood next to the sweet lady who was still holding his arm.

Voices coming from the room were only mumbles to him, except for one deep voice that he heard loud and clear: "Time of death, 8:17 P.M."

Ben closed his eyes and silent tears began to flow from the outer corners of his eyes, running down his cheeks and dripping off of his chin onto his shirt.

BUCK WAS WATCHING the rain come down in sheets as he breathed in the fresh air. He couldn't go back into the hospital right now. He had to get as far away as possible. With that in his mind, he ducked his head and ran out into the rain without an umbrella and toward his car. When he reached his car, he was soaked from head to foot, but he didn't care. He put the key in the ignition to start his dark blue Mercedes, pulled out of the space and headed out of the hospital parking lot. He didn't know where he was going, he was just going. He turned out onto the street heading north. The rain was beating down on the car and the windshield wipers were not sufficient to clear it, but he drove anyway. He turned right, not knowing where the street led. It didn't matter.

"Lord!" he cried out. "Can you hear me?" "Why have you forsaken me?!" he shouted.

Buck's body was trembling with anger, fear, sadness and guilt. His mind went back to Peggy, lying in the ICU on a respirator. Was the Lord ready to take her from him? He couldn't bear the thought. "Are you there, God?!" he screamed. "Please don't take her away from me!" he called. Again, he thought about what Edward Tarken had told him about praying that he would go first. "If you want someone, take me!" he shouted.

The raining was pounding the car. The night was darker than ever before. He had no idea where he was. It was a country road, long and narrow. There were no streetlights. Things were all blending together in Buck's head. It was so overwhelming it numbed him. He took a deep breath and blew it out, and then another. In a few moments he began to settle, knowing that he had to collect himself to be strong in this situation.

Buck shifted his mind to how he was going to handle this. He knew Ben was in his control, having already told him that he was requesting that Ben be transferred to another church. So that handled Ben. He would be rid of Ben, even if he was his son. He felt certain that since Katrina had not told anyone in all these years that Ben was his son, she wouldn't now. Nobody needed to know. He could keep this a secret and things could go on as he planned. He had his $8.5 million loan, and tomorrow they were getting ready to break ground, and he was only barely sixty-nine years old.

The rain was relentless, but Buck began to feel relief and in control again. He would go for a mile or so more and then turn around and head back toward town. He would need to go home first and change clothes before he went to the hospital to check on Peggy. He didn't want to have to explain why his clothes were drenched. He did not want to raise any suspicions that something was wrong.

Buck had regained his confidence and strength. Nothing could taken him down—not Frank Maddox, not a washed up old country church and certainly not Ben Montague. He was ready to go back and face them all. He sped up the car to find a place to turn around. It was hard to see in the rain and there were no lights except his headlights.

• • •

ONLY THE SLIGHTEST bit of pain pierced through Buck, and in an instant it was gone. Gazing down through a foggy haze, all he could see in the vast darkness was a tree across the road. He felt oddly separated from the scene. The light and dark blended into grayness as the sight became fainter. Crumpled against the tree across the road was a dark blue Mercedes deflecting the rain. As Buck tried to understand what he was seeing, the vision became more and more distant as he moved further and further away from the rubble, and then it all disappeared.

• • •

BEN SAT NEXT to his mother, holding her hand. He watched her face, how still she was. Confident that she was at peace, he stood up, leaned over, kissed her forehead and whispered in her ear, "I love you, Mom." Ben turned and walked over to the window and looked out. The sky was dark and the rain was beating down hard, but Ben could see beyond the darkness and there was light. He raised his arms and lifted the palms of his hands toward the skies and said, "Oh, Merciful God, I lift my eyes beyond the shadows of this earth to see the Light of Eternity. Into Your hands I commend Your servant and my mother, with hope and assurance of resurrection to eternal life through Jesus Christ. Amen."

Ben turned, took one last look at his mother and walked out the door. He walked over to the nurses' station. The sweet lady who had held his arm was sitting there. Ben said to her, "I am finished," and he turned and walked away.

Chapter Fifty-Six

THE LITTLE COUNTRY church called First Covenant Chapel was in a state of shock and dismay at the tragic death of their senior pastor, Bob Buck. For several days the doors of the church remained unlocked so that people could come and go when they needed. Ashley agreed to allow the church to be in silence for a week. With the silence came a reverence that had been long gone for the last several years. Each person that came to grieve was met with the Spirit of Peace as they sat in silence and prayed. There is an overwhelming acknowledgement of omnipotence that is present in the face of death, which escapes no one.

Chapter Fifty-Seven

BEN HAD NOT been to visit Peggy since she had come home from the hospital two days ago. He had faithfully gone to the hospital to be with her children, which he, alone, knew were really his own brothers and sisters. It was hard for him in the light of his own grief, having lost both of his parents in the same day. And what made it even harder was that he held the truth that would affect so many lives if it were revealed.

Once Peggy had been moved from the ICU to a regular room and it was clear that she would be fine, Ben slowed his visits in order to give his own heart a rest. But, she was home now, and as acting senior pastor of First Covenant Chapel it was his obligation to visit her.

Before heading over to the parsonage to see Peggy, Ben stopped in the church and kneeled at the altar. Then he walked out the front door of the church and slowly made his way through the parking lot and side yard that separated the church from the parsonage, taking deep breaths along the way. He walked up the front steps. Taped to the frame of the screen door was a note that said, "If you're here to visit Mama, please come on in." It was signed by Elaine, the Buck's eldest daughter. Ben pulled the screen door open and walked on in. He stepped lightly, but the floorboards still creaked beneath his feet. "Peggy," he called out softly. There was no answer, so he walked a little further down the hall. He called out again.

A soft voice from the distance called, "Come on in."

Ben turned the corner and peered through the door to Bob and Peggy's bedroom. Peggy was propped up in bed with pillows behind her back. The window to the room was open and a soft breeze whispered in the air. There was a chair sitting by the side of her bed to welcome visitors, and a tissue box sat on the table to the left side of Peggy.

"Come in," she said. "Sit down."

He walked into the room and over to the chair and sat down on the edge of it. Ben reached over and placed his hand on top of Peggy's, which was resting on the bed. "I am so glad to be visiting you here, rather that at the hospital," he said.

She smiled and gave a little nod that let him know she felt the same. "How are you doing, Ben?" she said, and before he could respond she added, "It is so hard on a child when a parent dies."

"I'm alright," he said, "but I am more worried about you. How are you?" He was thinking to himself, *If she only knew.*

Tears began to roll down Peggy's cheeks. She reached for a tissue. "If we could just roll back time," she said.

"I know," Ben said. It was all he had with which to reply.

"We try to do things the way we think we should," Peggy spoke softly, "but no matter what, the end is still the end."

Ben knew that Peggy was weak from her own health and still in shock from her husband's death. He smiled at her, not really understanding.

Peggy's gaze was distant, but she continued to talk. "It seems like yesterday you and Bobby were just little boys playing together on Sunday mornings in the nursery. I'm sure you don't remember. We were moved to another church before you even turned three. It's hard to believe that over thirty years have passed and here you sit again in front of me."

Ben smiled and squeezed her hand that he was still holding.

She moved her hand from underneath his, reached to the nightstand and picked up the Bible that was sitting there. She brought it close to her and held it next to her heart.

"There is no better place to look for comfort," Ben said.

She lifted it away from her chest and handed it to Ben. "I want you to have this," she said.

Ben looked down at the Bible. The black leather was worn from being well used. In the bottom right-hand corner was a faded, but still very visible, inscription. It read, "Reverend Robert B. Buck." Ben looked at Peggy with confusion across his face and said, "Peggy, I don't understand, why would you give this to me?"

Peggy gave him a weak smile, but it was the very best she could give. She told Ben, "Every child should have something by which to remember his father."

Ben's heart sank and a tear rolled out of the corner of his eye. "Peggy, how did you know?" he asked.

"I have known for years," she replied. "When you and Bobby were a little older than two, I received a letter in the mail from Stuart, who had been your mother's husband. In the letter he told me about the relationship that Bob and your mother had and that you were Bob's child. He said he felt that I had the right to know so that I could handle it however I felt I needed. I burned the letter and never said a word to anyone."

"So why are you telling me now?" Ben asked.

"Because we don't know what tomorrow will bring and I may not be able to tell you later," she replied. "There is so much I wish I would have told Bob, and now it's too late."

There was silence in the room for a moment.

"What would you have told Bob?" Ben asked.

"Well," Peggy said with a sigh, "for one thing, that I forgive him."

There was a very deep understanding between Peggy and Ben, much of which was unspoken.

"Would you be upset if I said I need to go right now?" Ben asked Peggy.

"Not at all. I understand," she said.

Ben got up, turned and began to walk out of the room. When he got to the door he stopped, but he didn't turn around. He didn't want Peggy to see the tears that were running down his cheeks.

"Peggy?" he said.

"Yes," came her voice from behind him.

"Thank you," he said softly and left.

Ben walked out the door of the parsonage, closing it slowly and quietly behind him. Holding the Bible, he ran his right hand across the front cover. He lifted the cover open and began to look blankly at several of the pages. One page was a family tree that was partially filled in. He saw the names of Bobby, David, Amy and Elaine. Above their names was his father's name: Robert Benjamin Buck.

He walked down the front steps of the parsonage and headed toward the path at the back of the church that led to the property that used to belong to Edward Tarken. In light of the events of the last several weeks, a hold had been placed on beginning the new sanctuary. The open fields were wide expanses, appearing void of anything except silence and beauty of the absolute basic: nature, just as God intended. *From the earth we all came and to the earth we all will return.* It was a phrase Ben knew very well, but really didn't understand at all. He stopped for a moment and gazed. His body was drained of strength and emotion. "Here I am, Lord," Ben whispered, knowing he was being heard.

The stillness of the atmosphere around him was deafening, except for the vibration in his head that sounded like the low murmur of a violin playing the saddest song on its strings. The sun was setting at the horizon, spreading glows of pink and orange through the sky, though it was fading rapidly. The violin continued and now began to fill his soul. He closed his eyes and began to sway to the music that only he could hear.

Interrupting the peacefulness of the soft violin and fading sunset were thoughts of reality. His mother was dead, and he had a new realization that the pain he endured throughout his childhood because a father he thought had left him was never real. The man he had grown to despise in the last few years was his real father, and he too was dead. Ben was now the senior pastor of a church that was in crisis both fundamentally, spiritually, and financially, he had two brothers who loathed him, and he was the only one of the three that knew they were brothers. He was left to deal with a music minister that most of the congregation loved, but Ben had the knowledge that his ministry was self-serving and corrupt. And on top of all of that, he could no longer deny it: he was in love with Sylvia DiLeo . . . deeply in love.

He placed the palms of his hands together and brought them to the front of his face, like a little boy first learning to pray. He slowly fell to the ground until his knees met the earth, then lifted his head toward the Heavens and prayed. A peace and acceptance came over him. He knew that he had to go on, and from this point forward, he would face things with a deeper understanding that nothing is fair on this side of Heaven.